The Shackled

Devon De'Ath

DEDICATION

In loving memory of William Leonard Barnes – RN and
Charles Thomas Mounteney – DCLI.

And for all those left behind:

May you find your way to where the light shines brightest.

CONTENTS

1

Liberation Time

SAMANTHA RILEY, 2019.

"Oh my God, it's found me." Samantha Riley stumbled against a dry stone wall. The jagged edges of upright 'cock and hen' capping stones grazed her tensed fingers. An undulating expanse of damp, bleak moorland unfolded beyond the man-made boundary. Overhead, an oppressive fake ceiling of gunmetal grey sky sandwiched all between it with the intimidating power of natural suggestion. A smothering blanket of heavy mist rose from patches of bog. Like smoke from the infernal chimneys of hell, it snaked in vaporous grasping fingers across the inhospitable wilderness. Dewy digits of doom, beckoning any unsuspecting beast closer for one terminal embrace. Woe betide the creature foolhardy enough to stumble into one of those saturated pits.

A thunderclap broke the unwanted solitude. The twenty-five-year-old woman twisted messy curls of her straw blonde hair between trembling hands, where the ends hung forward to grace the top of her chest. Lightning reflected in the deep pools of her pale blue eyes, raised skyward for one moment. A pause to catch her breath. The sense of loneliness flooded her being with a palpable ache, the way approaching sheets of rain would soon flood the sodden, grassy turf of the moor. But she wasn't alone. Samantha could handle emptiness and exile. She had learnt something of those states in recent months. Oh to be alone, rather than pursued by that thing.

Another thunderclap. This one bore the accompaniment of an unnatural timbre. Like some metal gauntlet dragged across a blackboard or sparking steel brake shoes reining in a speeding express train, the monstrous shriek cut crisp and powerful. The young woman gritted teeth - now set on edge - and threw her right leg across the rocky wall. Several loose stones broke away. Forward momentum from her frantic struggle carried her over the top. Beyond, the terrain sloped downward in a steeper bank than expected. She lost her footing and tumbled head over heels to land with her well-padded and rounded backside in a tiny rivulet of icy water. A heady aroma of peat filled her nostrils. Sam staggered to her feet, the light blue denim of her jeans darkened by muddy run-off from the ditch. An all-consuming dread caused her heart to pound. She twisted to gaze back up at the dry stone wall. Somewhere beyond it, The Entity approached.

Stabbing bolts of rain fired down from the

blackening firmament. Hard and chill, the precipitation bore all the hallmarks of hail, without producing any physical evidence of stones. Samantha ran, her medium-height hourglass figure out of place and character in that wild environment. Out of place to any regular viewer witnessing the scene. But there was only one witness, and it didn't care one jot for the oddity of circumstance.

Bedraggled locks of hair clung to the cheeks of the young woman's round face. She slipped and stumbled, trying to keep her footing. How could she run fast enough to escape this pursuer in an environment almost bent on thwarting her flight from peril? Whatever it was - that indistinct, formless shadow behind - nothing appeared to interfere with its single-minded purpose. It was after her and no-one would come to the rescue.

An inorganic shape faded into view from the billowing fog bank, interrupted by angled sheets of rain. Straight lines spoke of human intervention. A solitary act of defiance, erected to taunt the relentless dominion of nature in a place few people ever set foot. It was a rough stone livestock shed of some description. Samantha pressed forward through the stinging, blinding downpour, hands sweeping from side to side in a vain attempt to part the shiver-inducing veil. A simple crossbeam held the two-storey wooden double door fast from the outside, resting on wrought iron brackets mounted to the external oak frame. She attempted to lift the brace free. It didn't budge. All about the wind picked up like a whirling funnel. With it, an overwhelming dark foreboding conveyed a subliminal message that every route of escape had now been closed. Samantha squatted to set her left shoulder beneath the beam. She thrust herself upward with as much force as she dared: sufficient to dislodge the barrier, but not so much as to dislocate the joint or otherwise injure herself. A jarring shudder shook her bones, but the beam shifted. She tugged one door part way open, enough to squeeze through. Her shivering hands dragged the removed crossbeam along behind. It slid like a rigid snake slithering out of sight. The door closed again.

Inside, Samantha hoisted the beam onto two matching interior brackets, barring access. The effort drained what little of her strength remained. She sank down to rest on a dirty straw floor. Her eyes adjusted to scant ambient light that crept in from the odd crack and crevice. The structure comprised some rough, empty pens reeking of old manure, plus a rickety ladder to a hayloft mezzanine used for animal feed. Despite its ramshackle appearance, the building seemed sound enough. Rain hammered on the roof like a belligerent bailiff seeking to evict an occupant. But not a single drop of moisture leaked onto the panting woman from the well-constructed and installed shingles above. Samantha strained to listen. Her mind sought to filter out any other sounds above the din, as if she were a prospector panning for gold. No treasure did she seek; just the ominous rage-filled screams of that malevolent pursuer. If The Entity had no physical form, would the door, walls and roof of this structure even give it pause?

An ear-splitting thunderclap resonated overhead. The sound of rain ceased, as if God had got out the shower and turned off the water supply in an instant. Samantha listened. No sound, not even a whisper. But something drew near. Fine hairs rose on the back of her neck. The woman scrabbled forward on hands and knees, putting some distance between herself and the doorway. The ground vibrated beneath her palms. Its intensity grew, sending shock waves in a rising cascade from floor to ceiling. Within a minute, the entire livestock shed began to rumble and rock. Roof beams splintered. Samantha crossed arms to shield her head as the weighty supports caved in upon her.

Samantha Riley sat up in bed with a gasp. The entire room of her tiny rented attic studio flat shook like a leaf. If this had been another in a recent series of nightmares with a similar theme, she must still be asleep. From the floor below, a woman screamed and a baby wailed in fear. Shampoo and conditioner bottles clattered into the bathtub of Samantha's cramped washroom next door. Glasses tinkled in the cupboards of the vinyl-floored kitchenette occupying one corner of her carpeted living/bedroom. The items formed a chorus. They serenaded in the manner of vibrating tuning forks of the same frequency that resonate in unison. An unshaded, dusty light bulb hanging from what had once been a pretty plaster Victorian ceiling rose, swung like a pendulum. Samantha gripped the sides of the sofa bed mattress with intense pressure. She felt like her fingernails might sink into the material at any moment. The trembling eased and stilled. Her glassware ceased its tremulous soundtrack. The light bulb swung a few more times and slowed to a rest. But the baby wailed on. Its terrified mother attempted to still the outburst with unconvincing vocal assurances that all was well.

Samantha let out a sigh and noticed her clenched fists. She released the mattress and slid out of bed. There wasn't much space to stand in the attic studio. The slope of the roof meant anyone over six foot could only remain erect beneath the plaster rose in a narrow, level patch of false ceiling that ran the entire length of the flat. At five-and-a-half feet tall, Samantha had a few more options, though she still hit her head from time to time. The principal room was dual aspect, courtesy of dormer windows front and back: One above the kitchenette sink that overlooked a small park four storeys below; the other in the main living area facing the road of similar, tall, whitewashed multi-occupancy terraced seaside villas. She pulled open a thin, grubby curtain drawn across the front dormer. Down on the pavement, a growing assembly of residents spilled out onto the street, squinting at the early morning sunlight. All about, fallen clay roof tiles lay scattered in broken heaps. Vehicles parked on the road flashed indicator lights. Their car alarms rose into a cacophony that sounded weedy compared to the previous, rumbling din. Many of the inquisitive crowd still wore nightclothes and bathrobes. They jostled about, some with cups of tea in hand, in what you could only describe as a very British response to a shocking incident.

A pair of light feet thudded up the stairs to the flat across the hall. Samantha eased open her door enough to take a peek. A slim woman of Slavic appearance with short, tidy cropped black hair, inserted a key into her own door.

Samantha stuck her head further out. "Lena?"

The neighbour jumped and span. "Samantha. You scared me." She slapped one palm against the side of her face. "I must still be shaking from the tremors." An uncertain half smile crinkled the otherwise smooth face of the thirty-year-old Polish shop worker. "A little like the building."

Samantha wrinkled her nose. "What's going on?"

"Earthquake. It woke you, yes?"

"It scared the shit out of me. Earthquake? Are you kidding? In Folkestone?"

"We have them sometimes. Rarely. This wasn't as bad as the last one."

"Shit. I thought I was moving to the south-east coast of England, not flippin' California."

Lena took a step forward. "Are you okay? Not hurt or anything?" Her Polish accent was thick and pronounced.

Samantha shook her head. "I'm fine. A little startled, that's all."

The Pole stopped and retraced her steps. "That's a relief." She indicated her flat. "I must clean up mess inside. Not good." Lena's English grammar was also a little short of smooth, but Samantha had experienced no problems with her neighbour since moving in. At the rock bottom rent she was paying for digs of such questionable quality, things could have been a lot worse.

"Okay. Thanks for filling me in. Have a good day."

"You too. Bye now." Lena disappeared behind her door.

Samantha trudged into her windowless bathroom and pulled a light cord. A mandatory extractor fan clattered to life. Whether it vented air outside with any success was questionable. But it made such a loud and annoying noise that you forgot to worry about it. The woman fished her haircare products out of the bath and took a long, hard look at her reflection in the cabinet mirror. "If I don't get some normality back into my life soon, I'll look eighty before I reach my next birthday." She knew it was a stupid exaggeration, spoken to nobody in particular. Right at that moment though, Samantha Riley needed some gentle humour to calm the emotional storm that continued to rock her soul.

*   *   *

It was lunchtime before Samantha ventured from the flat into the outside world. After a shower, oatmeal, coffee and more self-assuring soliloquy, she had settled down at her battered laptop computer. The morning passed in the attic with a mixture of data quality checking she did on a piecework basis for an agency and studying the location of her (non-work related) afternoon appointment on an Internet map. About an hour before she needed to leave for that. Samantha always required a breath of fresh air before one of those appointments. Time, space and peace to get her head together. A necessary ritual before confronting whatever disturbance was on the cards this time. It had only been a few months since she fell into her new, bizarre lifestyle, but it got no easier. At least, there were no signs of that happening.

It was a glorious day in early May. A spacious blue sky hung dotted with several wisps of cloud, like blobs of cotton wool. A mere puff of wind disturbed the serenity. Out in the Channel, enough breeze ruffled the water to whip up a few white horses. The world's busiest shipping lane almost felt inviting, as it adopted the colour of the heavens. Twenty-two miles across the nation's natural moat, the French coast lay clear and visible. Samantha stood on The Leas near the Step Short Memorial Arch; a fourteen metre high commemorative stainless steel structure to honour First World War soldiers who once embarked for battle on ships in the harbour below. She took a lungful of the fresh, salty air and closed her eyes. A series of circular breathing exercises followed, to enhance relaxation. Agitation from her tense dream and shocking awakening during the morning's seismic tremor, lifted from her shoulders. Samantha swallowed, opened her eyes and proceeded west along the popular cliff promenade. A chubby, red-haired girl ambled past in the opposite direction, muffin top spilling over some shredded jeans. She was lost in whatever soundtrack blared from the earphones of her digital media player. Samantha smiled at the red T-shirt she wore, stretched tight across a bloated chest. It bore a crown and some white text in a parody of the popular *'Keep Calm and Carry On'* World War 2 slogan produced by the British government. Here the message read: *'Keep Calm and Eat Chocolate.'* Its wearer appeared to have taken that advice to heart. Samantha licked her lips. She could definitely go for a choccy bar right now, but the delicious little blighters always went straight to her hips. She attempted to distract herself from calorific mental images with visions of her father reciting *'and lead us not into temptation'* from the Lord's Prayer. *Not Dad. I can't be dragging thoughts of him up now. That's certain to screw my focus this afternoon.* Peace slipped away and her neck muscles tightened. Now she needed a distraction from her distraction. *Wonder if I should design my own parody shirt? I could replace the crown with a ghost and write 'Keep Calm and Cross Over.' Yuck, no. How flippant would I look then? Come on, Sam, pull yourself together.*

Ahead, a slim, elderly woman with neat permed hair stood near the entrance to the Leas Cliff Hall. Her elegant dress caused Samantha to check event posters outside the doors. There were no indications of a vintage dance in progress. The old lady touched her face and mouth with shaky fingers and bit her lip. A young couple leaned against the railings and scanned across the shimmering expanse of water. The man pulled his partner close for a full-on kiss, their busy tongues leaving little to the imagination. The elderly lady straightened her clothing and stomped up to tap them on the shoulder. Both smooching lovers ignored her. Samantha drew nearer and perched on one of several wooden benches nearby that faced out to sea. Across the road behind, more whitewashed terraced villas had been built to take full advantage of the view with five storeys.

"Excuse me," the old woman said.

No response.

"Excuse me. Would you mind not doing that in public?"

Still no acknowledgement.

The woman stepped back as the couple linked arms and strode off. She huffed to herself, loud enough for the bench witness to catch. "How rude."

Samantha watched her with unblinking eyes. She looked a charming lady who reminded Samantha a little of her late grandmother. Were it not for the modest legacy Nana had left her, she'd have to find steadier employment to pay the rent sometimes, even in her dingy dive of a flat. Agency data quality jobs didn't always meet expenses. That was the problem with piecework: feast and famine. You never knew which to expect in any given month. But it gave her the freedom to pursue other important aspects of her alternative lifestyle. They didn't pay much either. Those avenues might be profitable, but Samantha would never brook invoicing people for use of her unwanted 'gift.' As she observed the old lady attempt to flag down a passing gentleman to ask the time (and get ignored again), that gift set alarm bells ringing at the core of her inner being.

The pensioner sighed and turned to gaze at the young woman watching her. Samantha gave the old dear a gentle smile and patted the bench seat. The lady approached.

"Hello Miss, would you happen to have the time about you?" She reached the bench.

Samantha pulled out her phone and lit up the screen. "It's five past one." She had a handle on the time long before reaching for the device. Samantha used the action as a test to gauge the woman's facial expression. Her gift had never been wrong yet, but she needed to be sure.

Confusion and agitation flashed between the mature, half-lidded, wrinkled eyes. "Why does everybody have those things? I don't remember hearing about them."

Samantha sat back on the bench. "Would you like to sit down and rest awhile?"

The old woman fidgeted. "I don't feel tired. I used to feel tired all the time. Isn't that strange? But it would be nice to talk with someone. Thank you." She sat alongside Samantha, who caught a pleasant, subtle aroma of lavender water. "Don't get old, my dear. Everybody appears to ignore you when you're old." She rested a handbag on her knees and clasped the top with both hands. "Some days I almost feel invisible. The people who stop to chat, never hang around long. I can't recall if I've ever met any of them more than once."

Samantha watched her. "Do they always seem like they're heading off somewhere?"

The woman's face brightened. "Exactly. And why is everybody in such a rush now? I never noticed it before. What's happening to Folkestone? Where have all the English people gone?"

Samantha bit her lip. "Do you come to The Leas often?"

"Yes. I like a stroll, no matter the weather."

"Do you live nearby?"

The old face darkened. Cracked lips pulled back over yellowed teeth. "I can't remember. I hit my head. I get confused sometimes." She reached up to touch the rear of her skull.

Samantha noticed a dark area at the base, heavy with bruising. "What's the last thing you recall?"

"I was on my way back from voting in the general election. I'm a Conservative, you know. I've high hopes for the new leader, Mr Eden."

"Do you remember the date?"

"Of course." She stiffened and straightened. "I've had the date on my calendar ever since it was confirmed. 26th May."

"What year?"

The lady gawped. "What a silly question. This year, of course. 1955."

"I see. What happened next?"

"I tripped, or fell..." She rubbed her brow. "My head banged against a kerb. People gathered round. Someone ran for help. Things are a blur after that. It must have been nothing, because here I am. I come here every day. Always have. The Leas Cliff Hall is familiar to me. It still looks the same. But the cars and people..."

"Do you have any family?"

The old lady's head drooped. "No. Jim and I never had children. All my siblings have passed on. Jim died last year. I'm Ethel."

"Samantha. Pleased to meet you." She offered her hand, bracing for the inevitable jolt that would follow. The lady took hold and her mouth dropped open. A tingling sensation like static electricity flowed between them. Samantha locked her gaze onto the trembling spirit. "It's okay, Ethel. I realise it's a shock. I'm here to help you."

The old lady's eyes widened. "I died. When my head hit the kerb, I died. Why wasn't I aware?"

"Sometimes people don't realise. You have so much life in you, it's not surprising. But that life belongs elsewhere now."

"How long has it been?"

"Since 26th May 1955? Almost sixty-four years."

Ethel shook her head. "Sixty-four years. So much wasted time."

Samantha turned to glimpse the horizon. A flash of light appeared like the sun rising above the sea. She smiled to herself. The kind of smile you make after turning a corner and catching sight of something that reminds you of home. "No wasted time, Ethel. Not for you. Time doesn't exist where you're going. Events don't occur in a sequenced order. Years on earth have little bearing there."

Confusion returned to the pensioner's face. "But how will I understa-"

"Don't worry. It blows your mind trying to fathom it here. Everything will make sense when you arrive, I promise. All the answers you seek will come to you."

"How can you be sure?"

The light grew brighter but shone unnoticed by the occasional passers-by, pointing and smirking at Samantha with their companions. Samantha realised she must look like a madwoman, talking to herself. All part of the deal with her gift. She turned to Ethel, her voice flat. "Because I've been there. Been there and come back again."

"Why didn't you stay?"

Samantha's eyes reddened and watered. "I don't know. Look, someone is waiting for you." She diverted Ethel's attention with her left hand, pointing to the growing and approaching light.

Ethel jumped to her feet and clapped both hands together. "Jim." She moved with the agility of a young maiden; a spring in her step. Running and skipping, Ethel raced into the radiant brilliance to embrace the beautiful figure of a tall, shining man.

As the light faded Samantha watched Ethel turn, her face smoothing to resemble how she might have looked around thirty years of age or less. One grateful and contented smile shone back towards the young woman on the bench. And then The Leas returned to its ordinary self once more.

A man raced over to grab the arm of a wayward female toddler, on her way to study the curious blonde sitting on the bench. He scooped the child into his arms and handed her to his wife. A too-loud whisper betrayed his assessment. "Another one on drugs."

Samantha remained sitting on the bench a further twenty minutes, staring out at the bobbing waves. The encounter had drained her energy. They always did. That was the last thing she needed before her upcoming appointment. *So much for getting rested and 'in the zone.' Crap, I'll be knackered by nightfall. I hope I have no more nightmares about that shadowy thing.* She rose, turned and headed off back to the flat.

*   *   *

Samantha turned left off Valley Road in the picturesque village of Barham. Her black Ford Ka climbed deserted, single-track roads through isolated high valleys. She made a hard right at a crossroads to follow Covet Lane toward Westwood. A thick, ancient woodland ran along the offside, while an undulating field on the left sloped up to another ridge-top bank of trees.

A few minutes later the car slowed to a halt at the stone gateposts of a long driveway bearing the sign *'Westwood Dell.'* Several hundred yards beyond, stood a timber-framed hall house that must have been built by a Yeoman around the 15th century. It sat in two acres of meadow, surrounded on three sides by hilly woodland and a fence bordering the road on the fourth. Samantha put her car back into gear and rolled down the drive. A new, wooden triple car port stood to the left of the principal structure. A top of the range red Audi estate and brand new green Aston Martin filled two of the three bays. For the briefest of moments, the young woman wondered whether she ought to rethink her zero invoice policy. These people were minted, and no mistake. The Ka stopped in a turning spot to one side of the exquisite property. Samantha unfastened her seatbelt and took a long breath. There were no sensory indicators or alarms going off inside. All was calmness and serenity.

"Hello?" A woman in her late thirties called from a thick, oak-framed doorway. She fiddled with a dark brown, big French Braid, teasing the end strands between nervous fingers.

Samantha realised she'd lowered her passenger window to allow a through-draught. She turned the key back in the ignition and raised the powered glass pane, before climbing out of the car. "Mrs Walker?"

The verbal address caused the woman to drop her hair and advance down the front path. "You must be Samantha Riley." A young girl of five or six, ran from the front door to clutch onto her mother's legs. The woman placed a hesitant hand on her head. "Easy, Emily. This nice lady is here to help."

The girl pouted her down-turned mouth and gazed straight up. "Will she make the bad lady leave?"

"Yes, darling. I hope so." The mother turned her attention back to the new arrival. "As you can see, the disturbances have had a profound effect on our daughter."

Samantha nodded. "Your e-mail mentioned as much. And they've been getting worse?"

"Yes. More frequent and pronounced." She shifted on the spot from foot to foot, Emily still clamped onto one of her legs. "To be honest, you're not the first person we've had in to resolve this." She grimaced. "My husband wants to speak with you before we get started. He's particular about things, even though a friend of a friend recommended you. Shall we?" She motioned towards the house.

"Lead on." Samantha followed them inside with nonchalant steps. It didn't matter where in the paranormal pecking order her services fell. This was neither a business nor an ego-trip for her.

Westwood Dell had been fitted out like an interior design magazine spread. Flagstone and polished wooden floors, high-priced triple-glazed windows (custom made to blend with the structure), and a top-flight audio system with speakers connected to every room. Those were just some features. Samantha fidgeted. The place was so perfect it made her feel uncomfortable. She gazed around from floor to ceiling. *God, the flat will seem like even more of a shit-hole after this.* Her eyes fell upon a modern extension with plate glass, bi-fold doors that opened the rear of the property into a giant garden room. *How did they get permission for that eyesore? This place has got to be listed. I hate it when people dick around with historic buildings to make them contemporary.*

"Admiring the new additions?" A tall, thin-haired man about forty-two, wandered through a doorway clutching a scotch on the rocks in a crystal tumbler. He stopped and jangled his ice cube against the glass.

"Something like that." Samantha's voice was soft.

Mrs Walker got Emily seated on a long, low, blue Alcantara corner sofa. She rose to join her husband. "This is Samantha Riley, the-"

"Psychic. I guessed that." The man looked her up and down. "Martin Walker." He held fast to his drink and didn't offer a hand in greeting. "How long have you been doing this err... work?"

Samantha remained neutral of posture and body language. "A few months. It's not work and I don't consider myself a psychic. Not in the traditional sense."

"Oh, how so?"

"My focus centres on communicating with and helping earthbound spirits to cross over. Nothing more. I don't do readings or deliver messages from the dead. No parlour tricks." She caught his raising eyebrow. "And no charge."

Martin sipped his drink and loosened his erect frame. "I was going to ask about that. Polly here tells me you don't invoice anyone for your services. Sounds like a shoddy way to make a living."

Samantha allowed her eyes to sweep across the eye-wateringly expensive interior. "I'm sure it does."

Martin shrugged. "Still, I'm not complaining if it's free."

His wife tugged his arm. "It's not free. Samantha asks her clients to consider donating an amount that is comfortable for them."

Martin snorted. "Ever had anyone who found a quid comfortable? Doubt it would cover your petrol cost home. Where is it you live again, Folkestone?"

Samantha swallowed and tried not to reveal the gritted teeth behind her lips. "I've recently moved to Folkestone, yes."

The man smirked. "Where are you from originally?"

"Bath."

"A Somerset girl? Bath's a fine city. Beautiful architecture. Amazing Regency properties. Worth a fortune, some of them."

Samantha nodded. "Yes, our family live in one."

Martin jerked his head back and blinked. "Well Folkestone must have been a shock to the system. Whyever did you move away?"

The young woman sighed. "It's a long and personal story."

Polly played with her hair once more. "Martin's an architect."

Samantha clocked the ugly bi-fold doors in their out-of-place setting again. "I'd never have guessed. So, how can I help you today? Assuming you still *want* my help, that is?"

Emily swept a cushion off the sofa and clutched it to her chest. Her voice grew into a moaning wail. "Mummy, she's coming. She's on the stairs and she's angry."

Polly hastened to her daughter's side. "Now then, Emily, don't worry. Daddy and I are here. So is Samantha."

The piped media speakers crackled. Martin twisted

and bent over to examine his Hi-Fi system. "That's odd. The power's off."

A rapid series of bangs echoed across the room. Each plate glass panel of the bi-fold doors shuddered. Hairline cracks split the middle of every pane, giving an impression that the number of overall glass sheets had doubled. Martin dropped his tumbler, which shattered on the polished oak flooring. The speakers crackled again. A faint, faraway, disembodied female voice slurred from each device. "M-Y c-h-i-l-d."

Samantha's heart pumped. Butterflies filled her tummy. The familiar sense of a crackling electrical charge coursed through her limbs.

A plump, matronly figure of a woman in her sixties wearing an apron, strode out of the hallway. Round, black, thick-rimmed spectacles adorned her face, which appeared contorted with rage. She stormed past Martin - a man oblivious to her presence - and grabbed hold of Emily's right hand. Polly saw her daughter's arm fly up. She reached around the child's waist to restrain her. The podgy, bespectacled woman slapped the mother across her face. A crack of impact was plain for all to hear. Polly tumbled off the sofa and wailed. The spirit dragged Emily across the polished wooden floor. The child screamed and cried. She bumped up every stair, pulled by a force unseen to all except Emily and the visitor to Westwood Dell.

Martin knelt at his wife's side. Anger and frustration crumpled his usual facial expression of self-satisfaction and disdain. His eyes met Samantha's. "Can't you do something?"

The young woman remained silent, rotated on the spot and walked with calm steps toward the staircase. A door slammed at the far end of the upstairs hallway. Samantha ascended the stairs and wandered along the landing. The door handle felt ice cold to the touch as Samantha twisted it open. Condensation dampened her palm. She stepped into the child's bedroom and closed the door behind her with a gentle click.

Martin and Polly Walker sat clutching one another on the sofa an hour later, when Samantha Riley descended the stairs holding young Emily's hand. Polly jumped up and ran to meet them, her back stooped. "Oh my God." She bent down, hugged and kissed her daughter, then looked up at the quiet blonde. "Is she okay? Did it hurt her?"

"Emily's fine." Samantha glanced back up the stairs.

Martin joined them in the hallway with hesitant, stilted steps. "Has it gone? What was it?"

Samantha cringed at the term 'it' and pursed her lips for a second. "SHE was a farmer's wife who used to live here."

Martin noticed the emphasis in the young woman's voice. "What did SHE want with our daughter?"

"Maud had two sons, once upon a time. She always yearned for a daughter of her own, but never had one. Both her boys died at Waterloo. Neither had any children. Maud succumbed to grief a little after, but couldn't tear herself away from this place."

Martin coughed. "Waterloo? You mean the Battle of

Waterloo?"

"The same."

"And she's been hanging around here for two hundred odd years or more?"

"To her, it seemed like yesterday."

"But she's gone now?"

Samantha smiled. A faraway look glistened in her blue eyes. "Yes, she's gone. Reunited with her loved ones."

Polly stood to embrace the young woman. "Thank you. I can't tell you what this means to us."

Martin strutted into another room and re-appeared clutching his cheque book and a pen. "Now then, Miss Riley. You'll forgive me if I sounded sceptical earlier. We've had all manner of cranks try to help and fail, as I'm sure you appreciate. But, you name your price and I'll pay it."

Samantha gulped. It was an offer she could ill afford to refuse in the practical scheme of things. "I can't, I'm afraid."

Martin frowned. "Why not? You've provided an excellent service and should be rewarded."

"Something happened to me that set this gift in motion. Please don't ask me to explain, but I can't charge you for it. I'd appreciate anything you want to give as a '*thank you*.' But I'd take nothing at all and walk away content."

"I'd recommend you keep that last line to yourself. Okay, well it's no way to run a business, but I respect your integrity." The man rested his cheque book on a table and scribbled away with the pen. "Made out to

Samantha Riley?"

Samantha nodded. "Thank you."

Polly Walker looked over her husband's shoulder and hummed in approval.

Martin tore off the cheque and passed it across. Samantha took it and almost squealed at the four figure sum. "Are you sure?"

Polly led her by the arm to the door. "Yes, we're sure. Thank you for coming out, Samantha." She turned to her daughter. "Say goodbye, Emily."

Emily bounced over and flung her arms around the young woman's waist.

Samantha rubbed her hair. "She didn't mean to hurt you, Emily. Maud was frustrated, angry and confused." She shifted her gaze to the parents. "If it's any consolation, she loved your daughter - in a way. Even if it *was* borne out of an unrequited desire that followed her beyond the grave. I know these spirits seem like an *'it,'* because most people can't see them. But they're folk like you and I, minus the physical vessel we navigate this world in."

Martin tucked his pen into a pocket. "Have you ever met another kind? Something dark or inhuman?"

"No. But I've heard a few stories. Nothing like that was present here. You can enjoy your home now in peace."

Martin frowned. "Yeah. As soon as I write another cheque to replace those windows."

Samantha licked her lips to hide the grin. "Goodbye."

The drive back to Folkestone was peaceful to begin with. Samantha wasn't as tired as she'd expected. Watching Maud step into the light - released of her burdens - had invigorated the Somerset girl with renewed energy. She didn't know why she hadn't been afraid to enter Emily's bedroom. Was it because she could see that which was unseen by so many? Or did she simply appreciate how the spirits she engaged with were as ordinary as anybody else? There was love in there somewhere. Her gift was all about love, when you got right down to it. She loved helping others cross over. Helping them journey to a place she yearned for every moment of every day. *Oh to be back there again.*

The clear sky darkened within minutes. There was no rain in the forecast, but black clouds swarmed out of nowhere. A sudden, ominous, thick headache caused Samantha to pull over into a lay-by and clutch her skull. Fear welled up inside. The sensation was like that of a lone tree on a plain during a thunderstorm, waiting for inevitable lightning to strike. Ten minutes or more passed until the sky cleared and she could continue home.

2

The Rocking Horse

ROSALIND LAYTON, 1815.

"Have you finished your studies, Rosalind?" Barbara Layton tweaked an eyebrow as she sat at her dressing-table mirror.

A slim, ten-year-old girl with long, dark auburn hair dashed past the open door on the landing. A second later she re-appeared; large, close-set hazel eyes edging round the elegant white painted door frame. Warm spring sunshine slanted through an extensive upstairs Regency bay window, spilling onto the smart but modest green dress of the woman in the master bedroom.

The girl at the door bobbed on the spot. "Yes, Mama. I'm all done for the day. Governess Andrews says I can go out to play now."

"Very good. Don't overexert yourself. Your father should be home from London this evening. I'm sure he'd like to find you wakeful when he comes."

"Won't he feel tired himself?"

Barbara picked up a silver hairbrush and began attending to her copious raven locks. "Yes, I'm sure he will. But you know how he loves to have you meet him after a few days away."

A broad smile spread across the child's face.

Her mother paused from brushing. In the mirror, an eager reflection from across the room strained at the leash to play. "What game are you at this afternoon?"

"I thought I'd see what cook's about first."

"Don't get in her way." Barbara raised a gentle index finger.

"I won't. Then when I've been to visit Ned in the stables, I'll ride Nellie round the kitchen garden and back through the arboretum."

"Have you fed Nellie today?"

"She had some oats for breakfast." The child reached up to pat an imaginary horse at her side. "Are you hungry, girl?"

Barbara pressed her lips together, eyes half-closed with amusement. "You'd better get that horse off the upstairs landing, before she leaves her 'calling card' on our expensive Persian rugs. Imagine what your father would say."

Rosalind giggled. "Yes Mama. We'll go now." She hitched one stockinged leg up, as if straddling the unseen animal. Once settled (but still standing with both feet on the floor) she smoothed down her white cotton walking dress and clicked her tongue. "Walk on, Nellie. Walk on." The girl 'trotted' a few feet to the top of the central atrium. Around its four walls, stairs descended in a series of right-angled flights of low risers. Sunshine flooded down from an impressive roof skylight near the servants landing on the floor above.

You could become giddy leaning over the railing to look up or down. Rosalind bashed her heels together as if spurring her mount onward. Down and round each flight she went, past oil paintings of family portraits and hunting scenes. They hung in elaborate, heavy gold frames from sky-blue walls adorned with decorative plaster flourishes. Once at the bottom of the staircase she turned left down the main hallway. At the far end, French doors opened onto a sweeping lawn interspersed with Cedar trees. Sheep grazed in a paddock beyond a ha-ha that gave those livestock the deceptive appearance of keeping a respectful distance from the impressive manor. Behind her at the other end, the floor to ceiling double doors of the main house entrance stood fast, as if awaiting the master's return. Rosalind took another left and ambled down spartan corridors sporting tiled floors and dark, functional paintwork without adornment. Steam wafted from a room set below ground level. The child crept up to the doorway and peeped round. A plump cook in white overalls stood with her back to the door, kneading bread on a sturdy wooden table. To the right, a solid black range pumped out heat, as meat stew simmered in a hefty copper pot resting on top. Cupboards lined the walls, and hedges were visible through some ground-level window panes above.

Cook whistled to herself, sturdy limbs putting her back into the work. One muscular arm lifted a wooden spoon to clang against an array of copper pots and pans hanging from the ceiling. Lost in her busy reverie, she struck a note and began to sing.

"Courage, boys, 'tis one to ten,
But we return all gentlemen,
While conquering colours we display,
Over the hills and far away."

Rosalind snickered and brought the singing to an abrupt halt.

Cook spun with an expression of faux menace that didn't quite match her rosy cheeks and cuddly figure. "What's this, a spy near my kitchen? A dratted Bonapartist and no mistake." She waved a rolling pin and patted it against the fingers of one hand like a cudgel.

Rosalind coughed. "I should say not. Only the King's loyal subjects here."

Cook put the utensil down and folded her arms. "Is that so? You'll be wanting to join in the chorus with me then."

The child beamed. She entered the room and took hold of two large, flour-encrusted hands offered to her. Together they whirled about the kitchen to continue the song.

"Over the Hills and O'er the Main,
To Flanders, Portugal and Spain,
King George commands and we'll obey,
Over the hills and far away."

Cook released the girl's hands to open a stoneware pot. "Here's a little treat to take with you. Don't let it spoil your dinner later, or I'll catch an ear-bashing from senior staff." She handed over a custard tart.

"Thank you, Cook."

"You're welcome. Off with you now, Missy. I've a pile of work to do before your father gets home."

Rosalind took a bite of the tart and wandered past the butler's office to open a thick-panelled door onto the rear yard. Across the cobbles, a white dovecote crested the roof line of the stables. The grandeur of their windows spoke volumes about the esteem in which the animals were held. The girl continued to munch on her cake as she reached the massive entrance. A familiar heady smell of manure and straw greeted her nostrils, sweetening the aroma of the bakery treat.

Inside, a middle-aged man in a worn grey jacket and trousers brushed down a large, black stallion. A dappled mare occupied the stall alongside, but the others in the building were empty. He looked up and adjusted a flat cap as the child entered.

Rosalind flicked the last crumbs from her fingers. "Apollo looks resplendent, Ned."

"Why thank-ee, Miss. He has come up a treat, if I say so myself." The man stepped back to admire his work. "Just your mother's mount to sort out now, before Lord Layton returns with the carriage."

The girl turned to study the empty stalls. "Do Apollo and Athena miss their friends while they're away?"

Ned lifted his cap and scratched his head. "Well I don't rightly know. They don't pine like dogs or anything. I reckon they enjoy being the centre of attention for a few days. I'll have my hands full all right when the others return. This is the first patch of sun we've had in a spell. The roads will be a quagmire."

Rosalind stood on tiptoe to peer at her mother's mare. "Papa says if I'm a good girl, he'll buy me a foal for my birthday. Will it be a lot more work for you?"

Ned's face spread into an almost toothless grin. "No, Miss. It will be fine to see you learn to ride. How's old Nellie bearing up?"

The girl mounted her imaginary horse again. "She's grand. We're off for a hack around the grounds."

Ned rubbed some scratchy stubble on his chin. "Well now, don't push her too hard."

Rosalind bounced and lifted pretend reins.

The stableman strode over and gave the invisible beast two sweeps of the brush. "Keep your hands together. It'll give you better control. Have fun."

"Thanks, Ned."

The man watched her skip away in a fantasy gallop. He chuckled to himself. "Aye but she's an angel, that one."

Off through the formal gardens of peonies and roses Rosalind rode. She skipped across the gravel drive, through the walled kitchen garden past beds of herbs and vegetables, plus grapes and other exotic fruit under glass. At last her feet came to a rest beyond two tall rhododendron bushes in the arboretum. A tree to one side had taken a lashing from wind in the recent rainstorms. One low branch hung split and now sagged in a swaying motion. The child stood for a while, watching the wooden beam bob in a gentle breeze. An idea shone behind her playful eyes. She strolled across to the branch and pushed it down with both hands. The wood had dried in the sun. It bore a faint scent of coniferous needles. When Rosalind let go, the limb sprang back and nodded again. She lifted her walking dress high so that only her petticoat would suffer any stain from the platform and mounted the branch. At first the motion was gentle and relaxed. With rising confidence, the child called, "Giddy up. Ha. Ha. Let's ride," and threw herself into the game with more vigour.

Her reverie ended with a crack. The wood split without warning, toppling the girl onto the ground. Her left ankle hit first, twisting and snapping. She lay on her chest upon a sharp bed of fragrant needles, fingers pressed into the earth. A cry of agony tore from her lungs.

Light footsteps hurried from the orangery. One of the upper housemaids ran to her side.

"Good heavens, Miss Rosalind. Whatever have you done?"

Rosalind pointed at her ankle, unable to form words of any coherence.

The maid crouched and put a hand on her shoulder. "You hold on now. I'll fetch your mother and one of the footmen."

"Home at last. It seems like an age." Cecil Layton

stepped down from his covered carriage beneath a starry sky.

The coachman twisted to look back across flickering lamps. "Yes Sir."

A well-presented man in his late forties strutted with crisp steps from the welcoming light of the open front doors of the house. "Welcome home, Sir."

"Ah, Manders. I trust all has been well at Bridechurch in my absence?" The man slicked back a centre-parted mop of brown hair.

Manders shifted on the spot and flinched.

Beyond the hallway, Barbara Layton appeared at the foot of the staircase. Her eyes locked onto her husband. She lifted her dress to hurry down the hall in an uncharacteristic and unladylike fashion. "Cecil. Oh my goodness, thank the Lord you're home at last."

Lord Layton dashed to meet her. Barbara all but fell into his arms, face strained.

"Barbara, what on earth's happened?"

"It's Rosalind. She fell from a tree and broke her ankle. Oh Cecil, she's been in such pain."

"Have you sent for Doctor McPherson?"

"Yes, yes, he left a half hour ago. He's set her ankle."

"Well that's something. What was she doing in a tree?"

"Playing horses. She was bouncing on a split branch that broke. Sally heard her scream and ran to investigate."

Cecil released his wife and shook his head, fighting to conceal a smile Barbara might not appreciate. "Playing horses. I might have guessed. All right then,

I'd better go up and see her."

* * *

Rain returned with a vengeance in the few weeks after Rosalind Layton broke her ankle. As usual, her father had been away working in London with his tea import business. The ten-year-old yearned for someone to invent long-distance methods of communication that would enable him to stay home and work. Could such a miracle ever happen?

One stormy evening, she sat studying her Latin Primer by lamplight at a small, round mahogany table next to her bedroom window. Sheets of rain and lightning took turns in distracting her from declensions and conjugations.

A commotion sounded on the stairs. Under normal circumstances, Rosalind would have been off like a shot to investigate. Now she sat immobile, waiting for her mother or one of the staff to bring whatever news had caused such excitement.

There was a knock at the door.

Rosalind closed her book. "Come in."

A head covered with a mop of brown hair and thick sideburns poked into the room.

The child's eyes lit up. "Papa, you're home again."

"Indeed, I am." Cecil Layton strode into the room with a mischievous gait. His wife followed, and now Rosalind could see Manders and Sally out in the hallway.

"What's going on, Papa? Mama?"

Barbara clasped her hands together. "Wait until you see."

Cecil bent forward and lifted his daughter up as if she weighed nothing at all. He carried her back towards the door. "While I was up in town, something followed me home." They crossed the threshold into the upstairs hallway. "If I'm not mistaken, it was last seen entering the nursery. Isn't that right, Manders?"

"I believe so, Sir," the butler replied.

Rosalind clutched onto her father, countenance a mixture of confusion and excitement. "What? What's in there?" Her eyes fell on the flushing housemaid. "Do you know, Sally?"

"Ooh, I'm sure his Lordship wants you to discover that for yourself, Miss Rosalind."

Manders leaned forward, one white-gloved hand twisting open the brass doorknob of the nursery. Inside, lamps were already alight.

Rosalind's mouth widened and fell open. In the middle of the room amidst her dolls and games stood a gorgeous, glossy white rocking horse. Its mane hung with real hair. Glass eyes gave an almost lifelike appearance to the face. Upon its back sat a sturdy leather saddle and stirrups. All the other items of tack had been reproduced and added with the greatest attention to detail.

"Oh Papa." They were the only words the child could manage.

Cecil grinned. "I know it's been a chore stuck inside, unable to walk about and not 'ride' Nellie. But I thought you could sit on this new companion and rock without too much trouble. Would you like to try?"

Rosalind nodded, her eyes never leaving the breathtaking toy.

Cecil eased her down into the saddle. The girl winced as her left ankle pressed against one stirrup. "Easy. Try not to put pressure on that side. If you keep your left foot free and hold tight to the reins, you shouldn't fall off."

Rosalind eased back and forth, ecstatic fingers stroking the soft, plush mane. "Oh Papa, she's perfect."

Barbara hooked a hand in the crook of her husband's arm, where it rested on his hip. "You'll have to think of a name for her."

"Geraldine," Rosalind said without hesitation.

Barbara placed her free hand at the base of her neck. "My my, that was fast. Don't you need to think about it awhile?"

The child shook her head and continued to rock. "No. She's Geraldine, aren't you girl? See Mama, she's nodding."

Barbara laughed at her daughter pointing to the swaying head of the wooden animal.

Rosalind closed her eyes and coughed.

Barbara frowned. "She's been doing that a lot, the last few days."

Cecil leaned closer and placed one hand on her forehead. "I can't detect any signs of fever. Has her bedroom window remained closed during the rain? Perhaps she has a cold?"

Rosalind coughed again, lapsing into an extended fit of wheezing and spluttering.

Barbara pulled a handkerchief from her pocket. "Easy Rosalind, you've got yourself too excited now. Doctor McPherson says you still need to rest." She placed the hankie in front of her daughter's mouth. When she pulled the linen item away, her face fell. A patch of crimson blood daubed the material.

*   *   *

Bridechurch staff lined up outside the house entrance. Their faces were not the usual ebullient array that went with serving such treasured masters as the Laytons. A horse-drawn hearse stood before the front doors. Two heavy black shires fitted with blinkers drew it, their manes set in sweeping ranges of ebony flights. Pall bearers carried a small coffin from the hallway to load into the fringed carriage. Behind, Cecil and Barbara Layton observed the last journey of their only child, eyes red with grief.

In the staff line-up, Ned removed his cap and bowed his head, the gardeners alongside. Cook and Sally consoled each other with as much decorum as they could manage. Manders wrestled between two opponents: showing grief and maintaining the professionalism of his office.

Doctor McPherson - an elderly, grey-haired gentleman with top hat, round glasses and kind face - emerged next to the grief-stricken couple. He inclined his head closer to Cecil. "Take heart that God called her while she was asleep. It's a small mercy, I know. But there are fouler ways for Consumption to separate body and soul."

From underneath the tree by the orangery where Rosalind Layton fell and broke her ankle, and unseen observer witnessed the proceedings.

She had awoken one morning feeling dazed and lost. Her ankle and chest no longer pained her. Since then, she kept running from person to person in the house, trying to make anyone listen. Why did they all ignore her? Weren't they pleased to see her fit and well again? Who was in the coffin and what upset Mother and Father so?

Day and night became a blur. She lost all sense of the passage of time. One afternoon the girl stood by her mother's bedroom door, where she always watched Mama brush her hair. Gone were the raven tresses, now replaced by thin white strands. An old woman appeared to sleep in the master bedroom. And where was her Papa? Did business keep him from home longer than before?

At times Rosalind became scared. There was only one safe refuge when the fears came: Geraldine. She would sit and rock on the beautiful wooden horse to calm herself. On a certain morning, one of the housemaids came in to dust and polish. She took one look at the moving toy, screamed and ran from the house, never to return. Life was strange now and Rosalind didn't understand it.

* * *

"It's got an unusual history, Bridechurch." A portly Victorian gentleman with a tight crimson waistcoat (echoing bloodshot cheeks) waved his silver-tipped cane around the ground floor atrium of the manor house.

"Do all the furnishings come with it?" A slender crone of a woman with hair pulled into a dense bun, pursed her white lips. She gazed up to the skylight two floors above.

"They do. The previous owners died with no progeny to inherit. Their staff remained in service until the end. Quite remarkable. Now then. Where would you like to start, Mrs Snellgrove?"

The crone elbowed her bored-looking drip of a husband in the stomach.

He pulled at his mustard-coloured jacket, snorted and gave a disinterested wave. "Wherever you like, Lavinia."

The woman nodded to the cantilevered staircase. "We'll begin with the family bedrooms if you please, Mr Burthwaite. I'd like to spend more time examining the downstairs living spaces, so we'll approach those last."

"As you wish." The estate agent swept his cane in a polite gesture. "After you."

On the upstairs landing, Lavinia Snellgrove caught sight of the large west-facing nursery, flooded with afternoon sunlight. She hurried past the railings and what had once been Rosalind Layton's bedroom. "George," she called to her husband. "Come and look at this. What a perfect space for a needlework room. It'll need some decorative changes to reflect the latest trends. But once we clear out all these stupid toys, it will be glorious."

Mr Burthwaite wiped the corners of his mouth with a gentleman's handkerchief, pleased at this positive whiff of a sale. "I take it you don't have any children, Mrs Snellgrove?"

Lavinia scowled. "Perish the thought. Children should be seen and not heard. Ideally, not even seen. I can't stand them. Now, can we visit the master bedroom please?"

"Of course. Right this way." Mr Burthwaite retraced his steps to the atrium landing.

As the tour dragged on, the visitors' voices floated away downstairs at last.

Meanwhile, the sound of a little girl singing to comfort herself, drifted from the nursery.

"Over the Hills and O'er the Main,
To Flanders, Portugal and Spain,
King George commands and we'll obey,
Over the hills and far away."

In the middle of the playroom, a white wooden horse gently rocked by itself.

3

No Solution

ANDREW MILES, 2016.

"Mr Miles? Your wife is up and asking for you." A short, dark-skinned Ghanaian nurse with a warm and disarming smile approached.

Andrew Miles straightened from where he had leaned over the ward reception counter to seek attention. "Thank you, Nurse. How is she today?" He touched clumps of receding black hair, flecked with silver, clustered around his temples. Many chins wobbled beneath a plump face and faint five o'clock shadow. He fixed a pair of beady brown eyes - bulging beneath bushy brows - on the kindly little woman.

"She's slept most of the day. When I told her the time, Mrs Miles sent me to see if you'd arrived yet."

"Sounds like my Sharon." The forty-year-old man set off down the corridor with the nurse at his side. His plump and short stature added a slight waddle to those steps. He winced at a wall poster warning about the dangers of obesity. It featured a pile of chips, kebabs and several pints of beer. All that looked like a good and easy night in to Andrew, rather than the harbinger of doom. He coughed. "How are you settling in down here at Medway Maritime?"

The nurse nodded. "Very well, thank you. It's nice to be out of London. Your wife told me all kinds of places I should visit in the southeast."

"No surprise. She was office manager at a Tourist Information Bureau before she got sick. Is she well enough to take for a spin around the garden today?"

"I should think so."

They entered a private room on the Lawrence Ward.

"I've found Mr Miles for you." The nurse stood at the end of a bed, of which the top half stood raised.

Its occupant appeared so out of place in that setting. Despite a hospital nightgown and lack of make-up, she looked like a model in rude health. Big brown eyes shone from beneath a mop of layered, side-parted brown hair below shoulder level. White teeth and coral lips spread into a mischievous grin like some cartoon chipmunk.

Andrew's heart melted in an instant. "Hey love. How are you feeling?" He bent forward to kiss his wife.

"A lot better if they'd ease off with the tests. I'm so weak, it's maddening." Sharon Miles shifted as the nurse plumped her pillows.

The Ghanaian glanced at the window. "Mr Miles was wondering if you'd like to go outside?"

Sharon winked at Andrew, adopting a corny gangster accent. "Have you come to spring me, *Clyde*?"

Her husband joined in with the impression. "Not

today, *Bonnie*. We need a better plan."

The nurse appeared confused by the unfamiliar name tags, but sensed the healing presence of humour in their manner of conversation.

Sharon tilted her head to the nurse. "That would be lovely. But I don't think I can stand, Yvonne."

Yvonne clicked her tongue. "Don't you worry about a thing. I'll fetch a wheelchair. Mr Miles can push you around the garden in that."

"Oh Gawd, are you serious? You should see him try to parallel park his work van."

The nurse cackled and hissed to herself on the way out of the room.

Andrew pulled up a chair to the bedside.

Sharon studied him with soft eyes. "Thanks Andy. It'll be great to get out in the fresh air and sunlight. Flowers aren't allowed on the ward. I could use less clinical surroundings for a bit." She paused. "How's the latest client?"

"Nice enough. The bloke's a movie buff. He wants me to make and fit a range of shelves and cupboards in his new home cinema extension. His missus brews a decent cuppa. Great ginger nuts, too. The expensive variety. Not those rough supermarket own brand ones."

Sharon prodded him in the belly with a sharp fingernail. "How many have you had?"

Andrew diverted his gaze out the window. "Only one or two."

Sharon tickled him. "Yeah, yeah. At least one of us is putting on some weight. Mine keeps falling away like fat has become allergic to me or something. Don't think I'd recommend the cancer diet, even so. The 'after' picture from those 'before and after' shots is likely to be a box."

Andrew shot her a pained stare. "Don't say that. You'll get through this. You've always been a fighter."

Sharon reached forward to stroke one side of his face with the back of her hand. "Andy, we need to at least talk about the possibilities. The doctors said the prognosis didn't look promising."

Andrew pulled away and stood in a half turn. "No." He shook back a tear he'd earlier promised himself he wouldn't shed in front of his sick wife. "I can't lose you, Sharon. You're my everything. My life."

The nurse reappeared in the doorway, pushing a wheelchair.

Sharon swallowed hard and tugged at her husband's hand. "It does me good to hear you say things like that every once in a while. Now give me a cuddle, then it's time to play chauffeur. No handbrake turns though, okay?"

*   *   *

"Andy? The car's here, mate. Are you okay?" A tall, bald beefcake of a man knocked on the residential bathroom door with hesitant timidity.

A toilet roll holder rattled against the wall inside. Several trumpets of someone blowing their nose followed. Andrew Miles' muffled voice replied with a gargantuan, shaky effort. "I'll be out in a minute, Jake.

Let them know, would you?"

"Done. Look, I don't want to be a bastard and rush you, but some of those bloody crematoriums charge for even a ten minute over-run. Or so I read in the paper. It's a fucking conveyor in more ways than one. You want to give Shaz the best send-off possible, without rushing."

Silence.

Jake continued. "Hope it's not true here. Just saying." He waited a moment longer. When no response was forthcoming, the man shuffled downstairs to greet their limousine driver.

The crematorium chapel was rammed with attendees. Sharon Miles' coffin sat on the catafalque. A silver-framed photograph of her in happier times rested on top. In the picture, dark mascara traced those big brown eyes. A pair of her signature hoop earrings dangled from lobes either side of that classic, cheeky smile.

The celebrant adjusted the Windsor knot of his tie, where he stood at a lectern facing out across the throng. He scanned the front row, eyes falling on the puffy, reddened face of the grief-stricken husband. The official took a few breaths more. Space that might allow the poor fellow a moment longer to compose himself. He spoke into a microphone attached to a black, goose-neck holder. "Now I would like to invite Sharon's husband, Andrew, to come forward and say a few words. Andrew?"

Andrew pressed the sweaty palms of both hands against the tops of his knees. He rose without a word, head hot and pounding.

Beside him, Jake placed a supportive hand in the small of his back. He whispered as the bereaved man shuffled past. "Make her proud."

The celebrant stepped down to give the husband his place at the lectern.

For one agonising moment, Andrew stood fixed on the coffin. All the world and every person in that room seemed to fade away. He shut his eyes, then re-opened and lifted them to the white plaster ceiling. A subdued sobbing drifted towards him from the expectant crowd. He leaned against the lectern for support, eyes glazing over as he spoke.

"How do I cram my feelings about Sharon into words lasting a mere few minutes? I knew her for twenty of her thirty-six years on this earth." He waved one trembling hand at the photograph on the coffin. "As you can see from the picture - if you didn't already know - Sharon was an exquisite beauty. I was a young apprentice carpenter fixing up a shop window display, when a float drifted past carrying this sixteen-year-old carnival queen. She pulled a lambswool shawl close around her shoulders and gave me a huge smile and wave. That girl was the most beautiful thing I'd ever seen in my entire life. So much so, I struck my boss with a lump of two-by-four as I strained to watch the vehicle disappear."

A ripple of polite laughter, tinged with tears and blown noses, arose from the audience.

"I wasn't the chiselled Adonis you see before you today, back then."

More polite laughter.

"I was fatter and clumsier. What chance did I stand with a carnival queen? But I knew I had to meet her." He paused. "I won't bore you with the whole tale, but I did. And when I did, I found a young woman mature beyond her years. Someone who believed in me when I didn't even believe in myself." He swallowed. "All the local lads wanted to win that beauty, but she made a different choice." His voice cracked a little. "She chose me. Sharon had to scold me for asking her what on earth she'd been thinking. My girl was never fixated on the outward appearance, despite a face and figure no camera lens could resist."

A soft 'ah' murmured back this time.

"Everyone at work quipped that I must be holding her family to ransom or something. But her family became like my own. I'm especially grateful to my brother-in-law, Jake Baker, for his support today. He's always taken his wedding role as Best Man to be a lifetime commitment. Here at my parting from Sharon, he stands beside me still." Andrew stopped. He hesitated, tried to resist, then broke down into a heaving sob. His body rocked against the lectern, the wood gripped tight in his fingers.

Jake eased up from his seat and moved with fluid, cat-like steps to stand next to the weeping carpenter. His shiny, bald head leaned closer as he placed a mitt-like hand on each of the oscillating shoulders. Strong, banana fingers rubbed Andrew and guided him back to the front row.

The celebrant resumed his previous place, giving another respectful space before he spoke. "Would you all please rise for the committal song chosen by Sharon for her final farewell." Ushers removed the photograph as music played a melodious piano introduction over the chapel speakers. A singer's voice launched into a track called 'The Last Dance.' It had always been Sharon's favourite, despite her only being a child when the song came out. She discovered it later, and the song proved a love to last a lifetime. Curtains parted. The coffin rolled forward out of sight, accompanied by words that summed up the beautiful woman's fighting spirit. Words of hope about not giving up, when everything appears to have ended.

"How are you bearing up?" Jake joined Andrew at a rail overlooking the garden of remembrance, around twenty minutes later. Afternoon sunlight caused the well-manicured and watered lawn to shine like an emerald. All around the border beds, pink and yellow roses hung heavy with petals.

"I'm okay. Sorry about that in there, Jake. I just couldn-" His face screwed up again.

Jake held his gentle brother-in-law without flinching, as the podgy carpenter sobbed into his shoulder. "It's all right, Andy. No-one blames you. You loved Shaz with your whole heart. She chose well when she picked you. That's my sister, all over. God, I miss her too."

*   *   *

The dining room was quiet. The house was quiet. Somehow, the entire world was quiet. Grief, a sense of hopelessness and loss of control left Andrew Miles numb all over. He sat alone, staring at his half-eaten Sunday roast. Cooling gravy congealed into a sticky goo like engine sump oil. It clung to unevenly carved slices of beef, lumped without care amidst boiled carrots and cabbage, two Yorkshire puddings and a rough attempt at roast potatoes. Sharon had always fixed this meal to perfection. Her 'roasties' were crisp and even-coloured on the outside, yet soft and fluffy when you bit into them. Andrew's came out a mixture of dark and light patches (the ones that hadn't collapsed after he par-boiled them too long) and resembled odd miniature Friesian cows. In an attempt to make them taste reasonable, he added too much goose fat to the roasting tin. That and he had no clue how much was meant to go in, so opted for extra. Every window in the house now hung open, and his eyes smarted from the blinding smoke. He prodded one of the culinary disasters with a fork.

I'm amazed the fire brigade haven't run down the front path with an axe. Our neighbours must have taken one look at black clouds pouring out the windows and wondered if I was burning the joint down to finish myself off.

The last three words of that thought had been an almost constant companion in the weeks since Sharon's funeral: *finish myself off.* He vacillated from moment to moment over the merits and drawbacks of choosing such a path to end this mortal torment. Some days, every second became a gut-wrenching agony. On others - like today - he felt empty and dead inside. Why not be dead outside, too? Andrew let his cutlery clatter onto the plate and pushed it aside. He poured a sizable glass of Rioja from a half-empty bottle of the Spanish red. At first there came a long, savouring sip. The wine hung heavy on his palate with a musky finish of Tempranillo grapes.

It's all so bloody pointless. What does any of this mean? Sharon used to savour food and wine flavours. For what? A chemical reaction on a tongue now reduced to ash? Everything is transient. Why am I even bothering, without her here to share it?

He drained the glass with a careless slurp and re-filled it from the rest of the bottle. A light summer rain pattered against the window. Andrew left the half-eaten dinner alone and plodded over to a small stereo on the stripped pine sideboard. Blue neon lights flashed as he powered up the unit and inserted a well-used CD into the device. The piano strains of Sharon's favourite song struck up as they had that day at the crematorium. He leaned forward with one hand on the wood and his glass of red wine in the other. Andrew emptied the contents into his mouth, head thrown-back. Fruity liquid sloshed around and drained in a thick, alcoholic trickle down his throat. The man listened to the vocalist belting out those emotive lyrics again. He slammed the glass against the sideboard, causing its thin stem to shatter. Andrew sunk to his knees, allowed the bulb of the glass to fall and covered streaming eyes with one hand. Tears came in a flood but brought precious little relief from the vacant pit in his hollowed-out soul.

Later that afternoon the drizzle eased off. Grey clouds gave way to a pleasant brightness. After almost an hour slumped in a heap before the sideboard, Andrew had cleared away. The first traces of sun warmed his arms as he wiped down the draining board. He decided to get out of the house for a walk. The Sunday afternoon stroll was another tradition of their marriage. Andrew had read on-line that vitamin D from sunlight could boost your mood. Anything to raise his spirits even a notch was worth a shot. He'd read a lot of things in recent weeks. Almost every 'Near-Death Experience' blog and video he could find was ravenously consumed. Neither he nor Sharon had been strong churchgoers, but they lived by the general guiding principles of their ancestral faith. Now she was gone, Andrew needed to find some kind of reassurance that his wife was okay. How could such a vibrant life come to an abrupt end and then cease to be? No, he was sure there was something more. There had to be a continuation. Most of all, a growing desperation gnawed at his gut. He HAD to see her again. He MUST be with her, somewhere, somehow. Life without his soul-mate left the carpenter an empty husk of a man, devoid of power or purpose. The much-touted *'work will save you'* line hadn't helped either. Work was work.

He went out on a job, functioned on auto-pilot, and then came home. The only difference seemed to be the pretence that all was well, so as not to inconvenience or upset his clients. In emotional terms this felt like more outlay for less profit. How was that going to 'save' him?

Andrew slipped on a light jacket and stepped out into the street. A few minutes later he turned west down York Avenue, with Medway Maritime hospital on his left beyond a red brick wall. The thoroughfare formed a junction with Marlborough Road at Brompton Academy. He crossed near the hospital entrance, dropping an old shop receipt from his pocket into a black litter bin and taking the footpath alongside. At last he turned northwest across a high, green expanse of ground overlooking the ancient former ship-building town of Chatham. Ahead, the central Portland stone obelisk of the Great Lines Naval Memorial drew his focus. It rose surmounted by a copper sphere with four carved lions guarding the base. The central structure bore copper plates adorned with the names of Royal Navy sailors killed during The Great War. A surrounding wall was added as an extension to commemorate those lost during the Second World War. It had been a while since he last popped in for a visit. Andrew checked his watch. Four PM. The gates should remain open another hour.

"Good afternoon," he exchanged greetings with an elderly couple on their way out, as he crossed the semi-circular wall entrance. Sculpted statues of men in duffle coats and hats stood at various spots. Andrew hesitated, before heading along the right arm of the curved surrounding wall. As he ambled at a sedate pace, his eyes fell on some names of the fallen:

BALCOMBE A.J.
BARNARD L. A.
BARNES C.
BARNES F. A.
BARNES W. L.
BARTLEY T. J.
BATCHELOR D. W.
BAXTER J.
BEAN K. T.

What a waste; yet so precious and necessary. So many lives, each one leaving behind loved ones to soldier on without them. At that moment, life, death and the meaning behind any of it were concepts insurmountable to the tortured widower. "I can't do this anymore." He spun on his heel and marched back through the gate, shutting out a million racing thoughts.

Water gushed into the bath; the only sound in the otherwise silent Miles residence. Andrew wandered in from the landing, wearing only a pair of underpants. These he slid down and stuffed into a laundry bag hanging from a hook on the door. Next he leaned over the tub and tested the water by swishing it back and forth with his hands. The absurdity of those last two actions struck him. An ironic half-smile broke his vacant stare for the blink of an eye. Who would wash his underwear? What did it matter if the water in the bath was a comfortable temperature? Things were about to get uncomfortable for up to the next hour and a quarter. Unless he did it right.

A sharp, retractable work knife from his toolbox lay on the soap dish. At a mere six percent lethality and with high relative pain characteristics, cutting himself wasn't the smartest choice for a man at the end of his figurative rope. Being at the end of a literal rope was around ninety percent effective and took just seven minutes with a fraction of the pain. Somehow, Andrew didn't want to go down that route. Life after death wasn't the only thing he'd studied over the last few weeks. If the government had sought a report on suicide methods and statistics, the Medway carpenter could have delivered one by rote.

A bottle of vodka stood atop the toilet cistern. He'd already polished off the last half of another, before undressing. Was his head woolly from the alcohol, or grief and despair? Andrew didn't know. Right then, he didn't care. "Sharon." That single word whispered from dry, quivering lips. He reached for the vodka bottle and eased himself down into the tub. Steam rose from the scalding water. Unsure how long this would take, or if he might struggle with nerves at the last minute, Andrew had run the bath as hot as he dared. His resolve was strong, yet still the anxiety of it cooling quicker than the water caused him to take a long pull on the colourless spirit. Memories of blissful descriptions of the life beyond, wandered in and out of his foggy brain. Tales of boundless joy and reunited loved ones from those who had returned to earth, teased his anguished heart. Broken though it may be, his ticker still thudded with nerves at the thought of taking terminal action. He eased the pounding with another belt of vodka.

One shaking hand reached up to the soap dish. The razor-sharp blade glittered in a diffused ray of early evening sunlight through the frosted window. Andrew took one more swig. His breath blasted from both nostrils like a winded horse pawing the ground before a fresh gallop. The snorts increased in pace and frequency. He screwed his eyes tight and brought the blade down to press against his left wrist below the water line. "Agh," Andrew let out a desperate cry of pain and determination. The cold metal cutting tool crept up his arm, opening an artery lengthwise. Warm blood billowed in smoky clouds through the water. The agony of that incision fought with the emotional turmoil of his present mortal existence in some sickening internal rivalry.

Other images cavorted onto the stage of his memory from those NDE blogs and videos: Reports of those who witnessed successful suicide victims in the world beyond. Tales of them having to *go around again* as another person to learn what they should have received in their last life.

More thoughts arose of his early church upbringing: Sunday school stories of how suicide victims would go to hell.

What have I done? Andrew forced his eyes open to witness the full horror of the crimson lake in which he sat, and the gushing trauma wound that fed it. *I'll be separated from her for all eternity if I kill myself.* He gripped his wrist and lower forearm to stifle the flow. *I can't stop it. I'll die and lose Sharon forever. Help. I must get help.* Andrew fought against the pain and rolled over the top of the bath. His senses dulled and the world span. The desperate man crawled across the landing. Blood sprayed magnolia walls and spread like a blot across the beige carpet. The bedroom door was in sight. There was a phone by the bed. *An ambulance. I must get an ambulance.*

Andrew wasn't aware at what point the blackness came.

When the authorities kicked down the door a week later (after a concerned call from Jake Baker), they found the carpenter's naked and decomposing torso half-way across the bedroom floor. The house reeked with a pungent aroma to accompany that dramatic scene of gore. A snail trail of blood marked the last, heartbreaking physical journey of Andrew Miles.

* * *

There were no strong emotions that went with watching the house clearance people empty his home. Andrew Miles drifted from room to room in death, much as he had during the last few weeks of life:

aimless and dazed. Even watching Sharon's favourite dresses get loaded into the commercial vehicle outside, hardly provoked a response. She could no longer wear those clothes any more than he could put on his work overalls. Soon the building in which they had set up home as a happy couple, would be an empty shell. An apt metaphor for the hopelessness that transitioned out of the former carpenter's physical body, to haunt his frustrated spirit in the world beyond.

But what of the world beyond? He hadn't gone there. He remained on earth. Either that or Chatham was heaven, which seemed unlikely.

His first recollection post-mortem, was a sense of weightlessness. Free of that old physical shell, Andrew realised what an encumbrance it once proved to his real self. Senses were different, too. He didn't have a limited field of vision, dictated by eyes. Everything in every direction was visible at once, yet it all felt natural. There had been no tunnel of light. No throng of singing angels flocked to carry him away to pearly gates and bowls full of ambrosia. But there was no Sharon either. Some fears still clung to him, now that anxieties surrounding physical death had passed. They were the same fears that gave him enough strength to roll out of the bath.

What if I never see her again? What if I'm judged and can't be with her because of what I've done?

Somehow these grounded him like a tent peg on a guy rope, anchoring his spirit between realms. It seemed there was no way up and no way back. Yet with every eternal particle of his spiritual existence, he longed for her.

"Sharon."

4

Unwelcome Visitors

SAMANTHA RILEY, 2019.

As ever, the M25 lived up to its reputation as 'Britain's Largest Car Park.' Samantha pushed back into her car seat. One fed-up, stiffened hand pressed against her head, thumb digging into the flesh beneath her cheek. It was on warm days stuck in traffic like this, that she was glad to have bought a car with air conditioning. By the time she reached the turnoff for the M3 at junction twelve, Samantha thought to qualify as a master in the art of stop/start clutch control.

Ten minutes later traffic flow evened out, and the car picked up speed. She left the motorway at the A303. Off to her right, the famous, ancient standing megaliths of Stone Henge stuck out atop the rolling Wiltshire downland. Smaller, upright, indistinct objects shifted position. Squinting at the afternoon sunlight shining straight into her face, Samantha lowered her driver's visor halfway. The moving objects turned out to be the obligatory gaggle of tourists, performing a circuit of perimeter ropes at the monument. Beyond the historic site, a left-hand feeder lane at the next roundabout led to the southbound A360. This last stretch of road to where her sister lived, was always Samantha's favourite. The route flowed straight and undulating, with expansive views that dipped and rose.

Whenever someone asked where her big sister lived, Samantha always said 'Salisbury.' In reality, Rachel, her husband and two children resided in the delightful village of Middle Woodford. But since she'd tired of follow-up questions (trying to explain where that was) Sam's stock answer became 'Salisbury.' The picturesque cathedral city lay a little over four miles southeast, beyond Old Sarum, so it was a logical quick reply for the curious.

A directional sign announced 'The Woodfords' on the left up ahead. Samantha eased off the accelerator and indicated her intention to take the descending 'Church Bottom,' a lane connecting with one of several tiny villages nestled along the banks of the Wiltshire Avon. The road narrowed at a '30' sign. The woman slowed further, her tyres splashing in shallow run-off from the downs. Thick green hedges on either side gave way to a row of thatched and tiled cottages, before ending at a T-junction near white railings bordering the river. She hung a right and was soon rolling into the guest spot on the short driveway outside a characterful, converted agricultural building. Samantha switched off her ignition, raised the sun visor and sat in silence for a moment. She loved Rachel, but these occasional get-togethers could become fraught in no time at all, once the subject shifted to her unorthodox lifestyle. When you're having a catch-up with family, how do you avoid the inevitable question: *'So what have you been up to?'*

The white, glossy, painted front door swung wide. A five-year-old with bobbed blonde hair almost bounced down the front path. Samantha swung herself out of the Ford Ka and bent forward to embrace the delighted, squealing child.

"Auntie Sam, Auntie Sam, it's so exciting to see you," the girl giggled as Samantha lifted her to waist level and spun around.

"How's my favourite niece?" the woman gave her a squeeze.

"Aren't I your *only* niece?" the child blinked, as if about to discover she wasn't alone.

"So you are." Samantha caught sight of her sister strolling down the driveway, a boy toddler gripping tight to her hand. "Jane's sharp for five. How's young Adam?"

"Stumbling around and falling over every five minutes. No grazed knees today, but there are still a few hours until nightfall," the woman replied.

"Good job he goes to bed early then." Samantha let go of her niece.

The thirty-year-old mother stared at her younger sister with dark blue eyes. Her piercing gaze wasn't a patch on her sibling, but could still be difficult to read for strangers. Straight, pale-blonde, side-parted hair ran down to the base of her neck. A thin nose and flat mouth almost dissolved into a flawless, creamy complexion that suggested a need for greater exposure to sunlight. She hesitated without expression, then stepped forward to kiss her sister on the cheek. "It's good to see you, Sam."

"Likewise. How's John?"

"He'll be back from work in Salisbury soon. I've asked him to pick up fish and chips for supper on the way home." One eyebrow raised. "Oh, I hope that's okay? You must eat a lot of fish and chips down on the Kent coast."

Samantha smirked. "Only for a treat. I'm watching my pennies and my waistline."

Rachel swallowed and fidgeted. "Yes, well we'd better get you installed in the guest room before John arrives. I've got plates warming in the oven."

Samantha opened the boot and retrieved a small case. Jane tried to take it from her, much to the woman's amusement. "That's all right, darling. I've got it."

The child let go to chase a bumblebee in and out of rose borders on the front lawn. "I've drawn you a picture, Auntie Sam," she called, eyes never leaving the buzzing creature.

Rachel shook her head. "She's been a live-wire all day. Every time you come, Jane behaves like a coffee addict." They walked down the path.

Samantha compared the giggling, rambunctious five-year-old to the dour face of her sister. She resisted a pressing urge to point out it was nice someone here was pleased to see her. If she got out of this stay without a heated discussion or two, it would be a miracle. No sense getting things started before she'd even set foot in the house. She changed tack. "Have you heard from Mum?"

"Yes. I spoke to her on the phone this morning." Rachel stopped and eyed her sister for a moment. "We have a father too, Sam."

Samantha's face darkened. "Do we have to do this, Rach?"

Rachel sighed. "Mum sends her love. She told me to make sure you're eating properly. Not living on takeaways."

Samantha hauled her case over the front doorstep. "Mission accomplished. I couldn't afford that. Lots of fruit, veg and other produce in my diet these days. Even if it comes from the 'Reduced to Clear' bin at the supermarket. Did you know if you put eggs in water and they float, they're no longer fresh enough to eat? It might surprise you how little date labels mean in real terms."

Rachel shook her head. "Is that what your life has sunk to?"

"Sunk to? Rach, our grandparents did that kind of thing."

"In the war perhaps."

"No. People used their senses to tell if food was okay, way before then. Afterwards too, until we all delegated our common sense to massive grocery companies."

"At least you're getting a balanced diet. I can tell Mum that." She clicked her tongue. "You could tell her yourself if…"

"If Dad would let me speak to her?" Samantha huffed. "And so it starts. It might surprise you to learn

Mum called me a fortnight ago."

Rachel's face brightened. "That's marvellous. Have you extended an olive branch?"

Samantha folded her arms. "No. She snuck out of the house and spoke to me from a phone box. Mum can't call from the house, because Dad examines the itemised phone bill. He likes to check she hasn't been consorting with 'Satan's Daughter' and her debauched, evil ways."

"Now you're being unfair, Sam."

"Am I? You didn't hear him call me that, did you? And if you think I'm making up the phone call story, ask Mum yourself, okay? If I'm 'Satan's Daughter,' what does that make the religious bigot who supplied half my genes?"

Rachel noticed how her own daughter had gone quiet. The child stood next to Samantha on the doorstep, gazing up at her with a strained expression. "I don't want to fight, Sam."

"Good, that makes two of us." Samantha squinted at her sister and rubbed the little girl's hair.

Rachel reached down to toy with a small silver cross fastened about her neck. "Come on. John will be home soon with the food."

Samantha dumped her case in a wardrobe and plonked down on the soft, guest room mattress. Alongside her rested a picture drawn in colourful crayon. It depicted what she assumed to be herself, playing with Jane in a garden full of sunflowers. This was the first time she'd stayed in the new, upstairs suite. On her previous visits, 'bed' had been a blanket on the sofa. Now the house was modelled to perfection with every comfort for both resident and visitor. On the wall above the headboard, a framed photograph of a chocolate-box cottage hung emblazoned with a scripture slogan:

'As for me and my house, we will serve the Lord.' - *Joshua 24:15.*

A car drew up outside, its engine ticking over. Samantha rose and peered out of a small, leaded light window. Her brother-in-law, John Saunders sat at the wheel of a silver BMW 3 Series saloon. One of two electric garage doors rumbled open, and the car disappeared inside.

"Sam, John's home. Supper will be ready in five." Rachel's voice called up the stairs.

"On my way." Samantha opened the wardrobe to retrieve a compact bath bag from her case. Toiletries deposited in the cube-like, en-suite shower room, she descended the stairs.

John appeared with a briefcase in one hand and a white plastic bag full of bulging paper parcels in the other. Rachel kissed him and took the food. "I'll dish these up while you get changed."

The man set down his case on a table and removed a smart, grey business jacket, slinging it across one shoulder. "Good evening, Samantha." He didn't make eye contact.

71

"Good evening, John." The woman did her best to be a polite and patient guest. "Thanks for fetching fish and chips. I haven't had them in a while."

"Mmm." John grunted. "Well, fish on Fridays is one of many Christian traditions upheld beneath this roof. I'm sure you remember. If you'll excuse me, I need to slip out of my work attire." He brushed past and took the stairs two at a time.

Jane poked the bag of warm, delicious-smelling parcels. "I want the biggest chip, Mummy."

Rachel lifted the food out of her reach. "You'll have what you're given and be thankful for it. Why don't you help Auntie Sam get seated while I dish up?"

"Okay Mummy. Come on, Auntie Sam. Did you like my picture?"

The child's playful innocence took a bitter edge off the less than stellar greeting Samantha received from her brother-in-law. "Yes I did. It looked like you and I playing in a garden of sunflowers."

"Of course, Auntie Sam. That's what it is. Come on, I want to show you my goldfish, Jonah."

"Jonah?"

"Yes. Like Jonah and the whale. Do you know that story?"

"Indeed I do." Samantha allowed the exuberant little girl to drag her into the next room. "Won't Jonah get upset, watching us eat his distant relatives for supper?"

"Ooh, I didn't think about that. He's in the lounge, so I don't suppose he can see."

Samantha laughed.

Rachel flinched and disappeared into the kitchen to plate up.

John Saunders reappeared wearing a casual, open-necked white shirt and beige trousers. His wife wandered past with the first two plates of food, to set them on the dining room table.

Samantha half-stood. "Let me help you."

John halted her ascent with a raised, flat hand. "You are our guest. Rachel and I can fetch the rest." The thirty-three-year-old, sandy-haired man strutted to the kitchen in a business-like fashion. While he and his wife returned with the final plates, Samantha helped her niece and nephew open serviettes. The last thing she wanted was to feel beholden to John Saunders. That would make standing her ground in any upcoming quarrels even more awkward.

Rachel overturned a tumbler near her place-mat and motioned at two glass jugs next to the condiments. One contained clear liquid, the other a watery purple substance. "Sam, would you like blackcurrant cordial or water?"

"I'll take water, please." She had tried their blackcurrant cordial before. Despite a magnificent home and considerable wealth, the family always diluted fruit juice concentrate so much it tasted like water, anyway. She passed her own tumbler across for Rachel to fill. Pleasing aromas wafted from the serving of battered cod and chips on her plate.

Adam reached over to lift a chip with hesitant

fingers. John slapped his hand, causing the toddler to drop it and cry out. "We don't eat until we give thanks, son. You know that." The poor boy must have had scant idea what it was all about at his age. "Just because Auntie Samantha is here, doesn't mean anything has changed." He tried hard to disguise the barb directed at his sister-in-law, but it still found a mark. Now his attention turned upon their guest. "It's our custom to allow visitors the honour of saying grace, as you know. But since it's you, I supp-"

"Why don't you say it, John," Rachel interrupted with a flat tone, desperate to calm the waters.

The man frowned at his wife, then relaxed. "Very well." He bowed his head, followed by everyone at the table except Sam. She'd had enough of this nonsense already, and focused the full weight of her signature, unblinking stare on the family man for the duration of his prayer. "Lord, we know that every good and perfect gift is from You, coming down from the Father of Lights. Bless this food to our bodies. May it sustain our strength and drive out sickness from before us. Let nothing of our conversation be displeasing in Your sight. We thank You for providing our repast and a time of precious fellowship. Bless and keep each one here. In Your name we ask it. Amen."

Rachel, Jane and Adam all repeated, "Amen."

Jane nudged her aunt, innocent eyes bulging wide like saucers. "You're supposed to say 'Amen,' Auntie Sam."

"Thank you, sweetheart." She flicked the end of the girl's nose.

Jane grinned, forgetting all about the breach in religious etiquette.

Samantha reached for the condiment tray. "Would you like salt and vinegar, Jane?"

The child nodded, feeding a chip into her mouth by hand as her legs swung beneath the table.

John frowned. "Knife and fork, young lady." He picked up his own cutlery to stress the point.

Rachel helped Adam with his food while her sister applied the required additions to Jane's supper.

Samantha lifted the ketchup bottle. "Tomato sauce?"

Jane grinned.

Rachel coughed. "Only a little, please Sam. She plasters it everywhere and then I end up wiping sticky finger marks off every conceivable surface."

Samantha pursed her lips to avoid a chuckle she ached to let go. A small dollop of ketchup oozed onto her niece's plate. "There we go. All set?"

"Thank you, Auntie Sam."

"You're welcome." Samantha added her own condiments, and the family settled down to eat. After a few minutes of chewing, the guest thought it best to break the interminable silence with some polite conversation. "So how's the insurance business these days, John?"

John Saunders finished his mouthful and washed it down with some weak blackcurrant cordial. "Busier than ever, I'm happy to say."

"Does your firm have customers in Folkestone?"

"I'm not sure. Why do you ask?"

"Oh, we had an earth tremor last week. My

neighbour said it's happened a few times. There were broken roof tiles everywhere. Don't think our building suffered any structural damage, although the landlord would be unlikely to tell me if it had."

"I see. Were you scared?"

"A little. I woke up as it happened. The most frightening part? Not knowing what was going on. It took me by surprise."

Rachel gasped. "Any damage inside your flat?"

"No. Not that you'd notice the difference. A few shampoo bottles fell over, the glasses rattled and a light bulb swung. That was about it. Afterwards folk stood milling about the road in their nightwear, drinking tea and chatting. Funny, in some respects."

Rachel wiped sauce from her son's mouth. "I hope nobody was injured."

"If they were, it didn't make the news."

John squeezed a lump of cod onto the back of his fork. He hesitated to speak before poking it into his mouth. "And how is the data quality business? Are you still doing piecework for that agency?"

"Yup. There's not much to tell. Lately they've had me validating addresses on a relational database gazetteer for a local authority."

John nodded and swallowed. "I'm surprised they don't do something like that in-house."

"Turns out they used to. Had a three-person team once, before the austerity cuts forced them to let staff go. Now it's all contracted out. Budgets dictate priorities these days."

The family man raised an interested eyebrow.

"Tough times all round."

Rachel sipped her drink. "I don't know how you put up with doing that all day, Sam."

Samantha shrugged. "The thought of going hungry is a powerful motivator. If the agency offer me work, I can't afford to pass it up. Do that too often, and they'll send jobs elsewhere. Then I'd have to-"

"Get a real job?" John's eyes twinkled.

"John," Rachel warned in a disapproving whisper.

Samantha angled her head to smile at her niece enjoying the meal. "I suppose. Don't know what I'd do for a 'career' if it came to that. This work gives me flexibility for other things."

John's brow creased. "By 'other things,' I assume you're talking about your dangerous occult activities?"

Samantha bit her lip. "Are you serious? 'Dangerous occult activities?' I'm not quite High Priestess to the Prince of Darkness yet. But if you mean: Do I still help earthbound spirits find their way to the world beyond? Then, yes, I still do that."

John stared at his plate. "Spiritual deceptions then. Have you spoken with your father?"

Samantha remained silent until the man brought his gaze up to make eye contact with her again. "You don't speak with Matthew Riley, unless your life meets with his approval. That or you are seeking to 'repent of your sins' and become born again."

"So you haven't?" John fished some batter from between two teeth with his tongue.

"Haven't what: spoken or repented? Ugh. It's all the same. No on both counts."

Jane clasped a cup between dainty hands and drained it of cordial. "Please may I leave the table, Mummy?"

Rachel nodded. "Yes. Go and sit in the other room, while I bring your brother over."

The child slid down off her dining room chair and ran into the lounge. Rachel followed with Adam.

Once they were out of sight, John's eyes narrowed at Samantha. "How can you walk away from such a good upbringing?"

Samantha placed the knife and fork together on her empty plate. "I beg your pardon?"

"You heard me. The Bible says in Proverbs twenty-two: *'Train up a child in the way he should go; even when he is old, he will not depart from it.'* So what happened with you?"

"Either I haven't departed from the right way, but it's broader than you realise; or the Bible is wrong, and the truth is broader than you realise. Take your pick."

"I see. You think I'm narrow-minded? You think your sister and our children are all bigots?"

Samantha sighed. "John, you're free to believe whatever you want and raise your children any way you wish. You have a faith that gives meaning and purpose to your existence. That's great. But don't force other people to come along on a journey they're not ready or willing to take with you, okay?"

John clasped his hands together. "How can you sit there, knowing the penalty for forsaking the Lord, and appear so calm?"

"Because I'm a dirty backslider?"

John opened his interlocked fingers and closed them again in a matter-of-fact gesture.

Samantha took a mouthful of water. "Because I don't believe in those penalties. Because I've been where we're all heading and didn't witness tortured souls suffering eternal torment for not following your religion. Because I stood in the presence of the Divine and found acceptance rather than condemnation. Acceptance and pure LOVE."

"Whatever you imagined you saw, originated from your car crash injuries. The neurosurgeons explained to us that the brain does all kinds of things during a coma. Rachel and I sat with your parents at your bedside while he went through it. When God answered our prayers, and you regained consciousness, we gave you a lot of leeway to recover. We expected you might have a few mental issues to grapple with and resolve."

"Did the neurosurgeon also explain that I was clinically dead for some time?"

"Of course. It made the miracle of your return that much greater. The Lord extended His grace to uphold and send you back. Such a shame you can't remember what happened."

Samantha bristled. "I remember with absolute clarity, John. Would you like me to describe it for you?" Her face flushed. Enough was enough. "Or would you care to explain why (despite standing at the heart of what you call God), I never ran into Jesus or any of your other sacred figures?"

"Sam, please," Rachel slipped back into the dining room, closing a door to the lounge behind her. The words interrupted her husband, who was about to fire back a retort.

Samantha screwed up her serviette and tossed it on the table. "We go through this every bloody time. Is this why you invited me back to stay, Rach? So you could cram the stuff we've been spoon-fed all our lives down my throat, thinking I'd start swallowing it again?"

"No Sam. John didn't mean anything by it. You know how our beliefs are. We love you, that's all. We love you and feel worried you are being deceived."

"You think God will burn me, is that it? Where do you people get off?"

John cracked his knuckles. "You were going astray *before* the crash. If you hadn't been a passenger in the car with that boy, none of this would have happened."

"That boy was someone I liked. Just because Dad didn't approve, doesn't make me an enemy of The Almighty. The man might run a Christian publishing company, but he isn't the infallible mouthpiece of God."

Rachel shifted on the spot. "But the boy wasn't saved."

Samantha rolled her eyes and slapped her forehead.

John leaned forward across the table. "You *do* see what we're saying? Not only did you get involved with an unsaved young man; after you recovered you 'saw' him again."

Samantha crossed her arms. "You mean when Dad burst into my bedroom and caught him fondling my naked tits?"

John flushed. "Do we have to go into the graphic details?"

"I see. You're all up for lurid descriptions about how the Lord will see me doing backstroke in the lake of fire for all eternity, but mild ones about groping between lovers are taboo."

Rachel rested her hands on the back of a dining chair. "It's not only that, there was the Bible too."

"Yeah, my Bible was open on the bed. I'd cut a hole in the pages to hide my vibrator two years before. When Dad started searching my room for non-Christian contraband, it seemed like the last place he'd look."

"It broke Dad's heart when he saw it."

"So much that he threw me out of the house. Tells you what he values most, doesn't it?"

John growled. "His faith. As it should be. Samantha, it's been five years. If you were to return and ask forgiveness like the prodigal, Matthew would welcome you in an instant. Think how great that would be."

"I can't pretend to follow those beliefs, John. However much I love my parents, I'll never live a lie to placate them. Dad won't have it any other way than his."

John rolled up his serviette and slotted it into a silver ring embossed with an ichthus fish. "*Small is the gate and narrow the road that leads to life, and only a few find it.*"

Samantha leaned back in her chair. "How appropriate to use the gospel of Matthew, given our discussion."

Rachel smiled. "You remember some of 'The Word' then? It's not only the gospel of Matthew RILEY, Sis."

"Rach, I came back from the hereafter with a gift. I didn't ask for it and I still don't want it. But I can't ignore the things I've experienced. The stranded spirits I talk to and guide across to the light, are no deception. How can I sit by and act like they're not there, when each is as real to me as this table?" She drummed her fingers on the wooden surface. "John's right, in his way. I was 'going astray' before the crash, if 'going astray' means harbouring sincere doubts about our faith. It might surprise you to learn Mum shares some of those doubts, though she dare not speak her mind at home."

Rachel frowned. "That's not true."

"Believe what you want. But don't go repeating that suggestion to Dad, or Judith Riley will be in for a grilling at church. I can almost picture the elders encircling her to shout belligerent prayers, casting out the Devil."

John pushed back his chair and stood. "Your disdain for the religion of your birth is obvious. How long will this rebellion last? You're twenty-five now, not some wayward teenager."

Samantha rose. "My disdain is a response to that religion's treatment of myself and others, John. Or treatment by its adherents, at least. Nothing more. What I saw and experienced in the world beyond, defies description. If I learnt one thing, it's that no words can convey how that world IS or WORKS. Everything falls short, including religion. *All* of them. I don't want to attack what you believe. There's right and wrong in it, like most things. But I don't wish to partake of it either. Now, if you'll excuse me, I'm tired after a long drive." She turned to her sister. "Can I say goodnight to the kids?"

"Of course you can. Jane is hoping you'll read her a bedtime story."

*   *   *

"No!" Samantha sat bolt upright in the guest bedroom. Replayed events of her family split caused the woman to toss and turn, their power resurrected by that tense discussion over supper. Rachel and John's house stood dark and silent.

Something pressed down the end of the mattress. The room chilled as at the opening of a refrigerator door. A familiar, pulsating sensation vibrated her inner core. Soft, glowing fingers crept over the foot of the bed. An ice-cold, slender hand gripped her right ankle like a frozen vice. Samantha pressed both hands into the sheets behind her back, fighting to control pulse and breath. A head lifted as the apparition pulled itself up from the floor. Sad, empty eyes peered from the pale, mournful face of an unkempt young woman around her own age. She wore an old-fashioned farming smock. The wretched figure clawed her torso along Samantha's lower legs, bringing the pair eye to eye, mere inches apart. At this distance, a rough rope-burn across the figure's throat appeared fierce and fresh.

Those wistful eyes scanned the living, mortal woman. A dry, rasping, helpless voice gasped from between bloated, cracked lips. "Why are you here? What's happening to me? Have you seen Jethro? How I long for my love. Oh, how I wanted to go where he has gone."

Samantha required no further explanation. She took a deep breath and allowed the vibration to rise until it flooded into the pathetic spiritual creature clinging onto her.

Some depth flickered in the lifeless stare. "I... I wanted to be with Jethro."

Samantha nodded. "Don't be afraid."

Across the room, a growing light sparkled from a low glimmer to a strengthening flare.

The still night sky above Middle Woodford broke into a rising breeze. Bright stars dimmed as trails of shooting black smoke darted left and right above the cottage rooftops. Each trail moved with deft, deliberate intelligence. In and out they raced, striking windows and walls of every building in the village, then ricocheting back into the sky. Along the river, weaving and intertwining, those trails advanced south. Beyond the watercourse, a home built from a converted agricultural building lay in darkness. The swooping clouds coalesced into a single stream, tearing towards the structure at breakneck speed. The wind in its wake echoed with a supernatural roar. A furious tempest of pure evil. An evil that resonated with anger, frustration and hatred.

"All is well. You can go now." Samantha sat on the edge of the bed, the apparition beside her. That entire far wall of the bedroom glowed with a brilliant, unearthly light. Such incessant brightness in physical form on earth, would dazzle and cause pain. Yet its brilliance didn't hurt to look at. It appeared you could walk straight through the bedroom wall to a distant horizon and keep on going. Oh how Samantha longed to make that journey again.

The dead girl stood on shaky legs. "Will I be punished for what I did?"

Samantha rose in solidarity. "No. There may be some regret as your life is reviewed. Lessons your soul must learn. Nothing more. Then you will be at peace."

"But what of damnation?"

"Damnation is the fear that kept you here. Let go. Let go and be free."

A thunderous rumble echoed down the chimney. Something burst from the lounge fireplace on the floor below. Hairs rose on the back of Samantha's neck. A crash of overturned furniture caused a light to appear on the landing beneath the bedroom door.

John Saunders' sleep-addled voice broke the upstairs calm. "What the...?"

"Go now." Samantha's voice became insistent, though she wasn't sure why. "You MUST go now."

The girl edged closer to the spiritual horizon, fear holding her back like a child unsure about jumping into a swimming pool for the first time.

John flicked the landing light on, gripped the banister and took one step down. A black, whirling stream like directed smoke, blasted up the stairwell. It slammed the groggy man back into the far landing wall. A pounding roar shook the interior of the house, somewhere between a scream and a moan.

Samantha glanced in the commotion's direction. Doors banged open along the landing.

Jane screamed. Adam wailed.

"Lord protect us," Rachel's voice reached almost falsetto pitch. She stumbled along the hallway towards cries of "Mummy, Mummy," from both her children.

All lights in the house came on, flickered and extinguished.

The guest bedroom door blew open with such force, it walloped the wall behind. Hinges split and the brass doorknob punched through the plasterboard, anchoring the damaged portal in place. The astral gateway now provided the only source of illumination. On the fringes of its shimmering light, Samantha could discern a large, fathomless shadow figure in the bedroom doorway. Her stomach muscles clenched. It was no dream this time, but that entity - whatever it was - had pursued her night after night in the world of the unconscious.

From down the hall, Rachel's hysterical voice attempted to calm her children.

A torch beam scanned the landing walls, back-lighting but not piercing the heaving, ominous cloudy shape barring any physical escape.

John's voice rose in a shaky attempt to claim spiritual authority. "Begone, Devil. The blood of Jesus Christ is against you. I cast you out by the power of that blood and the word of my testimony. You have no dominion in this house. Depart, in Jesus' name."

The Entity remained resolute. There were no eyes, nor any facial features detectable in the bulge resembling a head. It reached out to study Samantha with its whole being. The woman remembered her experience of sight not limited to a field of vision, from life beyond. Every part of that shape could 'see' her.

"You must go," Samantha winced at the hesitant girl. She staggered against a nearby wall, burning pain searing across her skull. Relentless agony brought the young woman to her knees.

Several pairs of wispy black fingers reached towards the uncertain farm girl, teetering on the threshold between glory and the realm of mortals.

Along the landing, John shouted another attempt at spiritual warfare. "Nothing shall separate us from the love of God, which is in Christ Jesus, our Lord. Down on your belly, serpent. I crush you with the heel of the righteous."

Slithering smoke hands wrapped around the upper torso of the earthbound spirit, like a toxic lover.

Samantha crawled across the carpet, right hand outstretched. One final burst of energy poured from her flagging form, firing her gift like a spiritual missile. The clutching dark hands relinquished their hold for a few seconds, as if stung by an irritating insect. In those tense moments, the female spirit strode forward into the light.

The guest bedroom window blew open as the light faded. Samantha's sight faded with it and her head sank into the carpet. Blackness came in an instant.

* * *

"But she's my sister, John." Rachel's strained vocal tones drifted into Samantha's stirring consciousness.

"I don't care. She's not spending another night in this house. The Lord alone knows what kind of demonic forces she's mixed up with." The man spoke with subdued anger.

"I told her she could stay until Sunday night."

"And now you can tell her she's no longer welcome under our roof. Not until she returns to Christ and seeks deliverance from her occult ways."

"John-"

"Have you forgotten what happened last night? Do you not remember the cries of our children? Thank goodness the neighbours have agreed to look after them this morning. Rachel, Samantha is more than lost. She's in league with the enemy of everything we hold dear. When we invite her in, we invite the Devil and his cohorts with her. I want her gone. As soon as she's awake, get rid of her. I'm the head of my wife and this household. When I return from the DIY store to mend the guest bedroom, I don't want to find Samantha Riley in our home."

Samantha eased up in bed as Rachel padded through

the open doorway. The dazed younger woman rubbed her eyes. "How did I get here?"

"John and I lifted you off the carpet." Rachel perched on the mattress edge, fingers rubbing tense knees. She bit her lip.

Samantha studied the door, still smashed into the wall. "I'll pay for that."

"All the house fuses blew as well."

"I'll pay for those too. I've still got some of Nana's money."

"It's not about the cost." Rachel hesitated. "Sam-"

"I heard."

Rachel's eyes lowered. "Oh."

"So I'm not going to see my sister, niece or nephew anymore either."

"Sam, I'm frightened. How can you consider last night's episode anything but evil? What are you mixed up in? Talk to me. I want to help."

"It was evil all right, but nothing to do with me. At least, I didn't start it."

"Was it a demon?"

"What did you see?"

"A black cloud. John's torch couldn't penetrate or illuminate it. The furniture downstairs was all upended, our children thrown into a panic, and then this." She cast one hand at the damaged door.

"What about the light?"

"What light?"

Samantha sighed. "That's what I feared. You only saw the blackness. Nothing else."

"There wasn't a light, Sam."

"Yes there was." She rubbed her eyes. "You shared your former barn with a restless spirit. My guess is: she hung herself from a beam where this room now sits, long ago. A suicide after losing her love, Jethro."

"There's no such thing as ghosts, Sam. When you die, you go to one place or the other. There is no in-between. You're seeing hallucinations. Fake visions to keep you in thrall to that infernal creature that came for you last night."

"Is that John - the head of his wife and this household - speaking, or you?"

"You used to believe the same way too. Don't you remember how happy we once were? I know you'd just been born, but when I was about five, Mum and Dad used to laugh all the time."

Samantha wrinkled her nose. "I may not remember it, Rach, but I know enough to realise that was during the 'Toronto Blessing.' Half the worldwide church was rolling around laughing at the drop of a hat. If I read the old stories right, some even did involuntary animal impressions."

Rachel pulled at her blouse. "Perhaps God has a sense of humour? Mum said it was a period of great refreshing."

"God has a sense of humour? That's the first spiritual concept we've agreed on in a long time." She swung her legs out of bed. "I'd better get dressed and hit the road before his lordship returns. Guess he'll be checking your phone bill like Dad from now on. Wouldn't want you influenced by my demonic forces."

"I'll still call you, Sam."

"Give my love to Jane and Adam, would you? I heard they've gone to your neighbours while things settle down."

Tears brimmed in Rachel's eyes. "When I held onto Jane during the encounter last night, all she kept saying was, *'What about Auntie Sam?'* She loves you so much."

"The feeling is mutual. Shame I won't get to watch her grow up."

"You could if you wanted to…"

"If I repent and become an obedient believer?"

"Would that be so terrible? I'm afraid for your safety."

"I'm not too sure about it myself, but I've no fear of what comes next. It's one weapon this thing - whatever it is - can't use against me. My gift must offend it somehow. Its appearances and disappearances seem tied to the opening and closing of doorways into the hereafter. Were that not the case, I doubt it would've left me breathing last night. That's the first time I've seen it outside of a nightmare. The dreams were some kind of warning, I guess. If the manifestations get any more violent…"

"You could speak with our Pastor. He has a deliverance ministry."

"No thanks. I don't want some Charismatic Evangelical preacher clutching my head until it's fit to burst like a watermelon. All that shouting about the blood of Jesus worked wonders for John last night, didn't it?"

"The demon departed."

"After the astral doorway closed."

"But-"

"That's right, you didn't see an astral doorway." Samantha sighed. "We're going round in circles here. Give me fifteen minutes and I'll be out of your hair." She strode into the en-suite and shut the door behind her.

On the bed, Rachel cried soft tears into a tissue.

5

Foreign Fields

PETER HAWS, 1914.

"It's a fine evening. Won't you fall behind in your work, taking a stroll with me?" Peter Haws leaned against the crossbeam of a farmer's fence. Warm August sunshine reflected in his soulful brown gaze, resting on the eighteen-year-old, fair-haired beauty beside him. She fiddled with her hair bun and stared back, eyes matching the cloudless Devonshire sky.

"I can still sew by lamplight. My eyesight is better than Mother's."

"As long as the stitching is straight. Being a dressmaker in a village the size of Gateleigh, you'd soon run out of customers if word got round your work is shoddy. This isn't Exeter."

"Do I tell you how to bake loaves of bread? And what time of the morning do you start that?"

"I can knead dough with my eyes shut. A baker's work is less fine and precise."

"After we're married, I may adjust my working hours to match yours. Nobody cares when I sew, as long as I complete the work in time, up to scratch."

Peter rubbed his short, cropped black hair. "Once we start raising children, you'll be awake when I am, anyway."

"Once we *start*?" The teenager blinked. "How many were you thinking of having?"

"Oh, a baker's dozen seems appropriate."

"A baker's doz-" she stopped upon noticing the cheeky twinkle in his eye. "Well, if you want that many, we'll both need to work a lot harder."

Peter drew her close. "I love you, Mary Hutchings. On Saturday, before God and our families, they'll enter it onto parish records for posterity."

The girl sighed. "My heart skipped a beat whenever they read the banns. Soon we'll be Peter and Mary Haws. It feels like a dream."

"Have you finished your dress?"

"Yes. I can't wait to walk down the aisle in it. Have you finished the cake?"

Peter nodded.

The couple passed through a five-bar gate and descended a narrow track of deep red soil. All about, gentle rolling hills of the Devon landscape pressed together like buns proving on one of Peter's racks. A crystal clear stream gurgled and sang. It sparkled in glimmering shafts of light stabbing between gaps in the lush green tree canopy. The pair crossed the watercourse via flat stone slabs of an ancient clapper bridge. Ahead, the dark grey, granite tower of the village church poked into view between swaying branches. The building occupied the prime spot on a promontory, about which nestled abundant thatched cottages and other wonky buildings of whitewashed cob.

Peter and Mary walked hand-in-hand back into the village of their birth.

A crowd jostled around the open doorway of their local inn, 'The Wagon & Horses.' General murmurs of excitement from the men, mingled with less enthusiastic responses by their female counterparts milling about the street.

A farm labourer matching Peter's twenty years, stepped into the dusty lane clutching a foaming tankard of ale. The baker caught his eye.

"Ted. What's all the fuss about?"

"Fella arrived from Tavistock not ten minutes ago with news."

"What news?"

"War. The King declared war with Germany on Tuesday night. Chap says the First Lord of the Admiralty has already instructed the fleet to attack. Or so his story goes. If this carries on, they'll be wanting men for the fight soon enough, I reckon."

Mary squeezed tight to her fiancé's hand. "What about the regular army?"

Ted wiped some froth from his mouth onto the back of a shirt sleeve. "There's no way they'll be enough. Nation's going to need volunteers. Should be quite a lark. Might consider it myself. I've never visited foreign parts afore."

Peter read the fear flickering in Mary's sparkling baby blues. "Don't you worry none. We're getting married and starting a life together. The war won't touch us right down here in the West Country, love. Set your mind at rest."

A four-in-hand stood outside the parish church of St. Mark's the following Saturday. Its driver patted the horses as an organ played somewhere within the structure. The newlywed Mr and Mrs Haws emerged, surrounded by a cheering crowd of well-wishers. Gateleigh lay far enough away from the wider world's concerns, to miss developments of which the newspapers couldn't get enough.

Mary Haws (nee Hutchings) held a simple spray of wildflowers before her ivory dress. It was a garment into which she'd poured a tireless love that reflected her feelings for Peter. Disturbing events at the pub from the other night were now eclipsed by the joy of her wedding day. Yet an aching sensation tensed in the young bride's stomach. Something beyond the glare of conscious thought whispered troubling ideas of horror to come. Vague suggestions their quiet world was about to be overturned and tested by fire.

* * *

"They're pulling out all the stops for volunteers, aren't they, Mrs Rogers?" Peter Haws placed a granary loaf into the wicker shopping basket of a plump, middle-aged woman with greying hair.

Outside the bakery, a brass band accompanied soldiers marching past. Smart woollen khaki uniforms covered with single-piece pattern webbing were topped by stiff peaked caps. Each man carried a short magazine Lee-Enfield rifle against his shoulder. Officers accompanied them on horseback. The strains of *'It's a Long Way to Tipperary'* invaded the quiet of the shop.

Mrs Rogers lifted her basket off the counter and shook her head. "It makes me proud and sad at the same time, Peter. But enough of that. Is Mary well? How was your honeymoon?"

Peter snapped back from staring out the shop window in a daze. "Mary's fine. Thank you for asking. Our honeymoon was grand. We spent a few days by the sea in Ilfracombe."

"Oh, how lovely. I went to Ilfracombe many years ago. Such a pretty spot. The air was bracing back then."

"It still is."

"Give my love to your darling young wife."

"I will. Thank you, Mrs Rogers. Goodbye." After the woman left, Peter wandered round from his service position to stand in the shop doorway. Arms folded, he leaned against the frame.

Across the street, small folding tables were set up. Ted the farm labourer bent over one of them. A soldier perching on a stool opposite, motioned to the passing troops. He handed a pen to the stooping man. Ted scratched his head and signed a piece of paper. Peter flinched and rubbed his eyes. He stepped down into the dusty street and crossed between parade lines. Ted puffed out his chest, flat farm worker's cap clutched tight in both hands. The man adopted a swagger of confidence as he approached the baker.

"I've done it, Peter. I'm off to the war."

"Do your folks know?"

"Not yet. But they'll be proud of me, I'm sure. Are you coming into the pub for a spell?"

"I'd best not leave the shop. I wanted to check you were okay. A lot of people are getting swept up in the emotion of it all."

"We'll be heroes when we get back. Why don't you come with me?"

"And leave Mary?"

Ted batted the question aside. "Bah. It'll all be over by Christmas, anyway."

"So why take the risk?"

"To fight for King and country."

A young woman painted with striking red lipstick sidled up to him. "Glad to hear someone's got the right idea." Her accent bore a broad hint of cockney. She leaned close to Ted and plastered a kiss on one cheek. The resulting imprint appeared a deliberate ruse. A cross somewhere between branding and a badge of honour. She pivoted with a playful bounce to frown at the baker. "Are you going to follow this brave man's example?"

Peter drew himself up to full height. "If I'm called upon in person. I'll not rush out on a whim, abandoning my wife and responsibilities by enlisting though."

The woman raised one eyebrow and pursed her lips, disdain warping her countenance. "You *have* been called. Your King asks you to defend the homeland and defeat Britain's enemies. *Some* men have enough courage to answer without delay. How many lives could you save if you had the backbone and spirit to join them?"

Peter bit his lip. "Do they pay you to do this, or is it voluntary?"

The woman sneered and reached into a small cloth bag hanging from her wrist. "I have something for you."

Before Peter could resist, she stuck a white feather into his apron with a pin.

"That's your rank insignia. The mark of a coward. In this war, we should all wear emblems that distinguish us."

Peter's nostrils flared. "Get out of my sight, before my wife shows you how much fight and spirit a Devonshire lass can muster."

"Hiding behind your wife's skirts? What a surprise. If she wants me, I'll be over mixing with the *real* men."

Peter took a step forward, straining not to clench his fists.

The woman blew him a kiss and sauntered off into the crowd.

Ted fidgeted on the spot. "I know you're not a coward, Peter. You have other things to think about. It's a bigger decision for married folk. Everyone in the village realises that."

"You take care of yourself, Ted." The baker shook him by the hand.

"I'll be back afore you know it."

Peter pulled the white feather free and tossed it aside, before crossing back to the shop.

*   *   *

Mary Haws set her baby boy down in his cot.

Peter's voice called from the parlour below. "I'm back."

"Be there in a minute." The woman wiped evidence of tears from her eyes and eased down the steep cottage stairs.

Peter took his wife in his arms for a kiss. On his khaki uniform, the proud insignia of the Duke of Cornwall's Light Infantry gleamed in summer sunlight. "Is Jack asleep?"

Mary smiled. "Yes. Our son is such a good lad. How long before you have to go?"

"They've given us an hour until assembly for roll call on the edge of the village."

Mary swallowed. "I'm so glad we got to celebrate our second anniversary before they drafted you." She sniffed. "When they passed that act in January and exempted married men, I thought we may never reach a day like this. Then in June..."

Peter cradled her head into his shoulder. "Shh now. We knew it was only a matter of time until they amended it. Conscription of married men was inevitable. The cost in lives has been too high for any other course of action in this war. I'll come back to you both, you'll see."

"Like Ted?" Mary's eyes reddened.

Peter's face fell. "He asked me to come with him when he signed up. Said it would all be over by Christmas. But he never even made it to the first one."

"And now you have no choice but to go too."

"That's right. We're catching trains down to Folkestone and shipping out from there."

Mary reached into her pocket to retrieve a square of folded material. "I know you can't take much with you, so I made a special handkerchief."

Peter unfolded the item. It consisted of fine white linen embroidered with a scene of the village. In one corner, the letters 'M & P' flowed in blue script at a forty-five degree angle. "Mary and Peter?"

Mary couldn't keep the tears inside any longer. Her anguished cries joined with many others in the cottages of their little village. Simple homes where fine young men were setting off for battle in foreign fields. How many would ever return?

"Step short." The barked order caused every man in earshot to shorten his stride. Ahead, at the end of The Leas in Folkestone, Peter saw 'The Slope' for the first time. Already this road to the harbour (where boats awaited them) had become infamous among the troops. The instruction enabled soldiers to adjust pace for the steep downhill gradient. It was said you could have breakfast in Folkestone and be in the trenches of the Western Front by lunch. That sobering thought haunted Peter during his final moments on English soil.

Across the country in a pretty, quiet Devonshire village, his wife and young son were waiting for him. What would he have to face before earning the right to return home to them again?

* * *

"Stand-to." The call carried along snaking lines of a sodden trench.

Mist hung heavy in the air, creeping across the barren, shell-pocked landscape of no-man's-land. It reached down to wipe wet, invisible hands across Peter's face. He sat huddled with his back pressed against some rotten bracing planks. A pack of rats squeaked and scurried past, disturbed by the daily Five AM order to go on high alert. One rodent gnawed at a haversack. An item the soldier rested his feet on to keep them dry. Once you'd seen comrades suffer the agony of 'Trench Foot' you took every precaution to avoid being the next victim. Regular foot inspections by officers were superfluous after that. Peter slammed his boot into the disease-carrying vermin. It tumbled and ran away after its extended family. A Jack Russell Terrier darted along the curve, barking in pursuit of the pack.

"Looks like Scamp's after his breakfast." A gravelly voiced, ginger-haired infantryman hoisted himself up from the mud.

Peter examined teeth marks on his makeshift footstool. "Here's hoping he's got a big appetite for a small dog."

"Give me your hand, Pete." The fellow reached out one muscular arm.

"Cheers, Davy. Another day on our foreign vacation." He took hold and received a helpful tug.

"Yeah. I don't know about you, but when I get home, I intend to write a strongly worded letter of complaint to the tour company. The standard of their facilities is bloody appalling."

Peter forced a smile. "I'm looking forward to sleeping at night again. Even though getting up in the small hours is normal for me. It's going to sleep in the afternoon that mixes me up."

Davy Thompson picked up his rifle. "Oh yeah, you're a baker by trade. I'm not so worried about when I get some kip, but a real bed rather than a rat-infested muddy ditch would be nice. I can't even recall what a feather pillow feels like. Once I get home to Cornwall, I'll sleep for a week."

"When do you reckon the next attack will come?" Peter collected his Lee-Enfield.

The pair joined a short procession of men, slipping and sliding through a squelching bog towards the firing trench.

"No idea. I hope it's not before breakfast. If Fritz goes over the top before I get my tea and bacon, I'll spoil his prospects." Davy tapped his bayonet. "I'm good at filleting. You should see how many mackerel I can prepare in a day at work."

"Looking forward to that rum ration, too." Peter shivered, wishing the warm breath escaping his body in clouds, might remain inside.

Stand-down, rum ration and breakfast came and went without incident. Eight AM cleaning of self, weapons and trench proceeded as usual. Dinner at noon, the afternoon nap and tea at Five all blurred into another uneventful day on the Western Front. Each man pondered whether to be grateful for the monotony and discomfort, or frustrated by it. Everyone in the battalion had experienced a taste of action. When it came, the state-sanctioned mass murder was loud and brutal. Making friends during trench warfare proved a calculated gamble. On the one hand, it was nice to have a kindred spirit with whom to share the burden of suffering. On the other, chances were you'd end up wiping the residue of their brains off your face before the week ended. Peter and Davy had been through two such attacks: once as aggressors and the other, defenders. So it was that the Gateleigh baker and Polperro fishmonger formed a stronger bond than usual.

Stand-to and stand-down at dusk drifted past. At Ten PM, Peter and Davy took their places on a watch post. Davy propped his rifle against some sandbags. He leaned forward, clutching a dirty, hand-held periscope. In the distance, a rumble of artillery and the faint clack of machine gun fire carried on the wind. Explosions and muzzle flashes combined to light the barbed-wire-encrusted kill zone of no-man's-land.

"Someone's taking a pasting, Pete." He passed the viewing device across.

Peter lifted it and peered over the top of the trench.

"Can't tell who's attacking at this distance." He scanned closer to home. Between the swirling mists and the occasional half-light of thunderous illumination, something stirred in the vapour: Shapes. Shapes with arms and legs. "Davy, are those…? Oh my God." Peter shoved the periscope into his comrade's embrace and cupped both hands to his mouth. "Stand-to! Incoming!" He lifted a tin whistle to his lips and blew with every last breath his lungs might summon.

Davy raised the periscope again. "But they haven't softened us up with arti…"

Several more flashes lit up the night, like an approaching electrical storm. A screaming shell shrieked overhead, striking the gap between the firing and stores trenches. A plume of mud blew into the air. The explosion pinned Peter and Davy against the sandbags, ears whistling. Three more projectiles added their hideous music to the barrage song. British Army soldiers darted along the firing trench. Fifty yards down, a collection of Lewis guns roared to life, spitting volleys of searing lead in devastating arcs at the approaching German soldiers.

Peter shook, his ears bleeding. Sound became muffled, as if his body were tuning out the terminal theatre of terror to lessen its bite. Shell impacts ceased, replaced by a thousand whizzing puffs of mud from incoming small arms fire. The companions readied their rifles and began firing at any shadow looming out from the snapping barbed wire defences. A grenade sailed overhead and thudded in the trench behind them. Peter dropped his gun and pushed Davy aside.

The blast knocked him off his feet, but left only minor shrapnel grazes on his left upper arm.

Davy squatted to peer into the face of his friend. Words were mouthed, but Peter heard nothing. His limbs trembled.

Down the line, three German infantrymen rolled into the firing trench.

Davy Thompson fitted his bayonet, placed a reassuring hand on the baker's shoulder, and then stormed off to help repel the assault.

Peter staggered to his feet, groggy and confused. He couldn't recall how long he stumbled around. In his mind, a vision beckoned somewhere beyond the horizon: Mary and little jack waiting by the inglenook in their tiny cottage. He reached out quivering fingers to grasp the image, always too remote to seize. Frantic activity all about him lessened. The blood, screams and gore faded away. Then he was leaning against a fountain in the old Belgian town square. It was there his hearing came back with a terrifying rush, accompanied by the bellowing shout from a Sergeant Major.

"Arrest that man."

"Haws. Paper and pen to write a letter home. There's some rum too, if you want it." The military prison guard jangled a set of keys.

Peter took the stationery but waved the alcohol away.

His guard paused at the abattoir chamber door. The

place was set up as a temporary holding area for court martial executions. "Chaplain will be along to see you in a bit." He strode out and clanged the metal portal shut.

The condemned man sunk down onto a rough straw mattress. His defence had been sketchy in the ad hoc military court of justice. How could he explain leaving his post and arriving in town? He didn't understand it himself. Now the faintest sound caused his damaged and sensitive ears to jolt him like the recipient of an electric shock. A guilty verdict and sign-off for execution were arrived at in minutes. Peter pulled the decorative handkerchief from his breast pocket, fingering the couple's first initials. The embroidered scene of Gateleigh summoned memories of that vision from his unconscious desertion. Now he must find words to say goodbye to a wife and son he would never see again.

"Attention." The command resonated in a small brick courtyard outside the abattoir, during first light of the following morning. Twelve men assembled into a firing squad from Peter's own battalion, stood in a lacklustre line. Among them, a ginger-haired, Cornish fishmonger gritted his teeth as guards led their prisoner out.

Peter Haws fought against a rising scream that threatened to burst from his lungs with involuntary abandon. If nothing else, he would try to face the inevitable with dignity. A paper square pinned tight across his heart, now occupied the same spot a girl once attached a white feather. Hers was a symbol of cowardice. This new addition: a punishment for it. Something for his peers to aim at as they dispatched their comrade for supposed desertion in the face of the enemy.

A guard secured Peter's arms to a stake before a wall of sandbags. The condemned man's gaze fell upon the ginger-haired soldier. The reluctant executioner's eyes brimmed full of shimmering tears. Beneath the paper square and fabric of his tunic, Peter felt the faint shape of Mary's handkerchief comfort his breast. In this world of despair and madness it was the only thing to cling onto. And cling he would, whatever happened next.

The guard fastened a blindfold across his eyes, shutting out what little light already shone in this gloomy corner of the world.

A commanding officer stood next to the squad. "Company make ready."

There came a clattering of rifles.

"Take aim."

Peter's heart thudded in his breast, straining to connect with the simple fabric token of Mary's love.

"Fire."

His sensitive ears caused Peter to flinch at the gunfire. But the restraints secured him fast to the stake, lessening another unwanted jolt. One round penetrated his right shoulder, causing thick blood to soak his tunic. The wound burned, but he was still alive. Every other shot flew wide of the mark, despite the firing squad standing at close range. Widest of all and embedded deep in a sandbag, lay the rifle round of Davy Thompson. He couldn't bring himself to fire upon his friend. From the resulting lack of target impacts on the paper square, it proved a common sentiment.

The commanding officer glowered at his men and shook his head. Webley revolver withdrawn from a holster, he stepped forward and raised it to aim at Peter's right temple.

A flight of doves launched into the sky as a single shot rang out in the courtyard.

*   *   *

Mary Haws pushed her baby boy in a hand-me-down pram her mother had given. A week drifted by since she'd received Peter's final letter. About the same time, an official communication arrived announcing his execution for desertion. With it came his few personal effects. Among them, a pristine handkerchief made with her own fair hands. That it remained in such a condition, bore witness to the relentless care applied by its owner. No bullet pierced the paper square pinned across her husband's heart, so the treasured item survived intact.

"Good morning, Mrs Haws." Nellie Beamish, Gateleigh's fat, busybody postmistress greeted Mary. The young mother wheeled her pram next to the village post office counter.

"Good morning, Mrs Beamish. I understand I'm

supposed to draw a war widow's pension and dependent children's allowance."

Nellie placed a hand over her open mouth. "Oh my dear, I'd heard rumours the war took Peter. I'm so sorry."

Mary swallowed hard. "Thank you."

"Do you have your Ministry of Pensions, Widows-Form 1?"

"My what?"

"If the ministry have granted you a war widow's pension, they should write direct from Grosvenor Road, London."

"Err, no. This is the only letter I've received." She passed the death notification across.

Nellie adjusted a pair of large, round glasses and lifted the document for a closer inspection. Her sympathetic face transfigured into a scowl. "I see. There won't be any pension or allowance for you, Mrs Haws."

"What? But my husband was ki-"

"We don't provide pensions for the widows of cowards." Nellie slammed the paper back on the counter.

Mary fumed. "Peter was no coward."

The postmistress cast a nonchalant gaze at her fingernails. "Our government begs to differ."

"How am I supposed to live and raise a child alone on eleven shillings a week?"

Nellie slid the letter back to its owner. "That's not my problem. Now, if you'll excuse me, I see Mrs Jacobs is here to collect *her* war widow's pension. Her late husband did his duty. Good day, Mrs Haws."

Outside in the street, Mary clutched onto the pram handles for support. Any efforts at decorum and showing brave eyes to their neighbours vanished. Tears streamed down her cheeks as she pushed little Jack along. She'd lose the cottage - no question. Thank God her mother and father would take them in. The pain of that loss bore no comparison with her grief. A grief sharpened by the words of Nellie Beamish. That story must now blaze through the village like wildfire; there was little doubt. Her husband died, accused of cowardice in a time of chaos with no way to clear his name. The days ahead would bear telling witness to who among their community remained a true friend.

When the church bells rang out again during the 1918 armistice, Mary had settled back into life at home. The family's circle of friends diminished with the word of Peter's execution. The young widow challenged any man, woman or child who dared cast aspersions upon her late husband's good name.

Towards the end of November, a new face wandered into the tiny Devonshire village. A tall, muscular fellow with ginger hair and a Cornish accent enquired at 'The Wagon & Horses' for the widow of Peter Haws. The mixed response his question provoked, didn't surprise him. That was why he came. Mary at least deserved to learn about the man who'd saved his life from a German grenade. The brave soldier who once stood shoulder to shoulder with him in battle. To Davy

Thompson, Peter had kept his honour. For those who hadn't endured life and death in the trenches on a daily basis, his nervous injury was impossible to imagine. Peter Haws may have loved and missed his family, but he was no coward. Before the fishmonger left to continue his onward journey home, the dead soldier's widow listened to many stories of Peter's courageous actions. She also received a modest few coins. It was a small gift, but much appreciated. A donation Davy gathered from other comrades in their battalion who loved the Devonshire baker.

For Peter Haws, the final revolver gunshot never registered. His attention remained on the beautiful handkerchief and the woman who'd embroidered it. Now everything felt more of a haze than that day during the attack. Images of Mary and Jack flitted into his enlarged senses. Had he died and gone to Devon rather than heaven? Jack grew to be a man. Mary aged and remained a single widow. Where had his life essence drifted to and what was he seeing? Whenever Mary took out the handkerchief to touch it, she seemed so close. Then one day the visions faded. The old woman no longer reached for that touchstone of their love. She had vanished.

Peter's spirit endured, bound and yearning for a mortal life he would never lead. It clung fast to the one object into which he'd poured all his energy during life's final moments: Mary's handkerchief.

6

Spiritual Asylum

SAMANTHA RILEY, 2019.

Samantha's Ford Ka pulled into a parking space at
Fernhurst Village Hall in West Sussex. It had been a
hectic drive, delayed by an accident near the Gatwick
turnoff. There were still a few miles to go for this
afternoon's appointment. Samantha knew she had to
clear her head before things would flow as required.
She exited the car and stretched. A carved stone plaque
attached to a nearby wall drew her attention.

'BLACKDOWN AIR DISASTER
4 NOVEMBER 1967

In tribute to the 37 passengers
and crew who lost their lives,
the emergency services and the
people of Fernhurst who rallied to help.

4 November 2017'

Something tugged at the young woman's heartstrings. *Nana.* Memories came flooding back. Her grandmother used to tell stories of how her favourite actress, June Thorburn died when a flight from Spain crashed into a wooded hillside in the south of England. She recalled cuddling up to her grandmother and watching an old film version of 'Tom Thumb,' featuring the now-deceased star as 'Queenie,' fairy queen of the forest. Nana would approve of this recent commemorative addition to the village.

Samantha caught sight of nearby wooded hills in gaps between the red brick homes. She shuddered. Good job she hadn't stopped up there for a break. If restless spirits still lingered near the crash site, the need to help would see her drained of energy before ever reaching today's destination. That thought caused a flash of guilt to wash over her. It was a selfish notion, but how could one mortal woman help every earthbound spirit? She had to guard her health and sanity - such as it was. Eyes closed for a minute to centre herself, Samantha uttered a silent prayer that all involved in that horrible disaster would find their way to the light, if they hadn't already done so.

'Blackdown Lodge' was a large brick country retreat, off a no-through spur near the foot of the hills. It stood three storeys high, plus basement; an elegant yet rustic home of some long-forgotten landed gentry. The main structure formed a complete square with central grassed courtyard, either side of which accommodation wings wrapped round to meet an old stable and clock tower facing back to the principal building. A stylish billboard near the gatepost driveway declared:

'Linkletter Developments are pleased to announce the next phase of apartments at Blackdown Lodge. Please enquire at the sales office for details and a tour.'

Samantha took one look at the imposing structure and wondered if her entire rented studio might fit inside the bathroom of a single unit. She brought the car to a halt alongside several others to the right of broad stone steps. These ascended to an impressive, windowed, double-door entrance. Hairs rose on the back of Samantha's neck as she locked the vehicle. A nearby, single-storey outbuilding stood dark and derelict. Square, leaded-light windows hung thick with cobwebs like cataracts obscuring the eyes of some squatting, ancient beast. The feeling it engendered unsettled the Somerset girl. Something was very wrong here, and she'd yet to cross the threshold.

"Can I help you?" A smart saleswoman in a tailored grey jacket and skirt, swanned into the tiled hallway to answer the doorbell. Samantha wondered if someone had to stitch her into that outfit each morning, it was such a precise fit. Bottle blonde hair formed into a loose bun at the back of her head, with minor errant strands providing one carefree chink in that professional presentation.

"I'm Samantha Riley, here to meet Clive Linkletter."

"Ah yes, Miss Riley. We were expecting you half an hour ago. I'm Kate Horton, Mr Linkletter's personal assistant." She opened one of the double doors wider to allow their guest access.

Samantha stepped inside. "Sorry about that. Accident near Gatwick held everyone up."

"I see. If you'll wait here, I'll check if Mr Linkletter is available."

"Thank you." Samantha turned aside to conceal her frown. *If he's available? He'd better be available after that journey. I'm not coming back another day.* It was then she realised that might be a relief. The very walls of the place dripped with misery and despair. More than one lost soul roamed the rooms and corridors of that old lodge and its outbuildings. She could feel their listless anguish blowing through the structure like a spiritual breeze. Had Samantha bitten off more than she could chew with this one?

"Miss Riley. You found us all right then?" A bald, stocky man with a sandy-coloured suit and a dark blue polo shirt appeared from a side corridor. His semi-casual attire screamed 'mid-life crisis' and matched contact lenses which pumped his watery blue eyes to the size of tea plates (or so it appeared). Simple glasses might have been a less startling addition, even if the fellow wished to ward off the impending effects of age on a man's body.

"Mr Linkletter?"

"Please call me Clive."

"Samantha." She shook his offered hand.

"So where do you want to start? Can I offer you a coffee?"

"A glass of cold water would be nice. I like coffee, but caffeine messes with my sensitivity."

"Of course." He indicated along a corridor. "Let's sit down in my office a moment. Kate will fetch us some drinks and we'll devise a plan of attack. If that's the right turn of phrase?"

Samantha grimaced. "As long as it's the only 'attack' of the day. Your e-mail mentioned occasional violent disturbances, along with weird sensations experienced by your customers."

"That's correct." He ushered her into an office and closed the door. Sunlight streamed through two large sash windows opening onto the grass inner-courtyard. Outside, stone pathways from each of the four principal compass points met at a fountain in the middle of the spacious quadrangle. It was an area the size of a football pitch. Clive pulled out a leather, low-backed chair for the woman to sit on, then reclined into a spinning executive one behind his sturdy mahogany desk.

Kate Horton entered from the corridor clutching a highball of water and a small espresso cup and saucer. She was the picture of efficiency.

"There you go, Miss Riley. Some water for you."

Samantha took the glass, its chilled surface soothing to her fingers. "Thank you."

Kate deposited the coffee on Clive's dark green desk

jotter, then made herself scarce.

Samantha glanced around the high-ceilinged room. This chamber didn't feel so bad. She had a grim premonition it might prove one of few. "So what can you tell me about the history of the lodge?"

Clive cleared his throat. "It started life as a hunting retreat and country escape for a London businessman back in the eighteenth century. During the Victorian period, Blackdown Lodge became a lunatic asylum. One of those convenient, tucked-away places for families to incarcerate supposed 'loved ones' with socially embarrassing mental health problems."

Samantha sat upright, eyebrows lifting. "That sounded like a loaded statement."

"Forgive me. I had an aunt who was put away in a mental hospital as recently as the eighties. She had a nervous breakdown after losing her daughter, but wasn't mad. Not when she went in there, at least."

"I see." Samantha responded in a subdued tone, then sipped her water.

Clive went on. "The asylum closed, and this place remained empty until a religious organisation turned it into a church facility in the late nineties."

"What sort of church facility?"

"Word of Power - Bible Training Centre. Some kind of independent, born-again outfit with loose affiliations. They moved on to a cheaper property near the coast when maintenance costs spiralled and outstripped their student fee income. I bought the site from the Managing Director. A nice chap. Used to run a commercial machinery firm before he 'saw the light.'

It was when he took me on a stroll around the place, I first heard about disturbances in the north wing. Thought it odd for a holy roller to come out with an admission like that. But he seemed level-headed and straight-laced. I suppose I'm used to other stereotypes, you know? I'm sorry. I hope you're not religious."

Samantha shook her head. "Did any of the students live in the north wing?"

"No. It was still used as a bunch of empty storerooms back then. All student accommodation and most of the classrooms and kitchen were located here in the main building. It was the first area we developed. Some of our smaller, cheaper apartments occupy the two floors above us. A former 'Word of Power' student from a well-to-do West Sussex family owns one of them. I suppose he had good memories of the place. Plus a trust fund that enabled him to move back after the training centre closed." Clive lifted his tiny espresso cup with finger and thumb. "The MD told me they first got an inkling of spiritual disturbances, when some of their students used the store rooms for quiet personal prayer."

Samantha leaned forward on her chair. "What inkling?"

"There were reports of feeling 'watched.' Figures darting through empty doorways. Foul smells. Cold hands gripping and sometimes slapping people. You get the picture." He sipped his coffee and put the cup down. "To be honest, I didn't quite believe him. Struck me as odd that somebody wanting to sell an expensive property would even mention it. But I suppose honesty is a core part of their belief system." Clive swivelled in his seat to look at the courtyard through the right-hand sash window. "The disturbances only became a problem for us after we redeveloped and sold apartments in the north wing. We're quite an exclusive site. Many of our clientele are connected. If wild stories and rumours circulate about violent ghosts at Blackdown Lodge, it could bankrupt my company. Now with work on the south wing nearing completion, I want to get this whole mess put to bed with as little fuss and attention as possible."

Samantha nodded. "I have no doubt. What can you tell me about that small, derelict outbuilding in the car park?"

"It was the mortuary during those asylum years. Still has porcelain tables in there, complete with drainage holes. Even my staff hate going near that place. We considered renovating the crumbling stone shack as a sales office, but decided against it. I still don't know what to do with the structure. Why do you ask?"

"An odd feeling when I arrived."

Clive clasped his hands together on the desk jotter. "Which brings me to my next question."

Samantha sighed. "You want to know about my gift and how it all works."

"Are you psychic?"

"I get asked that a lot. I suppose in the sense I see and experience more than most, it appears that way. Are you worried I'll make a scene and scare your residents?"

"Not too much. An old architect friend

recommended you. He said you were discrete and effective. No theatrics."

"That would be Mr Walker, I assume?"

Clive eased back into his chair again. "Martin and I studied together. If he gave you a green light, that's good enough for me. You're the first person we've tried, because of the exact concerns you highlighted."

"That some crazy person would make a scene and scare your residents?"

"Yes."

"Are there people living in the north wing at the moment?"

"One couple left last week. The wife had a terrible scare in their bathroom a few months ago. She'd been on at her husband to leave ever since. I promised them both I would look into their concerns. The man got a new job in Switzerland, so they packed and moved out. I'm entrusted with selling the unit on their behalf. Beyond that, three other units are occupied. I've heard rumblings of odd happenings from snatches of conversations. None of the owners have addressed the matter with me in person."

Samantha finished her water and set down the glass. "People can be reluctant to talk about the topic. In my experience, they wait until they can no longer convince themselves it's all in their minds. That or the assumption they can ignore the disturbances and carry on regardless proves false."

"Has it ever been true for anyone?"

"I imagine so. But then they wouldn't have contacted me."

"Touché. If you'll pardon the use of another stereotype, you seem quite switched on for a young lady." He raised both hands. "I mean no offence to your gender. I wouldn't expect anyone - regardless of sex - to be so focused and savvy. Showing my age, I suppose. But, you appear mature beyond yours."

"No offence taken. Something happened to me I won't go into, that kicked all this off. Afterwards I became hyper-aware. I don't know if it's a gift, but nature balances everything out. Even one encounter can prove exhausting. I have a sense Blackdown Lodge will involve more than one."

Clive pushed back from the desk and stood. "We'd better get started without further delay, then. You've come such a long way and we're burning daylight. Where would you like to start?"

"Since your current concerns revolve around the north wing..."

"Ah yes. Sensible. Deal with the pressing and sensitive issues first. This way, Samantha." He paced back across the room towards the corridor. "I can let you into the vacant, troubled unit for starters. Do you need to be alone?"

"It helps. As long as you don't mind me wandering about the lodge?"

"Not at all. If you wish to go somewhere that's locked - other than our client's homes - pop back to the office and Kate will let you in. If we can avoid bothering residents, that would be better. I'll leave instructions with my PA. Please come and see me once you're finished, so we can *complete everything*." Clive squirmed over the last two words.

Samantha knew that face. He was a businessman used to paying for goods and services. No doubt Martin Walker had already appraised him of her curious penchant for not billing people. Commercial types were never keen on it. "Lead on."

Clive lifted a keyring off a hook by the door and strutted down the hallway past a broad flight of stairs. Despite great care and attention, the banisters still bore railings of utilitarian appearance. The spirit of Blackdown Lodge - the asylum - persisted in several fixtures and fittings. No doubt they had kitted out the apartments with no expense spared, to the latest in plush, modern taste. "That staircase leads to the smaller units I mentioned. The north wing begins at the end of this corridor."

She hadn't seen anything yet, but Samantha's body already tingled with rising static.

A blood-curdling male scream bellowed down the hallway behind them. The woman's shoulders rose to meet the back of her head in a shiver.

"Is something wrong?" Clive paused with a frown. He hadn't heard a thing.

Samantha cast a glance back over her shoulder. The corridor lay empty and silent. "No. Please continue."

"Left down here. The apartment is a ground floor unit. As you can see, the external passage is lined with doors and windows out onto the quadrangle. The apartment's windows face north to the hills on the other side."

Samantha wondered if this was an automatic mode

of speech for Clive, as if he were trying to make a sale.

Linkletter inserted one key into a door bearing the number '2.' He clicked the latch on the reverse side of the handle. "There. Release the bolt when you're finished and close the door behind you. Now if you'll excuse me, I've some important phone calls to make. Kate will help with any queries or concerns, back at the front office."

Samantha stepped across the threshold as the businessman pulled back into the hallway. "Okay."

"Good luck, Samantha. I appreciate you coming out to take a look. See you later."

She leaned round to watch him stride off down the passage. Glorious sunshine illuminated lush green fresh turf laid across the quadrangle. Out there, the feelings weren't anywhere near so ominous. Had times of exercise for the former inmates represented one moment of peace in their horrific lives? She re-entered the apartment and let the door swing to. No mistake about her suppositions on interior quality. The place was pristine and luxurious. For many, such a home might be an idyllic dream. Yet in that moment, the room's calmness gripped like a choke-hold. A suffocating silence assaulted her senses, now scanning on high alert.

"My art." A thin, reedy male voice drifted from a half-closed interior door. "I suffer for my art."

Samantha eased forward, reaching lithe fingers to push the obstruction open. It was a bathroom, tiled floor to ceiling with broad, white ceramics. Inside, an old man in a knee-length white gown knelt between the bath and a bidet. His back to the door, the fellow rubbed both hands across the wall, smearing twin trails of thick brown excrement. The smell hit Samantha's nose and caused her to recoil in disgust.

"My art. I suffer for my art," the man repeated. His bowels opened, dropping more 'paint' onto an already stinking pile. He scooped two handfuls from the floor palette and continued to daub a modern art masterpiece that was 'shit' in the most literal sense.

It was a pathetic scene, no less alive to all physical senses despite its spiritual origin.

Samantha took a step forward.

The figure span on his knees, wild but tearful eyes glaring at the intruder. "Have you come to take my paint?"

She shook her head.

The man reached his left hand up to stroke the improvised painting. "They always take my paint away and destroy my pictures."

"I'm sure they do."

"My art. I suffer for my art."

This bathroom must once have been his cell. In death he repeated the actions of life. Samantha had seen it many times before. She had no idea what caused the vacant old fellow to reach such a state. How often had he adorned the wall with his own faeces, before shuffling off this mortal coil? How often had the orderlies scrubbed the wall and cleaned him up again? The stench invaded her nostrils with repulsive insistence, but she pressed forward.

The man dropped a handful of poo and gripped hold

of her right forearm. "No. Don't take my paints." His other hand slapped Samantha across the face. It wasn't hard, but startling. "Don't destroy my painting."

A rising vibration kindled in the woman's breast. She allowed the stinking senior citizen to keep hold of her arm, as realisation dawned in his rolling eyes.

"Wha... what's happening. I'm..." His mouth dropped open to reveal several broken teeth.

Behind her, Samantha sensed an approaching astral horizon. A shimmering glow glittered with dust motes hanging in the air about her like an aura. The man let go of her arm. He gazed at the light as if it were the most exquisite thing his eyes had witnessed.

"Beautiful. Beautiful light. Such vibrant colours." The fellow climbed to his feet, stare locked on the scene occupying the opposite wall. "So much joy. Mother? Is that Mother?" His grizzled face broke into a blissful smile. "I'm coming, Mother. It's me, Gerald. I'm coming." He stumbled forward across the horizon like a giddy schoolboy, arms outstretched.

The brilliant illumination faded. Samantha found herself standing in a silent, spotless bathroom again. The only scent, a faint whiff of pine cleaner.

It was time for a ten minute break. Samantha relaxed on the sofa for a spell. The encounter with Gerald had been brief, but tiring. There must be several more to come.

The apartment door should have closed with a faint, well-oiled click. As the latch slid home, a deafening report accompanied it. So loud was the blast, Samantha performed an involuntary crouch in the hallway. Sunlight extinguished like the fading of a candle flame. Abundant, swirling thunderheads rotated in the sky above the quadrangle. Sturdy, double-glazed hallway windows facing out onto the grassy courtyard, rattled and cracked. A twirling jet of wispy smoke poured down from the heavens. It burst through a shattering, upper storey window of the main building.

Joshua Kingham opened his eyes at the sound of breaking glass. The twenty-eight-year-old had dozed off in an armchair of his apartment for a few minutes. To one side, still-packed suitcases bore airline bar code tags for LHR. He had slept little on the flight back from Atlanta, Georgia to London. A cheerful, pastel T-shirt creased across his upper torso, depicting a silhouette figure with hands raised in worship. Its bold logo declared: *'Persistent Praise Conference - 2019.'* Beneath it, a scripture read:

'Let everything that has breath praise the Lord. - Psalm 150:6'

A woman screamed in the hallway. Joshua hauled himself out of the chair and ran to unfasten his door. Out on the landing, shards of broken glass glittered in a flash of sudden lightning. It had been a perfect, warm and clear summer's day only moments before.

"Stay away from me. I don't want to go with you." A grizzling woman in her forties lay in a shivering heap on the vinyl floor. Tangled, unkempt hair hung across her face. She appeared to be wearing some kind of plain white nightdress.

Joshua lifted his head to examine the far window. Something obscured what should have been the view outside: a swirling dark figure, like billowing smoke in the shape of a human torso. "Lord protect us." The words came without thought. His mind grappled to fathom the scene.

The woman screamed again. "Help me. Somebody help me." She scrabbled at the floor behind her with frantic, twisted brown fingernails.

Joshua quelled his fear and ran to her side. One finger thrust forward at the shape, he let out a booming roar. "I rebuke you in the name of Jesus."

The smoky shape floated closer.

Joshua grabbed hold of one emaciated arm, to drag the shrieking woman along as he backed away. "I take authority over you by the risen might of the King of Kings. You have no dominion here."

The woman sobbed. "We must go. It wants me. Please can we go?" Overgrown, creepy fingernails scratched the Christian's arm.

The retreating pair reached the top of the stairs. Along the corridor, the shadow loomed nearer.

"Stay with me." Joshua attempted to comfort the panicked creature by making eye contact. He swept back the frizzy mane of her thick, brown hair. Half a face met his gaze. The woman's right eye and upper forehead appeared pummelled by some blunt, relentless force. How could such an injury not prove mortal? "Wha..?"

The object of his pity screamed again and let go of his arms. As the ominous dark creature whistled along the hall with a sudden burst of speed, she turned and ran straight through the wall.

Joshua staggered in shock. His left heel slipped on the top step. Arms flailing, he overbalanced and tumbled backwards down the stairs. Repeated impacts from the jagged, concrete flight against the base of his neck and limbs, caused the man's body to sag into a lifeless rag doll of splintering bones. A bent corpse with arms and legs pointing in unnatural directions, came to rest on the lower landing.

A woman in her mid-thirties opened an apartment door. She caught sight of the twisted body and yelled in a hysterical series of bursts, like an emergency siren.

The commotion set other doors opening. Clive Linkletter and Kate Horton ran up to the landing from the floor below. The businessman turned to his PA. "Call an ambulance at once."

Back on the ground floor, Samantha reached the junction of the north wing and main building. The male scream she'd heard earlier, sounded again. It echoed along the corridor walls towards her. This time a shape accompanied it. About her own age, with over-sized ears and disfigured face, a man wearing another asylum gown lumbered like a gorilla. Panic flashed in eyes that squinted with a nervous tick. Gobs of drool swung from the corner of a mouth it appeared he couldn't close. Samantha remained so transfixed by the approaching former inmate and his curious gait, she didn't notice a wild-haired woman appear next to her. Sharp, twisted brown fingernails dug into her arm.

"Please help us. It's coming and we can't escape." Samantha jumped and drew in a rapid breath, her eyes meeting the half-face at her shoulder.

Beyond the screaming fellow, the corridor darkened to pitch black. An ominous dread tightened in the pit of Samantha's stomach. The Entity had found her again. "Run." It was the only response left in her repertoire.

Back down the north corridor they raced: Samantha, the lumbering, disfigured hulk and half-headed woman. The escape bar clattered against a door into the quadrangle. Behind, a racing cloud of shadows clung to floor, walls and ceiling; swallowing up all light in a howling pursuit.

The fugitives reached the courtyard fountain. Samantha gasped for breath, sank to the ground and turned. Spine pressed against the stone water feature, she watched her legs lift as if sucked toward the closing dark nightmare. Her soul fought for purchase on her physical body. The Entity reached inside. Deep, spiritual fingers clawed at her life force to pin it in place. In the everyday world, Samantha longed to cross back to the endless bliss of what lay beyond. But the shadow creature wasn't attempting to take her there. This thing sought to hold her at bay. In that moment she understood its purpose. Whether or not hell was real, The Entity wished to deny anything that burned with the Divine spark, access to the light. How could she resist and fight back? Her mind returned to that night at her sister's house. When that girl crossed the astral horizon, The Entity had vanished. Samantha twisted her head aside against a raging wind. The half-headed woman flickered and struggled. On her opposite side, the panicked, disfigured man did the same.

"Take my hands." Her voice went hoarse with stress and effort to get the words out. She thrust both arms wide, fingers stretching towards her writhing companions. "Reach out."

A chunky mitt of a male hand and several slender fingers with ugly brown nails gripped those of the gasping woman. Above the courtyard, clouds parted. Light descended. Not sunlight or the orange hues of summer dusk; this was a light burning brighter and more constant.

Inside Samantha's being, a war raged. Energy almost spent, she reached down for every reserve drop. "I can't hold it back much longer. Let go. Both of you. Let go and be free."

The Entity roared.

Both earthbound spirits rose into the sky. Dark, grasping fingers snapped at their heels but gained no hold.

A thunderclap rang out, and the sky cleared. The pursuer was nowhere in sight.

Samantha touched her forehead. It would be an effort to find strength to stand. Plus something still wasn't right.

Out in the car park beyond the main building, an

ear-splitting spiritual wail cut through the temporary stillness. In her heart of hearts, Samantha knew no other mortal had heard it. The old mortuary shook, enshrouded by a cloak of darkness. Cobweb coated windows shattered as its roof collapsed. Stone walls - now devoid of mortar - sagged and dissolved. When darkness lifted from the resulting pile of rubble, no presence remained to trouble those sensitive to the unseen world.

A stab of pain seared Samantha's heart. The Entity had got one. How many would that make and where did they go? When you've been to the light and returned, the thought of eternity in outer darkness goes beyond agony.

Along the no-through lane to Blackdown Lodge, emergency sirens wailed and flashing blue lights drew near.

It was late when Samantha got back to her studio flat in Folkestone. Clive Linkletter did his best to downplay any weird noises or screams to his residents. In the ensuing commotion around the death of Joshua Kingham, there was no time for Samantha to deliver an after-action report. An initial assessment attributed the young man's death to an accidental tumble resulting from jet-lag. The businessman hoped it would end there.

His visitor slipped off to Kent during a quiet moment. If he e-mailed her, then she'd provide an update. Somehow Samantha didn't want to get paid for this job. When she collapsed into bed, sleep wouldn't come. Exhaustion failed to compete with the anguish of that final cry from the mortuary. She had failed. The memory was agony, and it haunted her. She must never fail again.

7

Timekeeper

SALLY NELSON, 1941.

"Is that clock new, Granddad?" A seven-year-old girl with a mop of straw-coloured, bouncing ringlets moved to the mantelpiece.

"Yes, Sally. Your grandmother always wanted us to have a fireplace clock." The old man smoothed strands of grey hair in a comb over of well-greased wisps. He leaned back in his rocking chair and let the natural motion move him like the cradling arms of a new mother. "Now she's gone, I thought I should buy one."

Sally peered into the shallow-domed glass dial cover with its elegant brass surround. The clock was set in a dark, shaped wooden base. It formed an organic curve from the horizontal, over the central timepiece and down the other side. A thin, red second arm moving with a gentle tick, fronted intricate black hands and elegant script numbers. "It's so smart. Is that the one Grandma wanted?"

Her grandfather teased out several strands of tobacco from a pouch and stuffed them into the bowl of his wooden pipe. "I don't recall that we ever chose one." He struck a match and puffed the mouthpiece for a few seconds. "Whenever we passed the jewellers in Chelmsford, she always reminded me we should get one, some day."

"I'm sure she'd like it." Sally returned to perch on a footstool next to him. "What's for tea?"

"Bread and preserves. I fixed a few jars of strawberry jam from fruit in the garden, last week. Saved up sugar from my ration to make it."

"Oh, delicious. Shall I fetch a jar from the pantry for you, while you finish your pipe?"

"If you think you can reach. Don't go tumbling off the steps in there."

"I won't." Sally skipped across the flagstone floor of the single-storey thatched cottage, to a broad, white wooden door. The Suffolk latch rattled in her hand and she disappeared inside another small room.

The old man continued to rock, blowing out long clouds of smoke. "If you fetch the loaf in, we'll slice it up right here and listen to the wireless," he called.

"I will. It's so good spending a few days with you. I know we live in the same village, but it still feels like a proper adventure."

The man chuckled and screwed up his eyes. "It'll make your mother's food go a little further, too."

Sally returned with a loaf under one arm and a jam jar in the opposite hand. "Do you think Father eats as well aboard ship?"

"I don't know, pet. The Royal Navy needs all its sailors to be fighting fit, so they must have reasonable grub. There now. Pop those items down on the table, and get a bread knife from the kitchen, would you?"

"Yes Granddad."

"There's a good girl."

Sally disappeared into the kitchen and let out a shriek.

The old man tapped out his pipe in a hurry. With aching limbs, he struggled aloft and hobbled towards the cry of distress.

A large, female Adder coiled at the foot of the cooking range. Waves of heat that made the room unbearable in summer, were attractive to the cold-blooded reptile. Its dark brown skin and diamond-backed body tightened. Red eyes glittered at the two giant creatures disturbing its impromptu basking session.

Sally pressed herself against one rough, stone whitewashed wall. "Will it bite me, Granddad?"

The man coughed and lifted a broom from the corner. "It will if you interfere with it. They come in off Danbury Common at this time of year, whenever I leave the back door open to let heat out. The females are bigger."

"Is that a lady snake?"

"That's right. Males have a grey body, with the same black diamond patterning." He leaned closer and pulled the hissing creature across the floor with gentle flicks of the broom. "Go on. Out you go." A few more encouraging shoves and the agitated reptile slithered off down the rear garden path. The man shut the back door. "There. Panic over. If it was the neighbour's cat popping in for a snooze, I wouldn't mind. A moggy you can stroke and make a fuss of. Can't say the same for an Adder. Right then. We were after a bread knife, I believe."

Sally rushed over and flung her arms around the old man's stomach. "I love you, Granddad."

"Aw. That's nice. I love you too, pet. Fetch two plates off the rack - almost forgot those - and I'll bring the knife in."

Back in the living room, the pair settled down to spreading delicious strawberry jam onto doorstep-sized slices of bread. The wireless warmed up and a BBC announcer relayed an account of action in the Mediterranean. The Royal Navy were engaged in an attempt to rescue as many British and Dominion soldiers as possible from the besieged island of Crete. They ferried evacuees to the relative safety of Alexandria in Egypt, their convoys dogged every step of the way by Luftwaffe aircraft. Ten thousand men got left behind, but the Navy saved fifteen thousand, taking heavy losses of both ships and crew.

Sally listened as she chewed. "I wonder if Father's ship is involved in that?"

Her grandfather rubbed crumbs from his fingers. "Don't you worry, now. With a name like Able Seaman Nelson, he's sure to win. Look what they did to the *Admiral Graf Spee* at the Battle of the River Plate."

"He was aboard *HMS Ajax*, back then."

"Now he's on another cruiser, *HMS Calcutta*."

Sally nodded. "Ajax needed repairs after the fighting in South America."

"She's been back in the fray. I heard she gave the German torpedo boats hell in the Med until a bomb damaged her."

The news report ended, and they finished their tea.

Plates cleared away, the old man deposited his kettle on the stove. Sally stood in the kitchen doorway watching him.

The man hooked a couple of cups and saucers from a cupboard. "I've never had you bring any of your friends round to visit. They're most welcome, you know."

Sally looked down at her feet, twisting them back and forth. "I don't like to play their games. I'd rather be home with Mother or here with you."

Her grandfather straightened and paused. "The other children aren't unkind to you, are they?"

"No, Granddad. They're very nice. But I get tired when I'm around them too long."

The old man licked his lips. "Your father was much the same as a boy. He could sit in the garden all on his own, happy as anything the whole day long. How he copes on-board ship, I can't imagine. It must be difficult for him."

Sally grimaced and intertwined her fidgeting fingers. "I would hate it. Cramped together with all those people and nowhere to get away."

The kettle whistled as a jet of steam escaped.

"Time for a nice cuppa, pet. Then it's off to bed so you're fit for school in the morning."

"Mother. I'm back. I had such a great time at Granddad's cottage. Apart from the snake. But otherwise it was like a magical holiday. Did you know Granddad has a new mantelpiece clock? It's so smart. He said Grandma always wanted them to own a clock for the fireplace. Granddad made some strawberry jam. It was so tasty. Mother?" The non-stop, excitable dialogue came to an abrupt end, moments after Sally arrived home a few days later. Her mother sat at the dining table of their tiny house on the other side of Danbury, Essex. Head buried in folded arms, her shoulders rose and fell in a series of sobs.

"Mother?" A flash of uneasy warmth throbbed in the seven-year-old's head. "What's wrong?" She approached the table. An official-looking piece of paper lay at a crooked angle, beyond the weeping woman's grasp.

Lucy Nelson pulled a handkerchief from her apron pocket to blow her nose. "Come and sit down with me a minute, darling." She patted a wooden chair next to her.

"Is something wrong, Mother? Has Father been injured?"

Lucy blinked. One tender hand stroked her daughter's right upper arm. "Your father's ship was sunk by aircraft, off the coast of Alexandria."

Sally's eyes reddened. "Did they pull him from the water?"

"No, darling. A bomb hit the ship. There wasn't time."

"So... He's..."

139

Lucy pulled the girl close. "He's not coming home to us, ever again."

*   *   *

"It won't be long now." Doctor Phelps clipped his leather case fastener shut as he entered the Danbury cottage living room.

Sally Nelson put down a June 1956 edition of the local paper. The attractive blonde - now twenty-two years old - stood and smoothed down a blue, full-circle skirt. Her mother rose to join her.

Lucy Nelson cleared her throat. "You've done all you can, Doctor. Thank you."

The physician adjusted a pair of wired-framed spectacles, removing them to clean the lenses on a cloth. "Was he your father?"

"Father-in-law. My late husband was killed in the war. He grew up in this cottage."

"Ah. I'm sorry. If you call me when... Well, you know. I'll see to the arrangements."

"Thank you again." Lucy escorted him to the front door.

Back in the living room, the only audible sound was a gentle ticking from a clock on the mantelpiece. Sally's eyes fell upon it. Memories of her childhood break came flooding back. Those halcyon days before her entire world crashed down about her ears. *Granddad should have the clock with him.* The thought appeared out of nowhere. She lifted the sturdy timepiece between delicate hands.

"What are you doing, Sally?" Her mother returned.

"This clock meant a lot to Granddad. I'll put it alongside his bed."

"What if he doesn't want it disturbing him?"

Sally frowned. "We can ask, can't we?"

Lucy gave a subtle frown. "Okay."

"I've brought the clock in for you, Granddad. Would you like to have it here?" Sally placed the item on a chest of drawers, where the bedridden man could see it.

A thin, drawn face lifted an inch or two from a pile of pillows. Breath came in wheezing gasps that descended into a rattling fit of coughs. When he found enough breath to speak, the old man smiled at his Granddaughter. "Thank you, pet." He lifted one bony, wrinkled, shaking arm.

Sally sat by his bedside and clasped it. "Is there anything I can get you?"

"The clock." The voice came faint and frail.

"I've brought you the clock, Granddad."

"I want you to look after the clock when I'm gone."

Lucy Nelson settled on the other side of his bed. "Now then, Dad. No need for that. You'll be up gardening in a week or two. You wait and see."

The man coughed again and shook his head. He aimed moist eyes at the young woman who had once come to stay in his home. That weak hand stroked her face. "Such a pretty girl. Is there no-one to tempt you as a husband?"

Sally swallowed. "No, Granddad. That's not for me."

He nodded in a slow sweep. "Still like your own company?"

"I'm happy as I am. Or at least, I would be less happy with someone else."

Lucy groaned. "Can't you talk some sense into her, Dad? I've tried everything. She'll waste her prime years at this rate. Twenty-two already and never had a boyfriend."

Bernard Nelson squeezed Sally's hand. He winced at his daughter-in-law. "Leave her be. I know you love her, Lucy. We all want what's best for Sally. But she has to steer her own course."

Lucy threw up her hands in surrender. "Fine. I'm going to fix a drink. Would you like a cup of tea, Dad?"

"Yes please."

"Sally?"

"No thanks. I'm fine."

Lucy left for the kitchen.

Sally leaned close to kiss the old man on the cheek. "Do you remember the Adder in your kitchen, Granddad? When I was a little girl, I mean."

The man spluttered, his chest rising and falling in a mixture of mirth, nostalgia and pain. "What a shriek you gave."

"I love you, Granddad."

"I love you too, Sally. Don't worry about being alone. I'll always be with you. Right until the end of time."

He closed his eyes, and the breathing came easier. In the stillness of that bedroom, the old mantelpiece clock ticked away the seconds. His hands went cold and the life force slipped free of its exhausted shell. When Lucy Nelson returned with the tea, she found her daughter washing his face with her tears.

Atop his chest of drawers, the clock ticked on.

*   *   *

1st June 2018 was a bright, sunny day at the Great Lines Naval Memorial in Chatham. At the foot of the hill, Friday lunchtime crowds walked with a spring in their step. That enthusiastic buoyancy of spirit that comes with the delicious anticipation of a weekend ahead.

Atop the hill, an eighty-four-year-old woman shuffled towards the prominent landmark. One hand rested with much effort on a simple wooden cane, steadying her frail steps. The other clasped tight to a wreath of poppies, in which was set a white paper circle featuring a printed blue anchor. She passed through the gateway and turned right along one of the curved outer walls. The span stood covered with plaques of names; each one a brother, son, husband, or father. The name she scanned for, met the last three criteria.

'NELSON H. J.'

The old woman stopped; arthritic body immobile, face mesmerised. Sally Nelson's eyes might have fallen upon the commemorative inscription, but her mind wandered elsewhere in dreams of yesterday: A young girl playing in the garden with her father. Carefree times, before his naval reserve status saw him summoned back to service. She had been five at the outbreak of war. One trembling, liver-spotted hand laid the wreath at the foot of the panel bearing her father's name. An attached card from The Royal British Legion contained Sally's simple, handwritten message:

'To Dad,
Lest we forget.
HMS Calcutta, 1st June 1941.
All my love,
Sally.'

The old woman straightened as best she could. Her hunched shoulders always featured a stoop these days; neck extending more horizontal than vertical. This was an annual pilgrimage from Danbury to Chatham, each June. Ever since the Commonwealth War Graves Commission added Able Seaman Harry Nelson's name to the monument, she'd never missed a year. The long and involved bus and train journeys from Essex, had proved more of a drain during the last five or six visits. Every step she took felt like someone strapped weights to her chest and legs. Simple tasks like getting up to put the kettle on, must be considered in the light of whether a visit to the toilet was the more pressing need.

True to her word as a young lady, Sally Nelson remained single. She moved into her grandfather's single-storey cottage when he died, and worked in a shop within walking distance until retirement caught up with her.

But it wasn't the physical toll alone that weighed heavy. The world had changed about her, and seldom for the better. In the last twenty years, the long-heritage local woman found it almost impossible to recognise her home. At the supermarket checkout, people pushed and hurried her. Sometimes she found herself the victim of verbal assault, while rummaging in her purse for the correct change or a coupon for baked beans. Common courtesy, patience and manners seemed to have vanished or gone out of fashion. Everybody hurried from moment to moment, glued to mobile computer screens. On the bus and train it was rare to hear a word of English spoken. And that in its namesake country; the birthplace of the international language of business and radio communication.

People's faces were different too. Sally got on well with some of her new neighbours. One jolly woman from Barbados always gave her a big hug and smile if she met Sally on the street. But they still weren't *her* people. Neither were they few nor scattered. The world had moved into her backyard, without a care for the homes, communities and traditions it displaced and destroyed. That centuries of generational history and local culture made Sally's home what it was, didn't seem to matter. For a lady who'd already lived a solitary life, being cut off from her own kind made her feel increasingly isolated.

The silver-haired pensioner tried talking about her feelings once, with a friend called Gill she used to meet in a cafe. Two university students overheard their frank discussion and hurled abuse at the pair, calling them *'racist, fascist, white-supremacist, Nazi pigs.'* They hassled the women all the way from the cafe to the bus stop.

Gill died later that month. Now Sally had no other contacts she could relate to. Even if she had, the encounter scared her so much it took every ounce of courage to open her front door and go shopping. A prisoner of fear in her own home and minority stranger in her ancestral land. Was this the freedom and liberation her father gave his life for?

At the bus stop near her cottage back in Danbury, Sally thanked the driver (as was customary in her generation) and alighted with her cane. The Somalian driver grinned and his bus pulled away.

A silver Audi with blacked-out windows cruised past, reverberations from bass on the stereo shaking the glass. Muffled strains of rap music caused the pensioner to stagger sideways. The lyrics were English, but not in a dialect she could understand. It all sounded so aggressive and violent.

Sally concentrated on putting one foot in front of the other, puffing at the effort. Combined with her walk to and from the memorial in Chatham, this had been an exhausting day. It was a great relief when the front gate and short garden path to the cottage appeared round the corner. Quivering fingers jangled a set of keys. The brass collection slipped through her fingers to land with a clink on the doorstep. Sally steadied herself against the porch and eased into a crouch to retrieve them. Getting back up again proved the harder task.

At last, after many missed attempts, the key went home in the lock. She tottered back into the familiar abode. The door closed on her sanctuary. Safe in the four walls where her father grew up and grandfather died, she breathed a difficult sigh of relief. At least the scant, secluded square footage of the old cottage was still 'England,' while she remained resident. Would that inherited home also be colonised once her time on earth ended?

After settling down with a bowl of soup and dry crackers for tea, Sally turned on the TV evening news. With the brief introductory headlines over, she switched it off again. The old woman couldn't watch full-length news stories any more. Even if they contained items of interest, each was always presented with the same awful bias and propaganda by political activists pretending to be journalists. Newspapers weren't much better, so she didn't bother with them either. Sally heard there might be places to read news of a more balanced nature on the Internet. But, she'd never used a computer and didn't know how. Nor did she want to.

The sudden absence of noise brought a welcome peace to the room. Only the slow, faithful ticking of her grandfather's clock - now back on the mantelpiece -

broke the stillness. It was a restful, almost hypnotic sound.

In that moment, a pang of loneliness throbbed deeper than ever. Her family and friends were dead. Her community obliterated. Every breath became a struggle. As an elderly woman she seemed invisible to others at best, and an unwanted burden at worst. One silent tear trickled down a dry and wrinkled cheek. What could she do? It was hopeless. She had no power to act or change a thing. Basic survival at her time of life proved difficult enough. Bernard Nelson's charge to look after his clock, bubbled up from her pool of distant memories. *I can do that at least.* She studied the timepiece from across the room, remembering her seven-year-old self peering at it. Granddad's later words of comfort drifted back from 1956, right before he passed:

'Don't worry about being alone. I'll always be with you. Right until the end of time.'

Until the end of time? What was this if not the end of time? *I love you, Granddad.* The recollection and her response restored some comfort to aching limbs, while Sally rested tired eyes.

As the clock ticked on, Sally Nelson wasn't aware of the moment her spirit departed. The old woman's will remained intent on caring for Bernard Nelson's timepiece. Her essence swam with rose-tinted memories of yesteryear.

The council discovered her remains some weeks later. Nobody attended Sally's funeral.

Someone bundled the old mantelpiece clock into a cardboard box, ready for sale. Whoever purchased it would gain an attractive, reliable instrument for keeping time. They would also gain a spiritual passenger, oblivious to her state. The lingering presence of a loving child at heart, who remained behind in this world to fulfil a promise to the grandfather she loved so much.

8

The Loner

ANDREW MILES, 2019.

Three years in limbo passed in the blink of an eye, for the wandering spirit of Andrew Miles. He remained near the Medway towns. Whether this was because of his association with them in life or a lack of imagination, the departed carpenter couldn't tell. He knew he was dead. Fear of judgement kept him glued to this earth. An existence based on cherished memories of the past with Sharon. But more than fear was at play. Andrew became angrier with every happy couple he witnessed. Folk enjoying their mundane lives in a state of carefree abandon. People oblivious to how lucky they were. Unaware how life could rip everything of meaning and purpose away from them in an instant. Beyond that, he was angry at God. What kind of sick puppet-master was the absent, cloud-dwelling smiter? Cancer struck Sharon down in her prime. A bright, beautiful, intelligent and loving woman, taken at thirty-six. Why? It became plain that time was an irrelevant concept in the life beyond. What did another fifty or sixty years matter to The Almighty, had God bestowed them upon his wife? Andrew was stuck, like a car spinning its wheels without traction. There was energy, force, desire, emotion. He wanted Sharon and their old life back. But how could such a situation ever come about?

That he wasn't alone in his stranded, aimless wanderings was also clear. Andrew never drifted much beyond Rainham, Gillingham, Chatham and Rochester. Even in the relative tight clustering of those overlapping towns, the world thronged with aimless beings. The restless departed going neither forward nor backward on their spiritual journey.

Andrew swooped low, heading southwest over the Medway City Estate one bright, early summer morning near the end of May. Beyond the rippling, muddy brown waters of the river peninsular, Rochester Bridge carried rail and road traffic in an unending flow as relentless as the mighty watercourse beneath. The ghost ducked low between wide brick pillars supporting the iron girder crossings resting upon them. Any novelty value from personal flight soon wore off when you had nowhere of interest to go, nor purpose for going. He rose to soar level with The Esplanade on his left. Castle Hill snaked up between the ancient fortress of Rochester Castle and its neighbouring cathedral. The damaged castle ramparts still bore testimony to a thirteenth-century siege of the keep. The result of attempts to hold it against King John after his refusal to abide by Magna Carta. In his fury, Andrew imagined a *'Great Charter of Liberties'* to free the hopeless, bustling deceased from their unseen perambulations among the clueless throng of mortality. It was a grand but pointless dream. Yet it served one purpose in adding fuel to the conflagration of his ire. That fuming furnace gave off showering sparks of life. Each one strengthened his resolve to take action, should he ever assemble a plan and find an outlet for it.

All along the waterfront, pale, listless, once-human creatures lingered. Sombre expressions spoke of the relentless erosion that came with unending hopelessness. Suicide and murder victims alike clustered near the water's edge. Spots where they met physical ends but their spirits went no further. Eyes as empty as their purpose for being, they watched Andrew drift by with vacuous, emotionless stares.

A broad, wooden pontoon stretched out across mud flats to where an array of moored white motor cruisers followed a lesser bend in the river. Andrew skimmed the head of a civilian captain, striding out to his vessel in a bright orange life jacket and dark blue peaked cap. The man puffed on a cigarette, oblivious to his presence. Most of the time, life continued that way: unseen and unfelt. Two realities side by side, yet worlds apart. There were those with a partial window into their existence. How 'fogged the glass' depended on the individual, their gifts and life experience. Some could feel you, others hear you. A precious few might see you. Andrew had never managed a conversation with one yet. Most tried to get away in a hurry. But if he did ever manage, what would he say? They couldn't bring Sharon back and he didn't want to cross over.

A dark green Mercedes van chugged down a side road to a small array of old, wharf-side warehouses that had somehow escaped conversion to upmarket housing accommodation. So far, at least. The sight of a dirty, commercial vehicle in such salubrious surroundings, piqued Andrew's interest. He couldn't make out the driver yet, but already a certain kindred bond based on his mortal occupation drew the spirit closer. The van pulled up on a short drive outside a set of sliding double-doors in a crumbling, multi-storey Victorian warehouse. The driver's door flapped open to allow a man in his mid-sixties to slide out. Thick white hair clumped either side of his head, but only a few cotton wool strands remained on top. Andrew descended to stand beside the fellow as he unlocked the double doors. When he turned, pale blue eyes gazed straight through the dead carpenter, as vacant as the waterside spirits. The creases of advancing age accentuated a broad nose and thin mouth. Those folds of cracking skin added interest to an otherwise unremarkable countenance, the same way dry-brushing techniques brought depth to a painted figurine. He inserted a key into the rear doors of the van. Gentle but straining arms flexed. He lowered a large object covered in a protective sheet to the ground. Andrew stepped back in surprise. A girl around ten years old with dark auburn hair, hopped down beside the warehouse owner. She was clad in an old-fashioned nightdress. Andrew recognised the telltale aura of the deceased in an instant. The white-haired van driver lifted the draped object with a puff. He carried it mere inches above the ground into the dark, cavernous maw of his lock-up. The child followed him without a word, neither acknowledging Andrew nor noticed by the struggling fellow with his curious burden.

For the second time that morning, curiosity got the better of Andrew Miles. It was rare to find something of genuine interest in his unending hell.

Inside the warehouse, the owner flicked on overhead lights of such low wattage they lifted the interior from pitch black to an indistinct twilight, and nothing more. For the departed, illumination mattered little. Andrew's gaze fell upon antique sideboards, boxes of silverware, elegant dining chairs, wardrobes, and even a stuffed tiger that must have dated back to the Indian Raj. History covering several centuries and notable periods crammed cheek-by-jowl in the open-plan interior. Only perimeter walkways and flights of rough wooden stairs occupying either end of the building, gave access to the upper levels. Faint glimmers of bright sunshine outside, poked through rare, clear patches in an array of dirty glass roof skylights far above. The owner set down his new acquisition with great care. The sheet rose in his hands to reveal an exquisite, antique white rocking horse made by a craftsman of considerable artistry. Glass eyes gave an almost lifelike appearance to the face. A sturdy leather saddle and stirrups still adorned its back. Tack and other accoutrements connected everything together. The mane hung with what must have been real hair.

Every item looked original, as though the animal had left the maker's workshop mere days before. Either that, or it appeared children down through many years had left the toy alone. How could that be, with such an inviting plaything?

The ten-year-old girl flung her arms about its neck and straddled the wooden creature's back. Outside, the building owner closed the warehouse doors and started his van engine to pull away. Inside, the horse rocked all alone in the dark, dusty storage facility.

Andrew paused for a moment, torn between wanting to make contact with the girl and follow the curious, white-haired fellow. In the end, the latter was too much of a draw to resist. After all - like himself - the spirit child didn't appear to be going anywhere. If his assumptions proved correct, she'd been in this restless state far longer than he.

* * *

Harold Jessop brought his dark green Mercedes van to rest on a steep gradient facing down Cookham Hill, Rochester. From outside his two bedroom, Victorian terrace near the bend into Hill Road, he could see the distant River Medway and buildings clustered along its far bank. Parking was such a premium on the narrow thoroughfare, he received constant flak from angry neighbours about the size of his vehicle. But Jessop didn't give a fig for their protestations. 1930s villas adorned one side of the residential street, while smaller houses like his own sat opposite. He switched off the ignition and retrieved a plastic dispenser of spearmint sweets from the glove box. The taste in his mouth on this sweltering day, brought a sense of freshness. He sucked and crunched, staring down at the broad, silent river on the horizon. To natural eyes and senses, it was another day alone in his sixty-five-year existence. Were his perception heightened in that moment, Harold might have considered his reflection of solitude a sham.

Alongside him - silent and unseen - sat a plump, short man with black hair and bushy eyebrows. At the time of his death, the curious passenger had lived through forty years. Another three passed after that fateful day when he'd opened his wrists with a knife, from grief and despair. Now he watched the driver chew on a sugary treat. Andrew Miles had forgotten the textures and flavours of food. It all seemed so pointless now.

Harold checked his mirror for passing vehicles, then hopped out of the cab. He opened a uPVC front door to his house, sitting three paces from the weed-encrusted footpath with its rusty metal railings. Inside, a hallway led straight into a front room with a fireplace, sofa, chair and TV. A wall separated this from a small dining room and galley kitchen. Between them, a steep flight of dark stairs ran up to the two bedrooms, one each front and back. Behind the downstairs kitchen, lay a ground floor bathroom and ramshackle conservatory fitted with a corrugated plastic roof. A door led down to a cramped cellar, impossible for a medium sized man to stand upright in.

Harold tossed his keys into a carved wooden bowl. His back arched and stretched while he studied his watch. He'd made good time collecting that latest trophy for the shop. A rocking horse of such age and quality was sure to fetch a decent price on the antiques market. At least he needn't rush today. 'Jessop's Antiques' was always closed on a Monday. He might have been a one-man band without staff, but Harold still appreciated the need for a rest. It was important to take a day off to compensate for every Saturday spent at work. He opened the fridge door to pull out a dark brown bottle of craft beer. There were no more journeys to make, so he intended to enjoy his break. A hiss of gas escaped from the levered crown cap. Harold took a swig from the bottle and wandered towards the back door. The rear gardens on Cookham Hill were of considerable length. Extensive, thin strips of land from an age when growing your own produce was a common fact of life. The antique dealer sauntered down a rough path of concrete slabs, glancing right across the river valley below. He savoured another mouthful of suds. At his feet, a Slow-worm slithered out of the compost heap and disappeared under damp boards of a rotting, half-collapsed shed. These legless lizards were a common sight in Rochester. Harold drained the bottle and strolled back towards the house. Some brickwork looked in need of serious re-pointing. He made a mental note to allocate funds from his profit on the rocking horse towards household repairs. Inside, the front doorbell chimed. Harold dumped the empty bottle in a glass recycling caddie by the back door, then hastened to see who was calling.

"Good morning. How are you today?" The forty-something postwoman clutched a rectangular brown package to her shapely chest. Two curvaceous lumps rippled through a bright red polo shirt summer uniform. Shoulder length, dark blonde hair gathered together in a loose topknot above her oval head. To Harold, this style choice suggested both practicality and a hint of naughtiness. Even a wild streak. Or was that what he wanted it to suggest? The woman looked hot for what he guessed to be her early forties. She gave him a wry smile, tapping fingernails painted with jade coloured varnish against the parcel.

The dramatic alteration of Harold's expression from grim emptiness to welcoming delight, made Jesus Christ's transformation of water into wine at the wedding in Cana look like a cheap card trick. Yet still the man did not understand why he reacted in such a manner. "I'm very well, thank you. Yourself?"

"Not too bad. Thank goodness we can wear lighter outfits in this heat. Shorts too." She twisted to show off a pert bottom wrapped in figure-hugging grey material. It defined the curvature of her tight buttocks with breathtaking precision. Either her job worked wonders on those buns, or they'd never suffered the strains associated with childbirth.

Harold inserted an index finger into his shirt collar and pulled the sweat-drenched material away to let in a breath of cool air. "That must be quite a relief."

"Yeah. After a few hours lugging the post around, I

can't wait to peel everything off and slip into a nice, relaxing bath. This job keeps me fit. I'll say that much for it."

The sixty-five-year-old wanted to add, "I should say it does," but his nerve gave out. Mild banter and cheerful greetings were as far as he'd ever got with the opposite sex. Before a familiar, inner voice could berate him for dropping the ball yet again, he changed tack. The volume of that inner critic sounded quieter these days. It became easier to justify inaction the older Harold got. The greater the difference in age between himself and anyone who caught his eye, the easier the justification. In truth, he didn't want to engage with women. But his frustrated, restless spirit still inhabited the flesh and blood body of a human man. "Do I need to sign for that?"

"Yes please." She retrieved an electronic signature pad and passed it across.

Harold squinted in the sunlight and scribbled an approximation of his signature with the black plastic stylus. "Don't think that would hold up in court as my signature, but there you go." How many times had he cracked the same old joke?

The postwoman presented a polite smile. "A formality. Here you are." She handed him the parcel.

Harold took it. For one delicious moment, their fingers met. The retiring, confirmed bachelor's digits tingled with excited electricity. Had she noticed? Did the woman feel anything at all, while staring into his ageing face with those big, soulful, baby-blue eyes?

"Have a good day." She bounced on the spot, span

and strutted back through Harold's front gate. It hung from loose, rusty hinges in a squat, ugly brown picket fence with peeling paint.

"You too," he called out late enough for the response to appear an exercise in soliloquy.

The woman pounded the pavement with firm muscular legs and toned calf muscles. She glanced back over her shoulder one last time, then crossed the road for her next delivery.

They have a short space in which to visit each address. Harold attempted to comfort himself with a true but unhelpful excuse for not pressing forward. Sure, he couldn't ask her *in* for a drink, but he could ask her *out*. Even the idea set his teeth on edge. *There's a good twenty or more years between us. Don't be daft. Open your parcel. You don't want all that nonsense in your life. Never have.* His mind returned to more comfortable topics. An Ipswich postmark caused his fingers to fumble. "It's the one I've been waiting for." Those words were spoken aloud. He might have been surprised to learn somebody nearby heard them. Harold ascended the stairs to the front bedroom which he used as a study. Floor to ceiling bookcases clung to three of the walls. Each shelf groaned under the weight of obscure, dusty tomes, rare arcane volumes, and first edition classics collected over a lifetime. The final wall featured an antique desk and chair. He flopped into his favourite seat, fingers swiping a brass letter opener from next to the dry ink well. Harold opened the package with care, to reveal a faded old book. It appeared a similar size and shape to the Anglican one of common prayer, though bound in cracked leather with yellowing pages. Gold-embossed spine lettering read: *'On Worlds Beyond: A Grimoire of Necromancy - Part I.'*

Harold peeled open the pages. His eyes scanned long-forgotten observations on communicating with spirits of the dead. Communicating and divining the future. The text was diverting, though written ages past using archaic English. His mind wandered back to the postwoman. Despite a life of romantic avoidance, basic biology still occasionally poked its head above the parapet of his attention. Down on the street, the attractive blonde postal worker finished her current bag of deliveries. She ambled over to where a Post Office van stood parked near the playing fields on the corner. Visions of those muscular legs wrapped around his upper torso, consumed the conflicted antique dealer. Thoughts of her *peeling everything off and slipping into a nice relaxing bath* followed. Their logical progression galloped into the jigging motion of her saucy topknot bouncing in time with the shapely breasts. All the while those jade painted fingernails dug into his back as she screamed for joy at his fantasy 'delivery.' Or was it the size and shape of his 'package?' Harold put his head in his hands, like a frustrated juvenile in an older man's body. He would never be able to concentrate until the call of nature diminished on its own or he pushed it aside. He left the book on his desk, rose and stormed downstairs. Another beer might help. Anything to provide a temporary distraction from the persistent one in his mind.

All the while this sequence of events played out, Andrew Miles looked on with interest. It was an interest growing at an exponential rate, now he'd glimpsed the man's personal library and the contents of his new book. This guy might be worth following around for a while. His collection was most likely full of ridiculous old superstitious guff, but still provided the first glimmer of hope in a heartless existence. Andrew couldn't open books on his own. He'd yet to master the trick of throwing objects about or interacting at a physical level. There didn't seem any need. Not until this morning.

His restless spirit drifted back to the ground floor. The householder seemed to live alone. From his body language, the man appeared to have a reluctant interest in that postwoman. He was watching her again before he ran back downstairs.

Harold Jessop stood by his fridge, knocking back another bottle of beer.

Andrew remained close by - a spirit perplexed. He studied the plain decor and simple furniture of the miserable little home. The place reeked of despair, shattered dreams, and a failed life longing for meaning and significance. Had he found and latched onto someone even sadder in life than *he* was in death?

* * *

'Jessop's Antiques' was situated down a quiet back alley off the quaint, pedestrianised and block-paved delights of Rochester High Street. The cathedral spire rose above rooftops, a short distance away. The shop was once a tumbledown, late seventeenth century timber-framed hovel. Someone attached mathematical tiles to the exterior a hundred years later. This form of cladding was common at the time in Kent and East Sussex. A way to modernise the appearance of buildings rather than tear them down. To the untrained eye, the shop was built of brick. In reality, the covering had more in common with the interlocking tiles of its own roof, as if time caused the shingles to grow and hang down over the eaves like hair reaching to ground level.

Harold Jessop inserted a thick brass key into an old mortise lock in a blackened, iron-studded door that could almost have been the original. It was older than some of the stock for sale inside. Warning tones pipped from a burglar alarm on countdown. The white-haired man tapped a sequence of numbers onto a keypad fixed to the wall. All sound ceased. He flicked an array of switches, causing dim, atmospheric spotlights to bathe intriguing nooks and crannies in a soft wash of illumination. A body on auto-pilot, he zigzagged down some rough stone steps to cross back and forth on a long, red carpet leading to his corner counter. Before reversing direction each time, he clicked on another light: the bulb in a free-standing, colourful art deco lampshade here; the bright, pooling beam from a green banker's lamp there. A gradual increase in light levels presented the full interior in an inviting manner. Small, hand-written white cardboard price tags hanging from cotton thread, were now readable without eye strain. Where certain shop corners appeared darker, Harold knew they would draw people closer to investigate the ageing clutter within. He sometimes placed pricier items there. If he had a piece that wouldn't sell, Harold liked to write a crossed-out higher price above his desired figure. That way customers not only believed they had discovered something tucked away that nobody else knew about, but that it was also a bargain. The tactic worked like a charm, especially on loud tourists with big cameras and little knowledge of the antiques market. Harold placed his Tupperware lunch box on a round side table next to a high-backed Victorian armchair by the counter. Loose papers cluttered the counter worktop. A solid collection of *Miller's Antiques Handbook & Price Guides* formed into a shelf of their own against the plaster wall behind.

Andrew Miles lingered at the shopkeeper's side. He had witnessed every movement in Jessop's routine. It was the first visit to a shop he must have passed a thousand times while alive. Sharon always liked to get crepes on the High Street, before they went shopping on Saturday mornings. During the nicer weather, they used to enjoy a good breakfast beneath blossom-heavy trees. A panorama framing the cathedral and castle a short distance beyond.

A vibration rippled through his innermost being. It always happened in close proximity to certain other spirits. He glanced around. Two steps led up to a corner alcove. An ethereal light glimmered from within. Andrew moved closer. Before a locked glass display case, stood a young man wearing what appeared to be a soldier's uniform from the First World War. His vacant stare remained fixed on an item within the case. Andrew approached. The unit contained fine pieces of rare Honiton lace and individual embroidered cloth. A sign fixed to the wall read: 'The Art of the West Country.' Andrew had seen this reaction in earthbound spirits before. They remained transfixed with complete focus on some item or other they could not relinquish. The soldier gazed at a small handkerchief with an embroidered scene of whitewashed, thatched cottages. It looked like the chocolate box beauty of a Devon village. The letters 'M & P' flowed in blue script at a forty-five degree angle in one corner.

Harold Jessop lifted the handle of a black Bakelite telephone resting on the counter. One precise index finger span the dial in a series of repeated flicks. He held the receiver to his ear and waited for a voice to answer.

"Eric? Harold Jessop. Very well, thank you. Yourself? That's good. I received 'On Worlds Beyond.' Yes, quite satisfied. You were going to track down the second volume for me. They are, aren't they? Very dark. My interest? Academic." Harold chuckled. "I sell enough possessions of the dead. I've no interest in raising the departed as well."

Andrew's ears pricked up at the curious statement. He drew closer as Harold rested against the counter. Its worktop provided welcome support to an elbow sagging under the weight of the heavy old telephone receiver.

"If you could. Okay, I'll wait." Harold drummed fingers on the surface for a minute or two. "Hello? You can? Marvellous. How much?" He listened then whistled. "Okay, well you can't take it with you, I suppose. Hang on while I fish out my credit card. Yes, first class - signed for - like the previous one, please. If you can send it to the shop this time, that's a better idea. I spend more time here during regular postal hours. Don't know why I didn't think of it before." He stuffed one hand into the pocket of a tweed jacket he'd hung from a wooden coat rack upon arrival. "Here we go. It's a Visa..."

Andrew returned to study the soldier again. The figure remained immovable and unresponsive.

Tuesday morning at the shop dragged on. Every twenty minutes, exclamations of happy surprise reverberated off the close alley walls. That sound itself acted in the manner of a shop bell, announcing more delighted potential customers who'd discovered 'Jessop's Antiques' for the first time.

At lunchtime, Harold sat down in the old armchair with his Tupperware box of sandwiches. Thick cut slices of honey-roasted ham poked like rude tongues between chunky slabs of crusty, wholemeal bread. The man sunk his teeth into the snack with carefree abandon. No customers occupied the shop at present, to be disgusted by his flicking crumbs and open-mouthed chewing noises. After another mouthful gulped down his gullet with cartoon-like exaggerated swallowing, Harold waved his left arm about. Pins and needles tingled the entire length, from shoulder socket to fingertip. He plopped down a half-eaten sandwich with his other hand, to rub some feeling back into the opposite limb. The action proved ineffectual. A stab of pain contracted his chest into a tightening grip of agony. Harold attempted to stand, clutching at it with both hands. The lunch box fell from his straightening lap. With laboured breaths, he staggered against the counter then tumbled forward to fall prostrate and unconscious on the red carpet.

More sounds of happy surprise erupted from the alleyway in a broad, southern US female accent. "Oh look at this, Ira. What a darling antique shop."

A gruff but friendly man's voice of similar extraction replied. "It sure is cute, Arlene. My Lord, I've seen bigger closets than this back in Texas. Let's go inside."

The door swung open with a slight creak of the hinges.

Two well-fed American tourists wearing shorts, T-shirts and bum bags peered into the shop, eyes wide in wonder. Extra light from the exposed doorway fell across the sprawled form of the shopkeeper.

The female visitor clapped both hands to her mouth. "The poor guy. Quick Ira, do something."

Ira lumbered towards the fallen man and attempted to rouse him.

Arlene ran to the counter. "There's a phone." She lifted the weighty receiver to listen for a dial tone. "It's working. I'll call for a paramedic."

It was fortunate that many years before, the British added '911' as a valid alternative to their own '999' emergency service number. Both connected through to the same place.

The kind American tourists stayed by Harold Jessop's side until two men from an ambulance crew raced into the shop.

Andrew Miles watched the green-clad angels of mercy perform CPR and attempt to restart the shopkeeper's heart with a portable defibrillator. Unseen to them - but not the departed observer - a portal of shimmering light expanded near the wall behind the counter. Andrew recoiled from the astral doorway, shivering and moving back like some vampire repelled by a holy symbol. A spectral shape in the image of Harold Jessop, separated from the motionless body on the carpet. For one moment it caught sight of Andrew, face puzzled. Without a word, the deceased antique dealer turned and flew into the light.

Andrew watched the man go without effort, reserve or inclination to remain in his shop. Jessop crossed over to a place he dare not follow. "Lucky bastard." The light faded, and the paramedics charged their defibrillator paddles again.

The taller of the two stepped clear. "Okay, Mark. One last time, then we'll have to call it."

Andrew watched his recent hopes about to vanish with the shopkeeper. Jessop had gone. Now he would never discover what secrets lay in the man's unorthodox collection of weird, occult literature. He reached out a spiritual hand to the corpse, as if in a soothing gesture. The defibrillator whined, ready to deliver one final surge of electricity. Andrew had come so close to a solution, or so it felt. Now it was back to square one. Unless...?

9

Maternal Charms

NADINE EVANS, 1983.

A ten-year-old girl with golden hair, triangular face, and perky, upturned nosed bounced on a padded seat before her mother's dressing-table mirror. Music blared from the single speaker of a small, Japanese radio/cassette player nearby. The angled, telescopic aerial jigged in time with a harmonica lick, as *Culture Club* filled the bedroom with a catchy melody. The child leaned closer to her reflection, fingers applying glossy red lipstick to a dramatic pout. Her face creased with concentration. She examined her handiwork, then put down the makeup item. Light from a ceiling lamp glinted on an expensive-looking gold bracelet, hanging loose at her wrist. A collection of charms in a variety of shapes from animals to high-heeled shoes, jostled as she clapped in time to the beat. Legs swinging, she swiped up a puce plastic hairbrush in both hands, clutching it like a microphone. "Oh, Karma, Karma, Karma, Karma, Karma-"

"Nadine?" Her mother's head poked round the bedroom door.

The child beamed at her. "Hi Mum."

Darcy Evans smiled back. "Look at you, all dolled up. It *is* a ten-year-old's birthday party you're going to, isn't it? Some fashion house hasn't poached you as a catwalk model and you forgot to tell your father and I?"

Nadine giggled.

Her dad squeezed into the room and stopped dead. "What on earth are you doing?" He stared at his daughter for a second, then frowned at his wife. "You're not planning to let her go out like that, are you?"

"Tim, relax. It's a one-off for Jo's birthday party at the burger bar."

"And what's Jo going as, a streetwalker?"

Darcy sighed. "Don't overreact."

"I knew that girl wasn't a good influence on Nadine. You should see the magazines she's got our daughter reading. Have you read the questions children her age write in to the agony aunt columns?"

Darcy squeezed some love-handles bulging over her husband's waistband. "No, and I hope you haven't been reading them either."

Tim pulled her hands free. "It's no laughing matter, Darcy. Nadine is at an impressionable age. We can't have our ten-year-old going to a place where there are boys, made-up like a teenager. Crumbs, I thought I'd lost a few years when I walked in here and saw her."

"Now you're being silly. Anyway, Jo's mother will be there the whole time. It's a kid's fried food and knickerbocker glory fest, not a Roman orgy, Tim."

"I don't like her wearing your bracelet. She's not going in that. What if she loses it?"

Darcy sat down on the edge of their bed. "I'll make her take it off."

Tim snapped impatient fingers at the young girl. "Now, if you please, young lady. We can't have you forgetting."

Nadine removed the charm bracelet. She lifted the item of jewellery to her father, but Darcy intercepted it en route.

"I'll take that. Thank you, darling."

Nadine's heavily made-up smile inverted. "I wasn't planning on taking it with me. I only like to wear the bracelet in here and look at the charms."

Tim turned down the radio. "Hmm. Well it's safe now. I suppose if your mother is adamant, you can go like that."

Nadine raised one eyebrow and tilted her head in the mirror. "How can Mum be *Adam Ant*; she's a lady?"

The man rolled his eyes. "*Adamant* means you won't change your mind."

A mischievous glint flashed in Darcy's eyes. She dipped two fingers into a pot of thick, white hand cream and smeared a broad line across her face below eye level.

Nadine doubled over in a fit of laughter.

Darcy leapt up, waving both hands around like imaginary pistols, before belting out some music lyrics. "Stand, and deliver-"

"Okay, okay." Tim's concerned face evaporated into

an expression of relenting amusement. "Like mother, like daughter. I'm in a jolly nut-house." He kissed Nadine on the head. "You have a good time. Stay safe."

"I will, Dad. Thanks."

Tim left to watch the Saturday evening football results downstairs.

Darcy wiped the faux war-paint from her face with a tissue. "I'd better not forget and go out like this. Whatever would Jo's mother say when I drop you at the restaurant?"

Nadine stood. "Everyone would think my mum is the coolest mum in the world."

"And they'd be right." One corner of Darcy's mouth crinkled. "Are you ready to go?"

"All set."

"Good. I'll fetch the car keys."

The Evans' blue Ford Cortina pulled up in a parking space on the street outside their local burger bar. Darcy dipped into her jacket pocket and lifted something free. Nadine's eyes bulged as her mother twisted to dangle the golden charm bracelet.

"Would you like to wear this at Jo's party?"

Nadine nodded but wrestled fingers together in her lap. "Are you sure, Mum? I love your bracelet so much, but I'm worried about damaging it."

"That's why I'm offering it you. A chance to learn a little responsibility. But, it's up to you. The bracelet will be yours one day, when I'm gone."

Nadine blinked. "Not for a long time. I'll be an old woman myself by then."

Darcy's eyes narrowed, her lips forming a thin smirk. "Thanks. Err, I think. Have you got Jo's present?"

"Yes."

A line of springing, excitable girls Nadine's age, followed a tall, slender brunette woman out of a nearby alleyway.

Nadine waved to them. "There they are."

Darcy fastened the bracelet around her daughter's wrist. "Right then. Have fun. I'll be back to pick you up later."

The girl gulped, tapped the swinging charms and opened the car door. "See you later." She kissed her mother and ran to join her friends.

"And then Mum smeared white hand cream across her face like *Adam Ant*. She started singing *'Stand and deliver.'* It was so funny, Dad gave up." Nadine squeezed a large, spherical red plastic ketchup dispenser in the shape of a beefsteak tomato. Sauce squirted across her beef burger, laced with caramelised onions. Giggling girls' faces - delighted by the tale - reflected in the polished, wipe-clean table surface. At the head of the group, Jo the birthday girl sat on a crimson vinyl padded bench seat. A pile of open gifts rested beside her. The aroma of sizzling meat drifted from a bustling hotplate. Cooks in small, white paper hats flipped burgers and assembled the next round of orders.

The party tucked into their food. With the main course behind them, they lifted sizable, laminated multi-panel menus featuring pictures of every dish. A plump youngster with pigtails grunted. "Is anyone else thinking of having the banana longboat for dessert?"

Jo's mother signalled at the serving staff across the room. "Before we get into that, there's another piece of business to address."

A waitress so thin she appeared to work there without ever having tried the food, waved back. She lifted a petite, round chocolate birthday cake from behind the bar. Ten candles blazed and flickered as the guests drifted into a chorus of 'Happy Birthday to you.' Well-meaning but off-key and out of time diners on tables either side, accompanied them. Jo extinguished the candles with a single puff, to much cheering and applause.

"Looks like your mother's here." Jo pulled on her coat and peered through the misting plate glass restaurant window. "I've had such a great birthday. Thanks for coming, Nadine. And for your gift."

"You're welcome." Nadine fastened her own jacket.

"You're so lucky your mother lets you wear her bracelet. I don't think mine would do anything like that."

"It's the first time for me. Do you like the charms?"

"I do. Which one's your favourite?"

"The heart. That's the first charm my dad bought for

her."

"How romantic."

Nadine joined her friend at the window. The blue Cortina sat outside, but a thick-set silhouette at the wheel couldn't be her mother. "I suppose he *was* romantic, once upon a time." She pulled the sleeve of her jacket right down to conceal the jewellery item. "I'll see you soon, Jo. Goodbye, Mrs Kelso. Thank you for having me along."

Jo's mother placed both hands on her daughter's shoulders to address the girl's friend. "My pleasure, Nadine. Say hello to your mother for me. Tell her I expect to see that *Adam Ant* impression, next time we meet."

Nadine let out an uneasy half-grin, then pushed open the sturdy glass door by its brushed aluminium handle.

"Mum had to go next door to look after the Swanson children. Their father was rushed into hospital with appendicitis." Tim Evans looked in his mirror to signal as Nadine got settled in the car. Before pulling away, he caught sight of her thick jacket. "You'd better take that coat off in here, or you won't feel the benefit."

"That's okay, Dad. We'll be home in ten minutes."

"Don't be silly. Ten minutes with the heater going and you wearing a winter coat? Take it off. We don't want you missing school with a cold."

Nadine undid her jacket. "There. That will be enough to stop me overheating."

"Take it off, young lady." Tim's tone grew severe.

Nadine slipped out of the heavy clothing. Try as she might, there was no concealing the shiny bracelet from her father.

"Where did you get that?" The man snapped. "Have you been into your mother's jewellery box after we told you not to take the bracelet?"

"No Dad. Mum gave it to me."

"GAVE it to you?"

"Well, loaned it."

"After taking it off you? A likely story."

"She did. Mum said I could wear it to the party and learn some responsibility at the same time."

Tim held out a flat palm. "Give it to me, this instant."

Nadine unfastened the bracelet and dropped it in her father's hand.

Tim placed the item in his pocket. "I'll have a word with your mother to see if that's true once she gets home." He pulled away from the kerb.

*   *   *

Wednesday, July 6th 2005 was a seasonable day all round. A heavy passing shower in a large, Buckinghamshire cemetery added an unusual but poignant accent to the sadness of mourners.

By the side of an open grave, two figures held hands beneath a large golfing umbrella. One a father and bereaved husband, the other his thirty-two-year-old daughter.

Nadine Evans kept her perky, upturned nose into adulthood. Piercing green eyes - more world-weary and less innocent these days - still glittered beneath her shoulder-length, layered golden hair. She squeezed her father's fingers as raindrops hammered against the fabric shield above them. "How long had you known, Dad?"

Tim Evans blinked back a tear. "No time at all. She kept her sickness from me."

"But why?"

"When I asked, she said it was because she wanted as many of her remaining days to pass as normally as possible. Not overshadowed by a cloak of sadness." He snorted and wiped his eyes. "Your mother was even cheekier than usual, the last two months. I should have suspected something was amiss."

Down in the grave, a fresh sheet of lighter rain tinkled against Darcy Evans' coffin lid.

Tim rocked back on his heels. "Looks like there's some blue sky up there, trying to peep through."

"Mum would petition God for at least a little decent weather at her funeral, if she could."

"Your mum and I had thirty-four wonderful years of marriage, Nadine. Did you ever think of giving that a try?"

Nadine sighed. "I don't know. My career and social life are on a stratospheric high." She paused and scanned around the stone markers. Each provided a stark reminder of how fleeting life was. "If I met someone at work, maybe I'd think about it. Or a nice guy in a wine bar whose career wasn't a competition with mine. Someone who didn't feel threatened by my success. Ugh, I've met a few of those."

"PR Manager at a London cosmetics firm. You always liked putting on your mother's make-up as a child."

"Mum's dressing table started a lifelong interest." She kissed her father on the cheek. "Come on, Dad. We'd better put in an appearance at the food spread, or we'll insult our guests."

They walked arm in arm along the path between row upon row of graves.

Nadine settled down in an armchair at her parents' old house. The post-funeral social gathering was exhausting. It was nice to find a moment of peace again. "I'll head back to my flat in the city tomorrow morning. The firm aren't expecting me until after lunch, so that allows a bit of space. I'm stunned they gave me compassionate leave at all."

Tim sat down opposite. "You work too hard."

Nadine shrugged. "Didn't you always tell me that hard work was the pathway to success?"

"Hard work, not work addiction, Nadine."

"I also play hard. That's how I compensate and balance life out."

"With wine?"

"No, not always. Sometimes vodka is involved, too." She cracked a weak laugh. Her father didn't join in. "Okay, so our crowd like a few drinks to unwind. I don't rely on it to get me through the day, Dad. If it ever reaches that stage, I'll quit. I promise."

Tim remained silent. He rose and disappeared

upstairs for a few moments.

Nadine studied her manicure, lips pursed in an uncomfortable sucking motion. She looked up as her father returned.

"Your mother wanted you to have this, one day." He held up the golden charm bracelet.

Nadine swallowed hard. "Dad, shouldn't you keep it? That bracelet is such a special token of your relationship."

Tim shook his head. "I can't even look at it since… Didn't I once take this off you, many years ago? What were you, twelve?"

"Ten. It was after Jo Kelso's birthday party. You thought I'd taken it from Mum's jewellery box without permission."

"That's right." Tim stroked his brow with an idle hand. "It all seems so long ago, now."

"Twenty-two years come winter. So yeah, it *was* a long time ago. That's the angriest I ever saw Mum, when she chewed you out for having a pop at me over the bracelet."

"I remember. She was looking after next door's kids when we got in. Crumbs, I got a pasting when she found out I thought you'd lied, didn't I? Anyway. Here." He handed her the bracelet.

Nadine's face softened. She took the item and fastened it to her wrist, stroking the dangling charms. "This way I'll always have Mum with me. Thanks, Dad." When her gaze lifted, unhindered tears drenched her father's cheeks. Nadine rushed to pull the sobbing man into a tight embrace. Both cried.

* * *

"Hi Nikki. Yeah, I left Aylesbury early." Nadine stared out the window of a jostling train as it approached London. She pressed a mobile phone tight against one ear. "I'll be at Marylebone in a few minutes. No, I've got the morning off." She listened. "Dad was okay this morning. As okay as you'd expect, anyway. Me? Surviving." She played with the charms dangling from the bracelet. Powerful thoughts of love and loss surrounding her mother, caused Nadine to stammer. "How do you put the pieces back together after something like that? I don't know where to begin, if I'm honest." Another pause. "Not a chance. I won't be staying in Friday night. I'd go crazy. Take me out. Drag me all over town. I know it won't help in the long run, but I've got a strong urge to get hammered. Shots are on me. Honest."

The overhead carriage speaker crackled to life. "We are now approaching London Marylebone. This train terminates here. Please be sure to take all personal belongings with you and mind the gap between train and platform when exiting the carriage."

Nadine flicked her head from side to side, attempting to find the correct door for the platform. She pulled the mobile close again. "I've got to go, Nikki. I'll call you later. Okay. Bye."

Disembarked passengers picked up pace in unison along the platform, evidencing the crowd mentality of lemmings. It was difficult to resist such a psychological urge, but Nadine forced herself to slow down. There was no rush to get home. Plenty of time to spare. The journey to Baker Street on the Bakerloo Line, then eight stops eastbound on the Circle Line to Aldgate, were so familiar Nadine lost track of where she was. Her mind drifted back to Jo Kelso's tenth birthday party. She shook herself down and checked her watch as the six car tube train pulled away from King's Cross St. Pancras. *8:41. I should be indoors by 9:15.* She clung to an overhead handle, packed like a sardine in a lurching tin with copious, early morning commuters. Any hopes of a seat were out of the question at that time of day. Seven minutes and three stops later, a decelerating whine and squeal of breaks announced their arrival at Liverpool Street. Nadine tightened her grip to avoid flying into someone as the train lurched to a halt. Twin sliding doors opened to allow one or two people off. Several more waiting, ambitious souls attempted to squash themselves into the heaving, sub-surface conveyance.

A recorded announcement blared: *'Mind the gap. Mind the gap.'*

A platform guard spoke over the station PA. "Please move down into the carriages, so people boarding can enter the train. Stand clear of the doors."

Bodies jostled and bumped together. Nadine fidgeted and shifted from foot to foot. The last few days already felt like the world was closing in on her. The sensation of being cramped in a claustrophobic tube train amplified her discomfort.

A rapid warning tone bleeped. Nadine made a snap decision and shoved her way through the throng to hop out onto the platform. Carriage doors clamped shut behind her. The train juddered and accelerated into the next tunnel. Railway staff glared at her for one moment, then went about their business. She had barely gone a few steps along the platform before a deafening bang caused her to slip on the shiny surface. Just out of sight in the tunnel darkness, a dark cloud of smoke wafted into the illuminated station. A faint series of human cries and screams echoed from the gaping black hole. Startled passengers looked from one to the other, then across at confused station staff.

Nadine kept moving up to street level. Whatever had occurred, she needed to get out in the fresh air. Her emotional coping mechanisms strained close to breaking point. It was a longer walk home from Liverpool Street, but she needed the space to clear her head.

Out on the road, emergency sirens wailed. Police, ambulance and fire service vehicles tore up to the station, lights and sirens blaring in discordant unison. The sight and sound itself wasn't unusual in London. If you'd been there more than five minutes and *not* seen or heard emergency vehicles on a 'shout,' something might be awry. To have them converge on Liverpool Street at the same moment, didn't bode well. Nadine glanced over her shoulder, head groggy and full of noisy thoughts all competing for attention. She didn't see the Land Rover bearing down on her at a pedestrian crossing. Its distracted driver - rubbernecking the action scene - didn't see her either. Not until it was too late and she couldn't stop the 'Chelsea Tractor.' The woman at the wheel screamed, her foot pressing the brake to the floor. A sickening thud rippled the car's bodywork. That sudden impact tossed the dazed pedestrian in the air like a rag doll. Her skeleton jellified upon impact with a pair of concrete bollards.

Nadine didn't know if she had drifted off into another reverie, or suffered some kind of oblivious psychotic episode. An unusual sense of lightness and peace came over her. The heartbreaking burdens of recent days seemed to fall away. Where was she? Down at her feet lay a familiar figure, one limp wrist dangling over the edge of a kerb. A hysterical brunette ran screaming from the open driver's door of a tank-like, expensive Land Rover. Passers-by rushed to the scene. Nadine turned her attention back to the lifeless crumpled form. Hanging from that flopped wrist, a golden charm bracelet twinkled in the morning sunlight.

* * *

Tim Evans expected to visit the grave of his wife regularly. Seeing Darcy's resting place would help him through the denial phase of grieving. But he didn't expect that grave to include the remains of his beloved daughter. Not in *his* lifetime. Nadine had left the family home the morning after her mother's funeral, a tower of strength and support to the bereaved man.

When Tim sat down to the lunchtime news of a co-ordinated terror attack at the hands of suicide bombers in London, his heart skipped a beat. The mention of one blast near Aldgate jolted him again. It sounded terrible, but surely Nadine wasn't in harm's way? How could God allow something like that, after everything the grieving man had been through? When his calls to Nadine's mobile, office and flat went unanswered, Tim swallowed hard and phoned the Casualty Bureau number given out on the television. A sympathetic operator recorded his concerns and information about Nadine. Yet it was some while before the police knocked at his door. As it happened, his daughter avoided the first horrific blast. She didn't fall foul of the terror plot that killed fifty-two and injured more than seven hundred. It seemed a cruel irony after such a near miss, to have then lost her life at the hands of a careless driver.

A temporary marker plate announced two people buried in the cemetery plot. Now, a week after the burial, Tim stood in silence staring down at the freshly covered earth. He'd always taken for granted that he would outlive Nadine. What parent expects to bury their own child? Vague visions of her coming to cheer him up in his dotage, or bring him a tin of biscuits at an old folk's home vanished. Those images faded like morning dew on the saturated cemetery grass. Greensward would soon cover the plot where what remained of his heart lay buried. A grave containing the two women who were once his life. Tim reached into his jacket pocket and pulled out the golden bracelet. The heart charm swayed in a place of prominence above its neighbours. That thing was worthless to him now. A memory yes, but an empty, haunting one as devoid of hope and warmth as the grief eviscerating his soul. Would he feel different in time? Doubtful. Should he put the trinket away, in case it one day proved to be a talisman against bitter loneliness? How could it ever be? Ideas that the universe might be a friendly and supportive place - watched over by a compassionate God - made him laugh. Not a hearty, hale and jolly laugh. This was the laugh of sarcastic resentment. It was a common sentiment among the recently bereaved. What were those secure and happy times past, but an illusion and prelude to unbearable loss? Like heedless children dancing on wooden boards above a disused mineshaft, all the joy of yesterday fell into a pit of despair when the rotten supports of Tim's world gave way.

At his side, shackled to the bracelet, the spirit of his loving daughter reached vaporous hands toward her father.

"Dad? Dad, don't you recognise me?" *Why can't he see, hear or even feel me?* Everything swam in a pool of confusion for Nadine Evans. Her one anchor and plumb-line for comparison was her mother's bracelet. If she let go of that, she might spin in a fit of dizzying confusion forever.

The pawnshop doorbell jangled. Tim Evans shuffled

across the threshold, eyes adjusting to a dim interior. He wiped his feet on a coarse mat, as sheets of light rain speckled the dirty window.

A middle-aged man in a navy waistcoat with a gold pocket-watch and chain looked up from reading his broadsheet newspaper. He pushed away from leaning against a dark wooden table. "Good morning. How can I help?"

"I'd like to pawn this bracelet, please." Tim retrieved the item from his pocket and placed it on a glass cabinet in front of the shopkeeper.

"I see." The man folded his paper and leaned forwards for a better inspection. "Vintage?"

"Yes it is."

"It's in good condition."

Tim sucked his teeth. "With everything it's been through, that's a wonder."

The shopkeeper raised a curious eyebrow. "Oh? How's that?"

"I bought it for my wife when we were courting. She left it to my daughter when she died."

"I see." The shopkeeper cleared his throat. "I'm hesitant to enquire about your daughter, or are you selling it on her behalf?"

"No. She passed away recently, too."

"Ah. I'm sorry to hear that. In my line, it's an all too common story. Are you sure you want to pawn it?"

"Yes."

The shopkeeper pursed his lips. "If you were sure you no longer wanted the bracelet, you might have taken it to an antiques dealer or auction house. To be honest, they'd give you a better price than I. But you brought it here instead."

"Err… I want to get it off my hands without a fuss."

"I see. Let's take a closer look then, shall we?" He pulled a magnifier on an arm across the counter, then retrieved a brass slide gauge from a drawer next to the till. "A vintage charm bracelet in 14K yellow gold. 7.5 inch medium size length on a two mil chain with five charms." He placed the bracelet on a set of digital scales. "24.3 grams in weight."

Tim fidgeted on the spot. "And?"

The shopkeeper bashed some numbers into a big button calculator. "I can do four hundred."

"Is that good for a pawnbroker?"

"It's fifty percent of the ticket price I'd pay."

"Eight hundred total ticket for a vintage charm bracelet? That sounds a little light."

"Like I said, other places would offer more. Can I be frank?"

"If you want to."

"I imagine you brought the bracelet here, because you're not committed to selling it. This way you've a chance to get it back for a time, should you change your mind. There's also a fourteen day cooling-off period, after leaving here today. This isn't about the money, is it?"

"Is four hundred your best offer?"

"It is."

Tim wrung his hands. "Fine. Do I get a receipt or something?"

"Of course. I would suggest you don't lose it.

Interest on the loan is eight percent per month, payable on retrieval - should you want the bracelet back. If you don't reclaim the item plus interest payments after six months, the goods will be sold. Given the value of the piece, I'll need to contact you fourteen days prior."

"Okay. Let's do that."

The shopkeeper filled out a receipt and completed the transaction.

The grieving man continued his journey home with a heavy heart. That pawnbroker had read him like an open book. Tim was trying to instigate some definite changes to save his own sanity. There was one more stop to make: the estate agent to request a valuation. He'd decided to undergo a complete new start: A new house in a new town and new county, if he could manage it. What was the alternative? Visit the grave of his departed wife and daughter every morning, before returning to a home filled with the agonising ghosts of yesterday? He knew he wouldn't be going back to the pawnshop. That financial loss didn't bother him. There was no going back to anything, now. Only forward.

Security shutters rolled down over the pawnshop windows that evening. The shopkeeper set his alarm, locked up and left.

Inside, a gentle sobbing from the confused spirit of a thirty-two-year-old female, echoed around a charm bracelet beneath the glass covering of a jewellery counter.

10

Ancient Hope

ANDREW MILES, 2019.

Saturday, 1st June saw Harold Jessop awaken as usual, ready for another day in the antiques trade. But something was different about the man now. To the outside observer, he was still the same, sixty-five-year-old balding loner. Clumps of white hair appeared to slide off the sides of his head like melting snow. Creases continued to highlight his thin mouth with the signs of mortal mileage. No remarkable changes on the outside. Inside that physical shell however, a new tenant had taken up residence.

The front doorbell rang at his Cookham Hill terraced house. Harold opened up to reveal the dark-blonde postwoman, clutching a pile of padded envelopes.

"Good morning." Her eyes shone as she handed the packages across.

Jessop studied the items for a second. Unless he was very much mistaken, the entire bundle would have gone through the letterbox in two bursts. "Is there anything to sign for?" He met her soulful baby-blues again.

"Not today." She half-smiled, fingering her bag strap with those jade painted nails.

The antique dealer shrugged. "Okay then. Thank you." He shut the door without another word.

Outside, the woman's shoulders sank. She remained on the spot for an uncomfortable minute, face a mixture of surprise and disappointment.

At the living room window, Jessop pulled pack his dirty net curtains enough to observe her turn and trudge across the road. Except he wasn't Jessop.

Nothing could have prepared Andrew Miles for the shocking sensation of his aimless spirit incarnating into the ageing man's vacated torso. With the final burst of defibrillator energy, he latched onto that serviceable 'flesh bag' using every ounce of willpower he possessed. The ambulance crew were startled and delighted at their patient's miraculous recovery. One for swapped tales with their paramedic colleagues at the coffee machine.

Andrew had forgotten the burden of 'driving' a meat suit 24/7. Senses dulled. Vision now only worked in a forward direction, unless you turned your head. Then there were extra, unfamiliar aches and pains. Wear and tear that came with living as a man far older than he had been at the moment of his regretted suicide. A few bonuses followed, though. Hunger and the delights of food and drink flooded back with everything else.

Jessop's craft beer supplies were now at an all-time low. He'd also put on a few pounds in weight, thanks to Andrew's penchant for fried food. A fit of over-indulgence spilled across his waistband, from binge-eating to celebrate like an inmate released from prison. As he watched the toned and shapely backside of the postwoman wiggle away, other appetites re-emerged. The burden of sexuality announced its return with a stirring in his loins. *That postwoman liked Jessop. There's no accounting for taste. The daft old bugger didn't even know. Either that or he couldn't find the courage to respond to her gentle, seductive hints.* For the briefest of moments, Andrew considered doing what the reserved antique dealer never could. Erotic daydreams of what it might be like to 'treat himself' as this new guy, played out their enticing drama in at least the first act. It was then the pain of Sharon's loss hit him afresh. Ever since the late carnival queen set her cap at the carpenter, he'd never desired another woman. Each day of their married life, he had to pinch himself at how lucky he was to enjoy loving Sharon in the most intimate ways imaginable. Now he had a physical body again (albeit not his own) those extra sensations of loss returned with a vengeance. He released the net curtain and clutched his heart. *Not this pain again.* Last time it was so strong, he'd climbed in the bath with a work knife to end his suffering. *Not this time. You've got another chance to fix things. This guy has a library of freaky shit. There's got to be something in there to help. There must.* He flicked through the mail. A few mid-season sales catalogues, other marketing bumf and a letter from the bank.

Nothing of particular interest.

The sun shone bright and warm as he headed into the shop. Rochester heaved like a kicked ant's nest. It was the summer Dickens Festival weekend. They held two such events every year; one in summer, the other at Christmas. Even at a casual glance, it was clear participating crowds had taken this year's theme of *'A Day at the Seaside'* to heart. Sailors, pirates and eccentric souls sporting Victorian bathing costumes joined the typical throng of characters from the collected works of famous local author, Charles Dickens. From Samuel Pickwick through Oliver Twist to Abel Magwitch and Miss Havisham, the cast of street performers - plus ordinary folk dressing up and joining in for the hell of it - provided a colourful, jolly atmosphere to the High Street.

Andrew unlocked 'Jessop's Antiques' and disabled the alarm, mimicking the procedure for lighting the space he'd observed from his body's previous occupant. The former carpenter didn't know much about antiques. This temporary identity was a means to an end. The sooner he found some way to connect with Sharon, the sooner he'd have an idea where he was headed. The shop lacked nothing in terms of stock. Every available space held curios of all shapes, sizes and for every price bracket. If he studied those antique valuation books, the man suspected he might gain enough insight to make a few canny purchases at auction, without suffering bad losses. It was a case of treading water in a metaphorical sense. Besides, from the bank statement he'd received that morning, Jessop had built himself a reasonable financial cushion against loss and slack trade. Andrew's only pressure appeared to be maintaining the fake facade of *being* Harold Jessop. Since the bloke was such a solitary hermit, his carnal usurper didn't reckon that too taxing a challenge.

With many visitors to the town, came increased footfall across the shop threshold. Bursts of trade were sporadic. It was a double-edged sword. The festival proved a magnet to people, but also a distraction from shopping. As a former, self-employed tradesman, processing payments and writing out receipts came as second nature to the intimate Jessop impersonator. He enjoyed tallying sales in an old-fashioned, hand-written desk ledger. Whether or not the shopkeeper was a technophobe, his commercial enterprise appeared to eschew many of the contemporary I.T. additions common to retail outlets these days. A credit card machine was about the only thing visible containing a microprocessor. Andrew imagined this to have been a grudging addition. In a world where chequebooks might soon become long forgotten stock items on display in one of his glass cases, Jessop must have cursed as the out-of-place modern box became a counter-top addition.

Andrew rested the shopkeeper's backside on the comfortable chair where the fellow enjoyed his last lunch. In the tucked away corner alcove, a shimmering light pulsed near the West Country linen display. He didn't need to investigate. While the everyday experiences of life in a mortal body returned, some things from his transition state had also remained. Most notable among them was the ability to observe earthbound souls. Andrew knew none of Jessop's customers could detect the catatonic First World War infantryman who occupied that quiet spot. Yet he could still see him, clear as day. He didn't understand why this should be, but then this whole experience wasn't part of the normal course of life and death as he expected it. Taking over another deceased body was like flying by the seat of your pants. Two faint concerns set his teeth on edge. The first was the state of Jessop's ticker. If eating a ham sandwich caused him a fatal heart attack, how long did Andrew have before this body suffered another? Not that his fried food banquets had helped matters. Even with his resolute spirit inside, if the doctors couldn't restart the physical engine he'd be back to square one. Chalk that up as a bigger pressure than pretending to be a sixty-five-year-old antique dealer. The second concern dovetailed in with his fear of crossing over into the light. If his suicide proved an offence to God - prohibiting entry to paradise and eternal life with Sharon - what was his almost necromantic occupation of Harold Jessop's physical body? Yet the paradox here was that necromancy provided the only hope in an otherwise hopeless existence. It was through that very arcane method he sought to find some answers.

The large, studded wooden shop door creaked open. A postman in summer gear whistled a jolly tune as he descended the short flight of stone steps to the main shop floor.

Andrew climbed out of the shabby, high-backed chair. "Good morning."

"Morning, Mate." The postman handed over a brown package, identical in size to the one Jessop signed for at home. He checked his bag for any letters. "Only the package today. Can you pop your signature on there please?" He passed an electronic pad and stylus across. "It's a proper party atmosphere out on the High Street. Have you had a gander?"

Andrew signed Jessop's name, correcting at the last minute an automatic urge to write *'Andrew Miles.'* He let out a sigh of relief. "Not since I opened up. The spectacle was already in full swing then."

"Gonna be a fab weekend." The postman retrieved the pad and tucked it away. "Cheers, Fella. You have a good one now."

"Likewise." Andrew watched him resume his happy ditty on the way back out. The door had only closed for a minute, before he tore the wrapping off that parcel. It contained a book of similar appearance to the one that excited the late Harold Jessop so. Gold-embossed spine lettering confirmed his suspicions: *'The Summoned Spirit: A Grimoire of Necromancy - Part II.'* It was the second volume Jessop ordered over the phone from his rare book dealer friend, the day the shopkeeper keeled over and died. Andrew sat back down to scan the contents. A few days of devouring tomes in the bizarre bedroom library at Cookham Hill, saw him gain knowledge of occult rituals he would once have scoffed at. His hunger and thirst for answers made the former carpenter an acolyte of unremitting zeal. How much of a master would he need to become, before gaining enough wisdom to take action? The final chapter opened in his lap: *'A Summoning Ritual for the World Beyond.'* It would take some study with a dictionary of Old English to get a proper grasp on the text. A contemporary of Chaucer could have written the prose, although lacking the same degree of literary flair. From the words that made sense, Andrew surmised it spoke of drawing on the power of earthbound spirits as a bridge. Their static energy provided some kind of vehicle to channel a departed being into the living body of a mortal human. The precise means and method he would decipher later. Five spirits whose energy remained focused on a central, material object were required. Each object to be placed at the points of a ritual pentagram, with the intended host occupying its centre. Could this be it? Were the unseen powers throwing him a bone at last? Further ramblings in the book, prattled on about divination methods for locating objects associated with earthbound spirit energy. Andrew smiled to himself and lifted his eyes to the glowing shop alcove. That part would prove easier than the long dead author anticipated here.

*   *   *

The rest of Saturday passed in much the same way, ringing up the odd sale at the shop. Sunday afternoon saw Andrew take Jessop's van over to the Great Lines Naval Memorial in Chatham. The place he'd gone after lunch on that fateful day his life ended. Somehow it was important to retrace those final movements. Inhabiting the body and life of another man, clouded the mind. He needed to focus and be clear on what his intentions were and why. Still, a nagging sensation that he was so much more than Andrew Miles pawed at his heartstrings. Was Sharon still Sharon wherever she'd gone? Had he departed this life and moved on in the usual manner, would his earthly identity cease to factor into who or what he was? A guy could go crazy thinking about all this stuff. Your mind went round in an endless loop. Instead, he pulled himself up short and resolved to concentrate on the next immediate steps. The visible and understood.

Back at the house on Cookham Hill, he spent the rest of the evening poring over that ritual text from the day before. Harold Jessop must have been straight with the book dealer, in that his interest in the occult was academic. If the man ever *had* been a practitioner of the dark arts, none of the required paraphernalia existed amongst the junk and clutter littering his home. Andrew's thoughts turned to the old warehouse. It was worth rifling around in there on his day off tomorrow. The ritual described a need for five items with shackled souls. He had already removed the embroidered handkerchief from sale at the shop. A thorough examination of stock around closing time, revealed no other pieces of note. That rocking horse with the young girl should still be at the warehouse. Plus, who knew what other antiques lurked away in its dark recesses? An entry in Jessop's diary noted his intention to attend an auction in Maidstone, Monday afternoon. Andrew put the leather-bound necromancy book aside and picked up the latest *Miller's Antiques Handbook & Price Guide* the old shopkeeper kept a duplicate copy of at home. The former carpenter was keen to turn his hand to bidding. It had always been intriguing. If an item or items of special interest for the ritual resided amongst the auction manifest and were in his price range, it was a good opportunity to acquire them. At that moment he could only account for two of the five.

Beyond that, he'd have to source a range of incense, special chalk and coloured candles to proceed. He could find those at some tucked away, flea market or new age emporium. The kind crumbling in a back street where business rates remained low enough to be affordable for geriatric hippies selling dream catchers, crystals and tie-dyed T-shirts.

But what of the host body for Sharon's spirit? That was another matter. A hopeless but enigmatic grin stretched across that old face. It was doubtful a classified ad in the local paper for someone who wished to be possessed by his dead wife's spirit would yield anything. An unwanted visit from mental health authorities, perhaps. Andrew's mind turned to the postwoman. *Should I ask her out on a date and make an excuse to visit the warehouse? What then; a bash on the head or something added to her drink? Could Jessop's old body overpower such a fit woman? She's attractive for her age, with a possible infatuation for the lonely shopkeeper. I could live with her, if Sharon was the one gazing out of those eyes. Is this deal a fools dream or errand? Oh, to spend a few more years as man and wife with my girl. If she passed away again, I wouldn't take my life next time. No matter what.* Statistically, given the age difference and Jessop's dicky ticker, it was likely he would die first of natural causes, anyway. Would God welcome him to the hereafter then? Andrew spat. *God. The same God who took Sharon away.* Did another ritual exist to jump spirits from host to host? Something to buy them time to find other, younger vessels of clay and so perpetuate their mortal existence? An endless story of two old loves, hijacking fresh, youthful bodies to re-consummate their union anew. So many questions. Only one way to find any answers: action.

A wall clock in the bedroom study showed ten PM. Andrew closed the antiques guide and rubbed Jessop's pale, tired eyes. The quandary over an available host could wait for now. He'd yet to assemble the other items. No sense trying to build a roof on your house before the walls were up.

Monday morning at the warehouse, Andrew flicked on the almost pointless lights. No matter how bright the sky outside, this space remained dingy. Cobwebs hung thick with dust between wooden beams. Their dark, unseen, fat-bodied occupants watched everything but remained still. The former carpenter rummaged around amongst the dirt and grime, senses straining for any hint of a shackled soul. Only the ten-year-old girl occupied this interior space at present, rocking on her horse in a sad, oblivious reverie. Filthy, stale air caused him to cough with a rattling chest. Andrew hoisted a rusty storm lamp from a rough wooden table shoved against one wall. He placed it on the floor to clear some room. The table surface lay strewn with yellowing papers, chipped crockery and an old, half-open wooden cigar box. The man lifted the lid. A disturbed spider scurried from inside, disappearing into a gloomy crack in the mortar between mottled brickwork. *This will do for now.* He retrieved the beautiful, embroidered handkerchief from his jacket pocket and placed it in the cigar box. Lid closed for safekeeping, he rested the container in the table centre. All other detritus he stuffed into an empty crate. Any more special items of lesser size than the rocking horse, he would gather here. With a bit of effort and some dragging of heavy furniture, there'd be ample space in the central warehouse atrium to conduct that necromantic ritual away from prying eyes. The ancient text revealed the need to inscribe a pentagram with purple chalk, inside a nine foot magic circle. One page illustrated many special runes and their exact placement for an optimum chance of success in summoning and containing a departed spirit. Andrew left the grubby storage space alone for now.

'Third Eye' was the type of place he'd expected. It lingered in a Gravesend back street between two empty trading establishments with whitewashed window panes. Andrew put his shoulder into opening the narrow door, swollen with damp. The heady aroma of incense and strains of a shakuhachi playing to a backdrop of birdsong filled the shop interior. A rough-shaven man in a frilly purple shirt, sat with his chin resting on one palm. With the other, he overturned a series of divination cards laid out across a counter draped in a pastel batik silk with yin-yang motif. His bored expression lifted to the potential customer for one moment. He returned to his cards without comment.

Andrew fished a shopping list out of his back pocket and the man sat up straight.

"Can I help?"

Signs of customer service at last. "I need several quantities of different incense," Andrew laid his list on the counter. "Plus three burners, a pack of purple chalk and five decent-sized purple pillar candles."

The shopkeeper scratched his coarse stubble. "Wild. You're planning a serious session then?"

Andrew frowned. "That's none of your business."

The man held up both hands in surrender. "All right, Man. I didn't mean to pry. Chill. Pretty sure I've got everything you need in stock. Bear with me while I rummage."

A few minutes later, Andrew watched the man key each of the assembled items into his till, before inserting them in a thick, brown paper bag. It bore a stamped environmentalist logo with the slogan 'Only One Earth.' A noble sentiment, though saving the planet factored least among his concerns at that moment.

"Gary, have you seen my aventurine pendant anywhere?" A slim, attractive redhead with long, tangled locks and faded jeans pushed her way through a bead curtain at the rear. Her grey eyes fell on their customer. She froze, fingernails digging into both palms.

"I thought I saw it over near the essential oils and soapstone diffusers." The man lifted his nose to indicate a direction. When the woman remained quiet, he twisted to face her. "Tanith? What's wrong?"

The redhead shuffled back several steps, eyelids flickering. Her voice creaked like the limbs of a thin sapling. "No. No, he must go. He shouldn't be here. Not like this."

Gary's brows knitted together. "Easy, girl. The guy's our best customer this week. He's picking up some ritual supplies. Nothing to freak out over." He winced and looked at Andrew. "Sorry, Man. She's sensitive."

Tanith's chest heaved. Her breathing became laboured, voice deep. "Abomination."

Andrew fidgeted. He caught the transaction total readout from the till display and dropped a few notes from Jessop's wallet onto the counter.

Tanith's eyes rolled back into her head, exposing their whites. One straight index finger pointed at the customer like a wand. "Abomination. Leave. Leave now."

Andrew grabbed the brown paper bag in both hands. "Keep the change." He swivelled to beat a hasty retreat to the shop door.

Gary called after him. "I'm sorry, Man. Please come see us again." His voice turned to an angry series of rebukes directed at his partner. The full force of their frustrated venom got cut off by the closing door.

By the time he arrived at the auction room in Maidstone that afternoon, Andrew had regained some of his composure. That encounter with the sensitive young woman proved unsettling. He reasoned everything out like a pragmatist. *It seems I'm an abomination. Isn't necromancy an abomination, too? So, who cares? Roll the clock back a few hundred years and mobile phones would be an abomination, causing religious types to throw a hissy fit.* The only problem with his logic appeared to be Tanith's obvious lack of religious affiliation. Her response wasn't based on discovering some nefarious, forbidden habit in his life, seen through a dogmatic lens of man-made holiness. She had done nothing more than occupy the same room as him, to provoke that reaction. He shook his head. *So what? I'm damned whichever way you slice it, aren't I? Sod 'em all. I want my Sharon back.*

It didn't take long perusing the auction inventory for one item to leap out at Andrew. An early twentieth century mantelpiece clock sat amidst several other timepieces. At its side, a determined, white-haired old woman watched the hands move with unblinking attention. Her semi-translucent and almost luminous appearance drew the pretend antique dealer across for a closer inspection. There was a good chance the price would fall within a comfortable range. Given how many other clocks of better quality and pedigree were due under the hammer, he might even get it at reserve.

That evening, Andrew placed the clock in the warehouse. It sat alongside the cigar box containing the handkerchief, and the bag of ritual supplies from that bizarre shop in Gravesend. Silent and immobile, a female pensioner and First World War soldier lingered near their significant keepsakes. Several feet away amongst some dirty furniture, the old rocking horse swayed back and forth. Andrew pulled the door shut behind him and locked it on the way out. *Supplies? Check. Shackled soul keepsakes? Three down, two to go.*

* * *

Clouds gathered in a velvet night sky over the Thames estuary. Streaks of light flashed and died all along the Essex coast. The residents of Southend and Canvey Island witnessed a dramatic thunderstorm appear out of nowhere. Sudden bursts followed sheets and forks of lightning in rapid succession. No distant rumbling approach heralded its arrival. Rain hammered down as the storm crossed the ancient river to Allhallows and the Isle of Grain, near the mouth of the Medway.

At Jessop's house in Rochester, Andrew sat down to a pepperoni pizza and a bottle of IPA for dinner. Local TV news ran a piece on how successful the summer Dickens Festival weekend had been. Images of the happy crowd decked out in Victorian fancy dress, flashed across the screen. The TV went dark and the words *'No Signal'* appeared for a couple of seconds. A minute later it happened again. Andrew clicked the remote *'off'* button. A loud bang echoed overhead. *Bloody hell, that storm snuck up without warning.* He lifted a slice of pizza and carried it to the ramshackle conservatory for a dry, front-row seat at the light show. Lightning arced high above the River Medway. A juddering crack of thunder followed without delay. An angled burst of dazzling light struck the mast of a compact vessel moored at Castle View across the water. More instantaneous thunder shook Jessop's conservatory windows. Andrew tucked into his slice of pizza. *Amazing. I suppose it has been warm and dry, the last few days.*

The Entity encircled the battlements of Rochester Castle. Its shadowy fingers reached out claw-like and grasping, counting ghosts like old Scrooge tallied his gold. It was a shepherd of lost souls that night. Or perhaps a prison warden to the stranded ones who milled about as always along The Esplanade waterside. The Entity brooded. She wasn't here tonight: that mortal creature who sought to steal his flock. A deep-noted voice boomed from the indistinct vaporous apparition, in time with the next thunderclap. "Pathfinder." It hated The Pathfinder from the deepest depths of its black, spiritual heart. If she appeared to guide more souls across tonight, it would fight her again like that day at the old asylum. Spirit them away as an offering to one who could hold them. The Dark Mistress welcomed lost souls. SHE always rewarded such a gift, in her fashion. Her hunger knew no bounds. Better Her to receive those lambs, than lose them to The Pathfinder. Lose them to the light and The One.

Lightning dazzled mere mortals in their little lives, peering out of tiny windows to watch nature's raw power at work in the skies above them.

Something stirred within The Entity. There was a change at play in the spirit realm. Someone had crossed over, while a stranded creature crossed back to the land of the animated clay ones. What trickery was this? A distant song from The Dark Mistress soothed The Entity's concern. She was amused. She wanted whatever this was, to come about. This time grief would serve Her purpose like never before. This time they would unleash havoc on The Shackled.

11

The Necklace

MATTHEW RILEY, 2008.

"It's a special day for you, Matthew," Pastor Mike Clarke adjusted a chunky pair of glasses that had wandered down the bridge of his nose. "Both your daughters will have followed our Lord through the waters of baptism."

"I'm proud of Samantha. Proud in a good way. Not the pride that goes before a fall, I hope." A tall, forty-nine-year-old man with dark, side-parted hair and a thick moustache placed both hands on his hips. He studied a group of baptism candidates clad in plain white robes, as they assembled on the river bank. His younger daughter stood among them, clasping and rubbing opposite shoulders with her hands. The fourteen-year-old girl sought to ward off imaginings of how cold the River Avon might be, even in summer. A hum of Bath traffic crisscrossing many bridges into the old city, disappeared beneath the repeated twang of a musician tuning his Fender Stratocaster electric guitar. Next to him a seated keyboard player with a Roland electronic piano, struck up a bright series of cheery chords. Behind, a bass player slapped and popped in time with an imaginary funk beat in his head.

Mike Clarke thumbed through several pages in a black, soft leather-bound Bible with gold leaf edged pages. "Don't worry, Matthew. It's the pride of a father at seeing his children walking in the light. Pride is the wrong word, in truth. Gratitude might be a better one. You have a thankful heart, directed at God for His blessings after raising your children right."

Matthew nodded. "I'd better get into my water robes. Judith won't be pleased if I help you baptise ten people wearing my Sunday best."

Mike chuckled. "Your wife is a lamb. A proper Proverbs 31 woman."

"And Proverbs 12."

"An excellent wife is the crown to her husband?"

"The same. Now we're past this hurdle, I'll have the usual worries of a father of two girls. Worries about the men who'll come into their lives."

"Rachel's nineteen now, isn't she?"

"That's right."

"I've always thought John Saunders seemed quite taken with her."

Matthew's eyebrows raised. "Is that so? I must have a word with my eldest about him. Find out if he's made an overture."

The pastor rested a light hand on his shoulder. "Why not let them have the chance to approach you first? John's a decent young man, committed to his youth work. Rare to find a twenty-two-year-old university student so stalwart and faithful. Once they go out into the world, they're never quite the same. Whenever John comes home, he's straight round to the youth meetings, rolling up his sleeves to help. Your Rachel might be a part of the cause, but only a part I'm sure."

A freckled, fair-haired man of about twenty broke into the exchange between church leader and lay preacher. "Excuse me, Pastor Mike. Joey wants to run his bass drum through the PA. He's worried it won't carry in the open air."

The minister shook his head. "Please tell him the sound will travel fine without. I'd appreciate it if you'd keep Carl's lead guitar volume under control too. Some older members of the congregation complained, last time we did an outdoor baptism here at the river."

"I'll try, Pastor. Carl mics the cab on his amp rather than using our foldback with a DI box. He says it provides a warmer sound that way. I have to turn everything else up so his guitar doesn't drown out the mix."

"You're a diplomatic sound engineer, Jake. I'm sure God will grant you words of wisdom to help Carl see the light and turn it down, if you ask Him."

"Yes Pastor. I'll try."

As the engineer faltered with an uneasy expression, the minister waved at him. "Oh, Jake?"

"Yes?"

"How are we going to amplify the professions of faith? Poor Harry Kemsley had to stand with us in the river last time, clutching a handheld radio mic. He ended up in bed with a shocking cold for a fortnight. His wife even had me round to pray and lay hands on the sick fellow."

The freckled man grinned. "Already thought of that. I've put together a temporary boom pole. An usher will swing it over your heads to capture each profession. It's far enough away from the speakers not to start a feedback loop."

"Good man." Mike clapped him on the back and Jake wandered off to disappoint their drummer.

Matthew finished changing into his water robes. "Are we almost ready?"

Mike Clarke glanced across to where their male praise and worship leader stood praying with the singers in a circle. The man looked up and nodded while the minister gave him a short wave. "All set, Matthew. Let's go." Mike strolled between rows of temporary plastic chairs, set out on the uneven grass surface. The seating snaked in higgledy-piggledy waves beneath a collection of riverside willow trees. Only two chairs remained empty at the front, reserved for both men. "Hallelujah." Mike spoke words to God under his breath as they went. "Thank you, Jesus. Praise your name. Glory to God."

Their beanpole-thin praise and worship leader took his place with two male and two female singers near the band. Shining white teeth glinted like a row of ivory piano keys, as he opened his mouth with a smile to speak into a mic. "Good morning, everyone. The Bible tells us in the book of Acts: *Peter replied, 'Repent and be baptised, every one of you, in the name of Jesus Christ for the forgiveness of your sins. And you will receive the gift of the Holy Spirit.'* Today we're here to celebrate with ten souls who, having found faith in our Lord and Saviour, are taking that important step. We're also believing God will fill them with the Holy Spirit, through prayer and the laying-on of hands afterwards. Amen?"

The assembled throng uttered a hearty, "Amen."

One of the female singers with frizzy brown hair and a generous, hourglass figure raised her left hand. The right hand clasped a mic near her mouth. She let out a flow of indiscernible words in tongues, followed by a prophetic translation of the utterance. "Thus saith the Lord: As you go through the waters of baptism you will clothe yourselves with Me. It is I who have saved you. I who will raise you up on the last day. You are My children; one family in God. Be not afraid. Stand strong in your Lord and the power of My might. For verily I am with you always, even to the end of the age."

The crowd cheered. Shouts of "Thank you, Jesus," and "Hallelujah" rang out across the riverside meadow.

Seated in the front row on the other side of Matthew Riley, his wife Judith uttered a quiet "Amen." The forty-four-year-old woman ran a distracted hand through short, neat side-parted brown hair. Her lazy right eye squinted, giving the appearance of someone half asleep. She shifted a round face and full figure, rubbing minor puppy fat on her upper arms. Proud like her husband though she might have been, something about the prophecy still grated on Judith Riley's nerves. Why did Christians always feel the need to speak in King James English when delivering a prophetic utterance? Did they think if you sounded like an old translation of the Bible, it lent more credibility to your words? It was an uncomfortable thought. One of several niggling criticisms forming on the inside over recent months. She shook such rambling concerns aside and mentally chastised herself, turning instead to the blonde nineteen-year-old girl seated on her opposite hand.

Rachel Riley toyed with a shiny silver cross necklace and gazed at her younger sister standing near the water's edge. Eyes brimming over with joy and wonder, Rachel watched Samantha lift a radiant face to receive the words from heaven with gratitude.

The drummer clicked his sticks together four times, and the band launched into an upbeat song of praise. Plastic chairs swayed on unsteady legs as the assembled congregation rose to their feet, clapping in time with the offbeat. The singers hit their first vocals of the chorus. People all about bounced, hopped and jumped for Jesus, singing with all their might. Every now and again, the electric guitar howled over the top of everything else. At a small mixing desk fixed into a black flight case at the rear, Jake moved his faders as high as he dared. A valiant attempt to compensate. Several white-haired folk (already half-deaf with age), twisted to scowl at him in response.

And so the service progressed, fast rhythms giving way to slower, more intimate songs of love and worship. The congregation raised their hands to the sky, swaying like pampas grass in a gentle breeze.

Mike Clarke and Matthew Riley climbed down into the river, shuddering at the sudden change in temperature. An usher extended a long pole from the edge of the bank. A handheld radio mic pointed downward at the far end, held in place by thick, grey electrical tape.

Mike spoke and his voice carried from the makeshift boom pole to blare out of the PA speakers. "Can the first candidate please enter the water."

A teenage boy slid into the river, hopping with cold shock. Eyes shining, he hobbled between the two leaders, hands clasped across his chest.

Matthew took hold of his right forearm. Mike put one hand up to support his left shoulder blade. "Please say your name."

The boy took a breath, feeling the weight of so many stares upon him. "Nicholas Gilbert."

Mike nodded. "Nicholas, do you believe that Jesus Christ is the son of God, your one true Lord and saviour?"

"I do."

"Do you believe He came down from heaven and offered Himself up as a willing sacrifice for our sins?"

"I do."

"Do you believe that He rose again on the third day, ascended to Heaven, and is seated at the right hand of the Father, where He will judge the living and the dead?"

The boy smiled. "I do."

"Then on profession of your faith, I baptise you in the name of the Father and of the Son and of the Holy Spirit."

The usher raised the boom out of the way. Mike and Matthew lowered Nicholas backwards under the water. His feet rose and bobbed, until they brought him back up with a shimmering spray, face elated. Along the bank, the crowd cheered. The worship team broke into the boy's favourite song of praise, chosen by him for the occasion. Mike and Matthew helped him toward the bank, hands extending to lead the next candidate forward. Matthew's heart leapt. A pretty, blonde fourteen-year-old girl (the apple of his eye), slipped into the chilly river. He led her by the hand to stand between himself and the Pastor.

Mike smiled. "Why don't you do this one, Matthew?"

His lay associate mouthed a quiet "Thank you."

The boom mic lowered again.

Matthew cleared his throat, voice trembling. "Please say your name."

The girl's face shone. "Samantha Riley."

"Samantha, do you believe that Jesus Christ is the son of God, your one true Lord and saviour?"

"I do."

"Do you believe He came down from heaven and offered Himself up as a willing sacrifice for our sins?"

"I do."

"Do you believe that He rose again on the third day, ascended to Heaven, and is seated at the right hand of the Father, where He will judge the living and the dead?"

Samantha nodded without hesitation. "I do."

"Then on profession of your faith, I baptise you in

the name of the Father and of the Son and of the Holy Spirit."

Happy tears stained Matthew's cheeks as his youngest daughter's face sank into the slow-flowing water. She came up wearing a huge smile, countenance aglow.

Rachel and her mother were first on their feet to clap. The strains of *'Here is Love'* - an old hymn from the Welsh revival - carried across the meadow and the worship went on.

"There she is." Mike Clarke clutched a paper plate loaded down with roast lamb, potato salad and lettuce. Matthew, Judith and Rachel Riley tucked into similar fare close by. Samantha emerged from a fabric screened windbreak, having changed back into dry clothes.

When the church leaders and elders laid hands on the new initiates after their baptism, the girl was one of the first to speak in tongues. Baptised in water and the Spirit, Samantha knew she could now consider herself a full-fledged disciple of Jesus Christ.

The service had been over some twenty minutes. Jake finally convinced Carl to stop playing endless rock riffs on his guitar and jamming with the bass player. He killed the mobile generator.

Crowds milled about, congratulating baptism candidates and enjoying their picnic lunch.

Rachel set down her plate on a table covered with a shiny vinyl fabric cloth. She rushed across to throw both arms around her younger sister's neck. "I'm so proud of you, Sam."

Samantha hugged her. "It felt amazing, Rach."

"I told you it would. Mine was the same. Are you all dry now? Come and have some food."

Samantha followed her back to the table where her mother delivered a hug of her own.

Matthew - having also changed again - reached into his jacket pocket and pulled out a small, oblong parcel wrapped in metallic paper. "This is for you, young lady."

Samantha took it. "Thanks, Dad." Rachel exchanged smiles with her mother as the girl opened her present. Inside, the lid came off a dark blue box to reveal a silver cross necklace. It was an exact match to her sister's.

Matthew sniffed. "We gave Rachel one after her baptism. Your mother and I agreed we should do the same for you. We hope you'll wear it always. Well done."

"Thanks again, Dad. Thank you, Mum." Samantha lifted the cross aloft. Rachel took the wrapping away, then helped her sister fasten the symbol about her neck.

Mike Clarke sipped from a cup of orange juice. "Were there ever two finer young examples of Christian virtue and beauty?" He raised his cup at Matthew and Judith. "My congratulations to you both."

* * *

"Where's your cross?" Matthew Riley looked up from the spacious, high-ceilinged kitchen of their multi-storey, late eighteenth century townhouse. The smart and expensive Bath property had remained in his family ever since its construction. Six years passed since the baptism of his wide-eyed, zealous youngest daughter. Now she stood before him, a blossoming twenty-year-old woman in a low-cut, little black dress so short it appeared to have had a row with her thighs. Waxed and tanned, muscular legs were pushed up by a pair of shiny, high-heeled shoes. Straw blonde waves in messy curls teasing her shoulders, became the way she always wore her hair these days. No silver cross nor any other adornment hung about her neck.

Samantha stopped in the kitchen doorway. Her father sat at the heavy pine table, reading from his open Bible. Shafts of sunlight streaked down through large sash windows above the sink behind him. Outside, a long, high-walled back garden hung heavy with lush foliage and blossoming apple trees. The girl pursed her lips in momentary thought. "I'm going out with some girls from work. If we dance, the necklace might get lost."

Matthew leaned back in the creaking chair and folded his arms. "Dance?"

"Yes. You know, Dad: moving your feet in time with music. Dancing."

"Moving your feet and gyrating your body, as flesh spills out of your skimpy outfit to arouse the passions of ungodly men, you mean?"

"I'm not responsible for their thoughts."

"Aren't you? Dressing provocatively and leaving little to the imagination, while seducing onlookers like Salome herself?"

Samantha frowned. "If I'm offered anything I want, I promise not to ask for the head of John the Baptist, okay?"

Matthew gritted his teeth. "This is no joking matter, Samantha. Have you forgotten the commitment you made to follow the Lord with your whole heart?"

"Dad, we're going to a wine bar for a few drinks and some girlie laughs. No biggie."

"Alcohol too?" Matthew flicked the pages of his Bible in search of a New Testament passage from First John. *"For everything in the world - the lust of the flesh, the lust of the eyes, and the pride of life - comes not from the Father but from the world."* He flicked back to Ephesians. *"Do not get drunk on wine, which leads to debauchery. Instead, be filled with the Spirit."*

Now it was Samantha's turn to cross her arms. "Finished?"

Matthew linked the fingers of both hands together above his open Bible. "You are a vessel of the Holy Spirit, filled and blessed with the gift of tongues as evidence."

"Wait a minute, Dad. I remember your testimony from church. When you were my age, you went right off the reservation - smoking and drinking."

Her father unlocked his fingers, made a fist and slammed it so hard on the table its surface juddered. "That's right. I almost became estranged from your grandmother and grandfather because of it. I questioned my faith, forsook the teachings of the Bible and got into a horrible mess. Mercifully I came to a place of repentance and was welcomed home like a lost lamb. The Good Shepherd didn't forsake me, and His faithful prayed daily for my salvation."

Samantha moved forward to rest her hands on the back of a chair facing across the table from him. "That's great. You found renewed faith of your own choosing. Isn't that how it should be?"

"But you've made the choice. You made it when you were fourteen." Matthew rubbed his forehead.

"I was a child at fourteen, Dad. Religion and church life were all I knew. You and Mum both made sure of that. If I'm going to continue with it, I need to do so in the full knowledge of what that means. I'm a young woman. I want to taste and touch the world around me."

"You can still be in the world but not of it. Don't be tainted by it, Samantha. That is the way of death. The second death."

"And I may very well arrive at that assessment. But only I can make it. Look, don't those Amish communities in America let their kids go off for a spell? A period to experience the world, before choosing whether to become active members? If they choose to, they're bound by their codes of worship and behaviour. What's it called again? Rum- something or other..."

Judith Riley strolled into the kitchen from the hall where she had overheard the entire exchange.

"Rumspringa. It means 'running around.' A rite of passage."

Samantha snapped her fingers. "That's it. Rumspringa."

Matthew's face darkened at the help provided by his wife. "But we're not Amish, Mennonite nor Anabaptist, Samantha."

The young woman leaned forward over her chair back. "That's not the point and you know it."

Her father sighed. "I would save you all that heartache and trouble. What if you fool around with a boy and get pregnant?"

Samantha shook her head. "Then I guess you'll be a grandfather. Jesus, Dad. Give me *some* credit, won't you?"

Judith gasped. "Samantha!"

Her daughter's shoulders slumped. "I'm sorry, Mum. I got frustrated, that's all."

"I'm not the one you need to apologise to," Judith said.

Matthew halted where he'd half risen at her blasphemy, arms pressed straight against the table. "You see how it starts? Already you are taking the Lord's name in vain." He sat back down. "Why can't you be more like your sister? Rachel didn't go through any of this. John finished university, and they got married. Look how happy she is. Now with their firstborn arrived…"

Samantha blinked. "I'm happy for her. Rachel fell in love with John and knew what she wanted."

"She didn't need to drink and dance or flirt with the

world," Matthew added. "Have you considered the roof under which you sleep?"

"It's a very nice roof, Dad. We have a wonderful home."

"And the history of its occupants?"

"I know, the family have been Evangelicals since the year dot."

Matthew straightened. "No. Our family's wealth originated from the slave trade, when they first built the house. Those forebears repented, like the slave ship captain John Newton himself. The man who wrote the hymn *'Amazing Grace'* about his conversion experience. From that time forward, the Rileys joined William Wilberforce and the abolitionists until they outlawed the trade and killed it. The rest of their fortune they invested in a wise and frugal manner. A mixture of ethical business ventures. Each successive generation grew up to follow Christ. THAT is the provenance behind the life you enjoy, and which you intend to squander in this stupid dalliance with sin."

A car horn beeped on the street outside.

Samantha half-turned. "I'm not those people, Dad. I can only be myself. Don't wait up." She strode into the hallway and left the house in silence.

*   *   *

"She's awake. Matthew, that was the surgeon on the phone. Samantha's come round from her coma." Judith Riley burst into the front room of their Bath home.

Matthew jumped up from his armchair, clapping

both hands together in a prayer-like gesture. "Thank you, Jesus." He hugged his sobbing wife. "There now, my darling. The Lord has been faithful. Like it says in Deuteronomy: *'The eternal God is your refuge, and underneath are the everlasting arms.'* He has delivered our daughter from death and offered another chance to make her life right."

Judith wiped reddening eyes and blew her nose on a tissue. "I'd better phone Rachel and John. They'll want to drive over to the hospital from Wiltshire. We can fix up the guest room for them and baby Jane."

Samantha Riley lay propped up against a mountain of pillows in her hospital bed. All manner of probes connected her to a series of monitors. Dark rings and copious bruising beneath her eyes, made the young woman appear a freakish, human/panda hybrid. Her straw-blonde hair spread out and matted into the pillow beneath.

Matthew and Judith hovered in the doorway of her private room beside a stern-faced nurse. The carer motioned to her patient. "She's still very weak and may tire if she talks too much. Don't expect a lot, so soon after a coma."

Judith pressed forward to sit at her daughter's side and squeeze her hand.

Matthew addressed the nurse. "Thank you. We've already received more than we dared hope."

"You're welcome. I'll leave you to it."

The patient's eyelids fluttered. Confused pupils fixed

on the new arrivals. They looked familiar, but she couldn't quite place them. "Hello." Her voice trembled and cracked with dry uncertainty.

Matthew took a seat on the other side of their daughter. "Thank the Lord you're alive and awake, Samantha."

The girl frowned. "Samantha?"

The married couple exchanged worried glances.

Judith kissed one of her daughter's hands. "Samantha is your name. Don't worry, darling. I'm sure it will all come back to you in time. You've been in a coma for a month."

Samantha struggled to lift her head. "Do I know you?"

Judith let out an involuntary sob, then sucked the following ones up.

Matthew swallowed hard. "We're your parents."

Samantha stared at the foot of her bed. "W-who's that?"

Her father looked round. "There's no-one there, Samantha."

Samantha watched the smiling figure of her grandmother place a tingling, gentle hand on her ankle. The vaporous old woman turned and walked into a growing doorway of light in the wall behind; her mission to escort Samantha back, complete. The patient thrust her upper body forward. "No. Please don't go. I don't want to be here; I want to go home. Take me with you."

Judith eased her daughter back against the pillows as the spiritual doorway faded. "Shh now. We'll take you home once you're strong enough and the doctors are happy to release you. Have patience, darling."

The pace of Samantha's breathing increased. She looked from side to side. "Tony. There should be someone called Tony here."

Matthew sighed and rubbed his eyes. "Great. She can't remember her own family, but the name of that unsaved boy comes right back to her."

Judith grimaced. "Tony is okay. He walked away from the crash with only a few scratches."

Matthew bristled. "Why did you have to get in that car with him? I asked you not to see the lad again. Three weeks after meeting him that night at the wine bar with your girlie friends, and you wind up in a car wreck. Then a month in a coma. The doctors told us you died, Samantha. Thank God our Saviour brought you back to us."

Samantha's brow creased, her eyes rolling from side to side.

Judith touched her husband's shoulder. "Matthew, not now. It's too much for her to absorb, so soon." She lifted a jug of water off a side table adorned with 'Get Well' and 'Be Blessed' cards from her husband's Christian publishing company. "Would you like some water, Samantha?" It seemed helpful to keep reminding their daughter who she was.

The girl nodded, licking parched lips.

Judith poured a cool drink into the patient's plastic cup. "There you go. Sip it slowly."

Samantha dribbled a little liquid into her mouth. Throat muscles took it down with an audible gulp. She eyed her father. "God. Is. Everything." The phrase came out like three individual sentences.

A wave of relief flickered behind the man's eyes. "Thank you, Jesus. It sounds like He's bringing you back in more ways than one."

Samantha shook her head in a vigorous motion. "No. Not Jesus. God. God is OM."

Matthew waved his fingers over and over, as if teasing out the rest of an unfinished word with the gesture. "Omniscient? Omnipotent? Omnipresent?"

Samantha rocked her head. "No. I mean YES - all those things. But that's not what I meant. God is OM."

Matthew looked at his wife, eyebrows lifting.

Judith shrugged. "She's groggy. It sounds positive, though. At least our daughter's talking about God. Do you think she stood before the Lord?"

Matthew raised his eyes to the ceiling. "What must she have seen? This will make some testimony back at the fellowship when she's restored to faith. We might even publish a book about it. *'Prodigal in the light,'* or something of that nature."

Samantha coughed. "Darkness."

Matthew studied her. "Excuse me?"

"Darkness, not light. There's light beyond. Amazing light. But when you stand at the heart of God, you are in total darkness. It's beautiful; not frightening or evil. Every answer to every question you ever wanted to know, comes to you in an instant. It all makes sense." The suddenly coherent young woman frowned at the surrounding room. "But nothing in this world does."

Matthew smoothed his hand across her brow. "There

now. You're still confused, trying to process it all. Let's pray to the Father that your memory will recover intact."

Samantha locked her eyes onto him. "Not a Father."

Matthew's brow furrowed.

The girl went on. "You're a father, but God isn't. Not in the same way. OM is an IT. Both father and mother, yet neither in isolation. It's the only way I can explain things with human words." She gasped. "I must get this out before the memories fade. Oh please don't let it all slip away." She lifted one shaking hand to touch Matthew's cheek, her blue eyes filling with tears. "I wish I could make you see, Matthew. God is so much more than we've ever dreamed."

Matthew baulked at his daughter addressing him by his first name, even if he was glad she remembered it. She'd never done that before. He pulled her hand away but held it tight in one of his own. "I wish we could do the same for you." He reached his other hand across to take hold of his wife's offered fingers. "Let's bow our heads in prayer."

*   *   *

Matthew Riley stared with vacant eyes at the page-a-day calendar on his desk: *Monday 3rd June 2019.* Nothing remarkable about the day or date, yet he would never forget it as long as he lived. As long as he lived? That turn of phrase adopted a new significance after he went to collect results from his medical check-up that morning: Terminal Cancer of an advanced and aggressive nature. His doctor recommended tests after Matthew experienced repeated bouts of indigestion and trouble swallowing. The now sixty-year-old man thought he had a gluten or dairy allergy developing. Being told in no uncertain terms he could expect to be dead by Christmas at the latest, hit him like a lightning bolt. Not that anything prepares you for such news.

His side-parted hair had long since turned grey with only a few dark streaks hinting at its original colour. He wiped slow fingers across his thick moustache and stared at the company logo bolted to one office wall. *'Agape House Press.'* Intense graft to grow this firm had been his life's work. The galley proof for a new book on divine healing sat next to the desk calendar, awaiting his approval. Matthew couldn't even bring himself to look at it. Inside, a nagging voice berated him for not swiping up the text like a gift from heaven. A spirit-filled Evangelical, this was the moment he should name and claim his healing from the cross of Christ. Instead, an all-pervasive dread and despair hollowed out the shell he knew to be filling with murderous, alien cells. Pastor Mike and the elders would pray for him when they found out. They'd lay hands on him in front of the whole congregation, believing in the power of corporate agreement. They would cast the devil of sickness out with dramatic, faith-filled shouts. Yet why did he not find any comfort in something he had been a part of for others, on several occasions? One even lived and went into remission.

Matthew stood and stretched. A plain, circular wall

clock announced it to be one PM. His slim, thirty-something secretary, Emily Killick poked her head around the door.

"I'm going to put the kettle on, Mr Riley. Would you like a tea?"

"No, thank you. I'm clearing my schedule for the rest of the day and leaving early, Emily."

"As you wish." She caught the distant, glazed expression in his eyes. "Is everything okay?"

Matthew stepped aside from his desk and wheeled the leather chair back into place. "Oh, thoughts of this life in corruption. Nothing to worry about." He managed one fraction of a smile.

"Thank goodness our corruptible will put on the incorruptible, one day." Emily tilted her head. "That's what I tell myself whenever I have aches and pains, or find a new wrinkle in the bathroom mirror reflection."

Matthew nodded and donned his suit jacket. "Thank you. It's good to remember 1 Corinthians 15 on a day like today. If my wife calls, please tell her I've gone for a walk and may be home early."

"I will. Have a good afternoon."

Matthew took a casual stroll up Gay Street to the circular, Georgian architectural grandeur of The Circus. He was aware from spiritual warfare aficionados in the church, that The Circus, Queens Square and Gay Street formed a key shape when viewed from above. Masonic architect, John Wood added many other such symbols in carved relief on his building parapets. Once, Matthew might have prayed a quiet prayer, rebuking and binding the Devil. Today, none of that seemed to matter. They were beautiful buildings and streets. Nothing more. Part of the Bath Stone grandeur of his ancestral haunts. He headed west down Brock Street to the peaceful splendour of Royal Victoria Park and a world-famous view of The Royal Crescent. This five-hundred-foot, semi-circular row of thirty terraced homes with Ionic and Palladian features, never failed to make him pause for breath. It was quite a sight, standing on quite a site.

The reflective man walked along the broad, straight path running parallel to The Royal Crescent, across the park. A light-brown dachshund scampered over to sniff his trouser leg.

"Tolly, come here." A blonde girl, about fourteen, called to the inquisitive animal from the shade of a nearby tree.

Matthew's thoughts drifted to his youngest daughter. His heart sank like a lead weight, pulling down on a sore and wheezing chest. Ever since the results of his medical exam, the man already noticed niggling pains he may have once dismissed. Was it that, or were they psychosomatic reactions to the news of his supposed, imminent demise? Matthew couldn't tell. He'd always assumed there would be time to make things right with Samantha. The day he found her half-naked in their family home with that boy who caused the car crash, his temper got the better of him. Then there was the pink, vibrating sex toy, hidden inside her hollowed-out Bible. The word of God, cut away and discarded to conceal that hellish tool for indulging her sinful desires of the flesh. No, he'd been right to throw her out of the house. Samantha was old enough to understand what they expected if she wished to remain in a Christian home. Now, if God didn't deliver him from terminal cancer, there was little time to help her repent. She must escape that special place reserved in the lake of fire for backsliders from the faith. Anguish brought one numb hand up to clutch his ribcage. He would pray. That's what he would do. Not for himself, but for his daughter. Warm sunshine fell across his brow. Matthew closed his eyes and sniffed the clear air, pointing hungry nostrils aloft. "Not my will but Thine be done, Lord."

"Judith, I'm home early." Matthew let the dark front door with its central brass knob swing wide. Behind him, the glorious buildings of Bath unfolded at the foot of the hill on which the old Riley house stood.

Judith appeared from the kitchen. "Emily said you might be home early when I called. Pastor Mike was wondering if his house group could meet here this evening? I told him I'd check with you, but thought it would be okay."

"That's fine, my love." Matthew closed the door and stood his briefcase next to the doormat.

Judith stepped forward, wobbled, then grabbed onto the stair banister for support.

Matthew rushed to catch hold of her. "Are you all right?"

Judith touched her head. "I keep getting these weird dizzy spells. One minute I'm fine, but the next I lose my balance. Age, I suppose."

"Fifty-five is no age. How long has this been going on?"

"Only a week or so. Must be a virus or something. Anyway, enough about me. What did the doctor say?"

Pastor Mike Clarke stood in the Rileys' front room, hands resting on Matthew's shoulders. Ten other men and women of various ages gathered around, the members of a weekly cell church group from the main fellowship. An acoustic guitar rested against the sofa. Bibles of all shapes, sizes and colours lay discarded on tables, chairs and the cream, thick-pile carpet. Judith leaned against an ornate, white marble fireplace topped with a huge, brass-framed mirror. Her feet pressed up and down against the hearth fender in a series of nervous twitches.

Mike Clarke cleared his throat. "Stretch out your hands, Brethren. Let's pray for our brother, that he may be delivered from all sickness and the machinations of the evil one."

The crowd obeyed.

Mike gripped Matthew's shoulders tighter. "Lord, we thank You for our faithful brother, Matthew. We thank You that he is a good servant and disciple of Christ. In Your mighty name, we declare this sickness of cancer null and void. It cannot hold sway and remain in his body. The body of a man delivered from sin and baptised with the Holy Spirit. Lord we thank You that Isaiah tells us: *by His stripes we are healed*. We claim that healing now in Jesus' name. Devil, you have no authority here. I cast you out. Begone from this body and return no more. In Jesus' name we ask it. In Jesus' name."

Judith watched the crowd stretch their arms out in dramatic shakes, repeating "in Jesus' name" over and over like a mantra, or the act of waving some invisible magic wand. Ever since her husband laid out the tale of his medical results and prognosis after returning home, her already quavering faith collapsed about her ears. For some time, certain aspects of that familiar religion had felt as shaky as her legs did of late. Now the fabric of her world came unglued in such a way those heartfelt efforts to secure divine healing seemed almost repugnant. She remained silent, her own prayers a hollow, inner pleading.

Matthew awoke with a start. Beside him in the darkness, his wife fidgeted in her sleep. Indistinguishable words drifted from her parted lips, as if she were praying in the Spirit. Yet lines of concern creasing her face suggested troubled dreams instead.

The man slipped from beneath the sheets. Samantha's face was all he could see when he closed his eyes. Questing feet located his slippers in the blackness. Matthew didn't wish to turn on a light and disturb Judith, despite her repose appearing less than restful. He fumbled around for the door handle and edged along the upstairs landing in the moonlight. It was some time since he last ventured into his youngest daughter's bedroom. Christian rock group posters still adorned the walls. One throwback, never removed, from her on-fire days in the faith. A small jewellery box rested on the nightstand beside her bed. Matthew sat down on the mattress and opened it. Samantha's silver cross necklace glittered in the wash of headlights from a passing car outside. The man lifted that token he had presented to her, the day of her baptism. Hands pressing either side of the cross, he prayed with fervent intent for his daughter's immortal soul. The early church Apostles prayed over handkerchiefs that brought healing to the sick when laid upon them. He wished his prayers to strike Samantha in such a manner whenever she connected with her necklace. Even if he were long gone, it might be his last chance to save her.

Shooting pains burned through his chest. Matthew let the necklace flick across the room, hands clawing at his body as if to drive out the rising agony. His head pounded, heart fluttering in irregular beats. Was this the beginning of the end or the grand finale? Surely there would still be a grace period in which to tidy up his affairs? Another chest pain. His throat contracted. Matthew slipped from the mattress to kneel on the floor. A second car passed on the street below, its sweeping beams illuminating the fallen cross on the carpet. Spasms of shock dropped the man onto his chest. *Not yet. I haven't finished my prayer yet. Samantha must hear the Lord's call. I can't let her go. I must stay.*

Must save her. He crawled hand over hand across the floor, talon-like, trembling fingers stretching for the necklace. All sight faded as his fingers connected with the cold silver emblem of faith. *I love you Samantha. I can't let you go.*

When Judith awoke next morning, it surprised her to find her husband's side of the bed unoccupied. *Maybe he got up early for a quiet time with the Lord? Goodness knows the news from yesterday must be testing his faith.* She slipped on a dressing gown and stepped onto the landing. Samantha's old bedroom door stood ajar. "Matthew?" A kind smile spread across her pale face. Despite his righteous indignation at Samantha's behaviour and the manner in which he'd ejected her, Judith knew the man loved his youngest daughter more than life itself. He always had trouble expressing emotions. A bizarre paradox. Faith was everything in the Riley household. Samantha cast aside that faith. Now she didn't fit in the puzzle picture of their day-to-day life. It was as if someone had altered her connecting edges. Yet without her, a gaping hole remained. It left an impossible choice: Cast aside their daughter for the faith that ruled their lives, or cast aside the faith that ruled their lives for their daughter. A daughter who might one day find her way back to that faith again. More than anything, Judith wished she could share some of her honest doubts with Samantha. She'd tried to. First on the phone at home, until Matthew got uppity about it. Then from a kiosk. But that wasn't conducive to a proper discussion. Was there not some middle ground to be found that didn't lead to an unacceptable compromise for both sides?

Her fingers pressed against Samantha's bedroom door. It slipped open to reveal Matthew's prostrate form, clutching their youngest daughter's baptism necklace in one firm fist. The man lay motionless and ashen, like a toppled wax effigy. "Dear Lord, no." Judith crouched to touch her husband. His pallid skin chilled her quivering digits. "Help. Somebody help." The words were addressed to nobody in particular. Judith Riley staggered downstairs to the phone. Another fit of dizziness sent her stumbling from wall to banister, but she somehow called for an ambulance.

Back in Samantha's old bedroom, the stunned spirit of Matthew Riley watched men zip his body into a bag and haul it away. Judith stood in shock, Samantha's silver cross resting in her upturned palm, chain drizzling through loose fingers. Matthew leaned closer to his wife. *She can't see or hear me. Why haven't I crossed over? The Lord must be giving me a chance to reach Samantha. I can't move on until I know she's safe.*

12

Relative Problems

ANDREW MILES, 2019.

On the one hand, Andrew Miles found it bizarre to live another man's life. On the other, it was nice to interact with the mortal world again. Possessions which meant nothing surrounded him. To Harold Jessop, each might glow with meaning, purpose and sentimental significance. Or would they? From what Andrew gathered, the loner was a ruthless businessman, not above taking advantage of people or ripping them off to line his own pockets. Would such an unscrupulous character 'do' sentiment? Was any object in his cluttered house above the right price, if offered? It didn't bother the usurper. All bets were off, after everything he'd been through. What cared he for admirable behaviour, now? Anybody was fair game if it served his purpose to summon Sharon from the afterlife. *Sharon.* He sat down at the breakfast table with a bowl of soggy honey flakes, their edges as limp as the fabric of his present morality. *Whatever would she think of me?* Canny wheeler-dealer though Jessop might have been, Andrew was once the opposite. Carpentry never made him rich, but not once did he struggle to find work. The principal reason was an unflinching honesty and desire to go the extra mile for his customers. Word of such behaviour followed him like a lengthening shadow. It wasn't that he'd been born an extra-decent person. Sharon always kept him honest. She was so full of love and kindness, he did everything for her. Each freebie he supplied in work or materials, he undertook to make himself a better man for his wife. Every virtuous action - irrespective of whether Sharon saw it - he performed to deserve her. Andrew owed it to the universe somehow. Though he never vocalised that, even as an inner dialogue.

The doorbell chimed. The man dropped a spoonful of soggy honey flakes back in the bowl and wandered into the hall. *Could it be the postwoman? Another two items to find for the ritual. But, it wouldn't hurt to test the water. I still need a host for Sharon's spirit.* He worried once again that Jessop's ticker might be on a short fuse. Sometimes a ball of dread scrunched up in his belly. He imagined the Grim Reaper standing in one corner of the room eyeing an hourglass, while tapping a bony, impatient foot.

"Surprise." A beaming face, the spitting image of an older Harold Jessop met Andrew as he opened the door.

The home-owner stared with blank, confused eyes, unsure how to react.

The visitor gaped. "Jesus, Harold you look awful. Have you been ill?"

Andrew thought fast. "Lot on my plate right now."

"Well, aren't you going to invite your big brother in?"

"Yes, of course. Silly me. Come in then." Andrew flushed. *How did a hoarder like Harold Jessop fill his house with bizarre junk, yet not keep a single picture of any family?* The carpenter had assumed him to be an orphaned, only child with no friends or relatives. This latest development might complicate matters.

"Thanks, Harold." The man stepped across the threshold. "So, you've been keeping busy then? What is it, a lot of summer custom at the shop?"

"Something like that. Are you stopping long? Can I offer you a tea or coffee?"

The older Jessop folded his arms and stared. "Tea? Since when have I drunk tea?"

"Okay. Coffee then. Unless you'd like something a little stronger?" Andrew considered there might be another beer lurking at the back of the fridge.

"Nice thought, brother dear. But, I need to get back to Bristol before nightfall. The firm had me on a buying trip in France. After I got off the Eurostar at Folkestone, I thought I'd take a quick detour off the M20 when I reached Blue Bell Hill. Haven't seen you in a while. M25 will be a zoo this time of the morning, anyhow."

Andrew breathed a sigh of relief that this sibling lived on the other side of the country. That took the pressure off, if he could keep up the show for now. "Instant coffee all right?"

"Sure. I've never known you to serve posh coffee. You're tighter than a gnat's arse." He coughed. "Speaking of which, Margie tells me you didn't even send her a birthday card last week. What's going on with that?"

Andrew walked to the kitchen, accompanied by Jessop's big brother. Who the hell was Margie? "Err, it must have got lost in the post."

"You might have at least called her. She's our only sister, Harold. What would Mum and Dad have said?"

A sister too? This was getting worse by the minute. Andrew made a mental note to scan Harold's address book later. What if she lived close by and dropped in at a moment's notice? "I'll send her some flowers later."

"Better. Are you sure you're okay? There's something different about you."

Colour drained from the pretend home-owner's cheeks. He filled the kettle and set it to boil. How long could he get away without addressing his brother by name? The question of his health provided a flash of inspiration. "I'm fine, MARTY. Been overdoing things a little. At my age, I should slow down. Either that or hire myself an assistant." He stressed the name 'Marty' with enough emphasis to be noticeable but not deliberate.

"Marty? Who the hell is Marty?" The man touched Andrew's sweating brow. "You feel a little hot. Sure you're not coming down with a fever? There's some weird stuff going round at the moment."

"I'll be okay." He lifted an instant coffee jar down from a cupboard and spooned some of the contents in to a plain, china mug.

"If you say so. But I'm still your brother Chris, not Marty. Let's get that straight at least."

Andrew parted his lips and bowed his head. He let out a faint, pretend snigger. "I'm a daft bugger. Sorry, Chris. Speaking of which, I'm so much at sixes and sevens, I can't even remember if you take milk and sugar?"

Chris shook his head. "White and one. Ta."

Andrew let out a faint sigh at having dodged another bullet. He poured out the water onto milk and sugar, then passed the mug across.

"I see I've interrupted your breakfast." Chris deposited himself at a dining chair opposite.

"Nah, I'm done with it. Didn't feel much like honey flakes this morning." Andrew cleared the bowl away and sat down to sip a cup of tea he'd fixed earlier. "How was it in France?" If he got Chris talking about himself, the guy might ask fewer questions. He must know Harold would have to go into Rochester town centre to open the shop before long. Now it was a juggling game until he left.

"Great. A lot of promising new clients. Still takes me ten minutes to switch my mind over to driving on the other side of the road. I never will get used to going anti-clockwise at a roundabout. Thought I was about to have a head-on, at one stage."

"Oh dear."

"No harm done. My French has improved a lot, ever since they made me principal buyer. I suppose it's had to. Right in time for my impending retirement. Carol keeps nagging me about when I'm going to take her along. Can you imagine the wife on a business trip? Like I need all that extra stress."

Andrew shrugged. He realised Harold couldn't *'imagine the wife on a business trip,'* although *he* could. A business trip including his late partner seemed like a dream. Christopher Jessop was so lost in his non-stop prattle, the irony of that statement when applied to his bachelor, younger brother passed him by. And so the one-sided discussion progressed, much to Andrew's relief.

The doorbell chimed again.

"Excuse me." Andrew stood and walked down the hallway.

"Good morning," the fit postwoman handed over a small parcel; tone even, face nonchalant.

Andrew put on the best smile Jessop's face would allow. It must have been an unusual expression for the deceased antique dealer, because his muscles struggled to comply. "How are you today?"

The woman pursed her lips, that usual glint gone from her eyes. "I'm fine."

Andrew realised his previous dismissive demeanour with her had not done him any favours. "I'm glad you rang. I thought I saw you down at 'The Man of Kent' when I went past yesterday."

The postwoman adjusted the weight in her delivery bag. "No, that can't have been me."

Andrew leaned against the door frame. "It's a nice place. Cosy."

"Yes, I've been there before. But not lately."

The man folded his arms. "Would you like to?"

"Excuse me?"

"Would you like to go for a drink there sometime?"

The postwoman shifted from foot to foot. "Err, that's nice, but I'm seeing someone already." She picked her red polo shirt and delivered a forced attempt at an appreciative smile. "Thank you for asking. Have a good day." With that, the woman turned and marched double-time to the next address on her round.

Andrew blew out his cheeks. *Great. She's a shameless flirt. One of those people who feeds off turning heads and exercising her power. Scratch that possibility as a host candidate.* He raised his eyes to a cloudless sky and muttered under his breath. "Fortunate you never took the initiative there, Harold." He closed the door. *Poor bastard died with the romantic imaginings that she might like him. And who'd blame the fellow?*

"Well that has to be a first." Chris stood in the hallway, mug of coffee in hand.

Andrew opened one palm out flat. "What?"

"You know what." Chris burst into a half gasp, half snort. "Asking a woman out for drinks."

Andrew frowned. "A first?"

"Unless there's something you haven't been telling me." Chris walked to the living room window to watch the postwoman trot down the hill, toned backside wiggling. "Not bad taste, little brother. If a tad young for a creaky, solitary old miser like you."

"You're all heart," Andrew snorted.

"Knock it off. You're not upset." Chris gulped down the last of his coffee. "What would you have done if she'd said yes?"

"Spent an enjoyable evening with a beautiful woman."

Chris screwed up his eyes. "Sixty-five years with precious little interest in relationships or the opposite sex, and now you're developing an appetite for women?" He grinned. "Okay. Who *are* you and what have you done with Harold Jessop?"

Andrew bit his lip. This guy would never know the accuracy with which his joking question represented actual reality. He thought it best to downplay the situation, lest the interrogation start up again. "A moment of pure insanity. I never had a midlife crisis."

Chris nodded. "That's more like the little brother I know. I'd better let you get off to work. Thanks for the coffee, Harold." He passed the china mug to Andrew.

"Have a safe journey home."

"Ta. Don't forget those flowers for Margie."

"I won't."

"Take it easy. Stop overdoing it. You've accrued more assets and resources than you'll ever need in your old age. It'd be stupid to keel over from exhaustion and never enjoy the fruits of your labour."

"Fair enough." Andrew opened the front door. Yet again Chris had nailed the absolute truth down in an oblivious fashion. Shame it was too late for Harold to heed his warning.

Chris slapped him on the shoulder, jangled a set of keys and stomped off down the road to his parked car.

Andrew rifled through Harold's address book. It relieved him to discover Margaret Jessop - a spinster - lived in Cromer, Norfolk. Closer than Chris but far enough away to avoid the likelihood of an unannounced visit. Later that day he paid a visit to the local florists and arranged delivery of a late spray of birthday blooms. If his luck held, she would be the kind of person who preferred to write letters, rather than talk on the phone. He'd got away with things for now, and the game was still afoot. Who would believe the truth if they ever found out? All he had to do was avoid unwanted attention and interest in his life and activities. That and keep Harold Jessop's body breathing until everything was in place.

*   *   *

Samantha Riley clicked 'Apply' to complete a set of changes to the last address record of the day. That final one was a pain to verify. She resorted to tracking down a phone number and gave the occupants a call. It turned out the property had been subdivided into two flats. Problem solved at last, Samantha logged her time and signed-off.

A smart-phone screen lit up on the shabby desk beside her laptop. She rubbed her eyes and squinted at the caller's name: *Rachel Saunders*. Samantha lifted the device and swiped to connect the call. "Hi Rach."

There was a moment of near silence accompanied by a faint, slow intake of breath.

"Rachel? Is everything okay?"

"Mum phoned me this morning." The voice came shaky and hesitant.

Samantha's eyes narrowed. "Oh? Mum hasn't called

me this week. Our last chat was brief. Some yobs started hammering on the phone kiosk while she was talking."

"Where are you, Sam?"

"I'm at my flat. Was about to unwind after a long data validation session for the agency. What's up?"

Another hesitation. "Are you sitting down?"

Samantha swallowed. Her voice grew stern. "What's happened, Rachel?"

"Dad passed away in the night."

In her attic studio flat, the young woman held the phone clamped to her head, eyes staring through the wall as if it weren't there.

Rachel's voice started after an uncomfortable pause. "Sam?"

"I'm listening."

"Mum found him dead on the floor of your old bedroom. She called for an ambulance, but it was too late."

Samantha's eyes glistened and her breathing intensified. She wrestled with memories of Matthew Riley throwing her out in the street for transgressing his religious standards. "That's a shame."

"A shame?" Rachel's voice steadied and rose in pitch.

"A shame for Mum."

"Is that all you can say? It's a shame for Mum?"

Samantha clicked the tensed muscles in her stiff neck. "I suppose it's a shame for the church. Dad's tithes alone must have paid for their new welcome centre."

"Sam, how could you? He was our father. Aren't you in the least bit upset?"

Samantha ran her free hand through the messy curls of straw blonde hair. "I may be, in time. It's a shock reaction. This news has got to process."

"Process? I broke down in tears the moment Mum told me."

"You got on all right with Dad. Of course you're upset."

"And you're not? All those years of love and care."

Samantha sighed. "Rach, I'm not sure what you want from me, or what you were expecting. I loved Dad, once upon a time. But he was a cold fish. Love and care? Try indoctrination. The moment I coloured outside the lines he drew for us, that was it for me. I'm persona non grata at the old family home, if you recall? At least I was until last night. I haven't heard from Mum yet. Shit, I'm not welcome at your house either. Pardon me if I don't break down and bawl my eyes out because Matthew Riley's gone."

"How can you be so unfeeling?"

"I'm a chip off the old block."

"Oh, Sam." Rachel's voice trailed away into a soft sobbing.

Samantha closed her eyes and tilted her head back. "I'm sorry, Sis. Thanks for filling me in. How's Mum bearing up?"

"She alternated between stunned, slow speech and tears when we spoke. Pastor Mike and some women from the church are at the house consoling her."

"Any idea what caused it?"

"Mum said he came home early from work yesterday, after a check-up at the doctors. They diagnosed terminal cancer. He received prayer last night, but was dead by morning."

Samantha bit her lip. The rejected, offended woman inside her wanted to lash out; to strike with a sarcastic barb at those unanswered, ineffectual prayers. She sucked it up. Rachel didn't deserve that. Samantha loved her sister. Those folk from the church didn't deserve it either. She knew enough to realise the sincerity of their faith and concern for her late father. This whirlwind of thoughts and emotions lasted longer than she realised.

"Sam?"

"I'm still here."

"Are you going to call Mum?"

"Later. First thing in the morning might be best. If the God Squad are round there, they won't leave her alone for hours. Mum and I wouldn't be able to talk properly. I'll wake her up tomorrow. Try to start her day off with some encouragement."

"I doubt she'll sleep much. Don't think I will either. Mum might have the funeral service date by the time you call."

"Yeah."

"Sam?"

"Uh, huh?"

"You will drive over for the service, won't you?"

There was a long silence. "Let me talk to Mum first, okay?"

Rachel allowed a long stream of breath to escape.

The sound itself spoke more than a thousand words ever could. Her sister picked up on each nuance before Rachel spoke again. "Okay. Take care. Talk soon?"

"We'll talk soon. Bye."

Next morning, Samantha arose early. She didn't want to speak with her mother from the confines of that attic cubbyhole. With the sea breeze only a gentle whisper, she took her favourite walk along The Leas from the Step Short Memorial Arch. The promenade lay still and empty, except for the occasional passing car. Samantha deposited herself on a bench looking out across the channel. The name 'Mum' came up on her mobile phone address book and she initiated the call.

"Hello?" A thin, tired voice answered with a yawn.

"Mum?"

"Samantha?" The tiredness gave way to a sudden burst of renewed energy. "I'm so glad you called. Rachel must have told you the news."

"Yes, she phoned yesterday."

"I was hoping to speak with you last night. But by the time Pastor Mike and the church crowd left, I almost collapsed with exhaustion."

"Did you sleep?"

"To my shame, yes."

"To your shame? Mum, that's good."

"I meant it made me feel guilty, that's all. A wife shouldn't have a good night's rest straight after the death of her husband."

Samantha groaned. "Is that a scripture I haven't

read?"

"No, darling."

"Mum, I wish I had words of comfort to offer."

"It's all right. I've had enough of the Bible quoted at me in the last few hours to last a lifetime. I'd rather hear how you're feeling. Tell me something honest. Something real."

"How *I'm* feeling? What about you?"

"Numb. It hasn't sunk in yet. Your father came home yesterday, having been told by the doctors he was dying of cancer."

"Rachel said something like that." Samantha hesitated. "How did he die?"

"I woke to find him out of bed. When I walked onto the landing, your old bedroom door was ajar. He'd collapsed and died on the floor in there during the night."

"What was he doing in my bedroom?"

Judith Riley choked back a rising wave of emotion. "I believe he was praying for you."

Samantha attempted to disguise the disdain in her voice. "Praying I'd repent and go back to my old life like nothing had ever changed, you mean?"

"I realise your father could be hard, Samantha. He was uncompromising in his faith."

"You think?" Samantha fought hard not to spit as the words came out.

Judith's kind tone softened further. "Are you so very different with your own experiences?"

There was truth in that statement and it stung. Samantha wanted to counter with: *'But I'm not a bigot, cutting people off who disagree with me.'* She couldn't bring herself to say it. Besides, she had no intention of attending the funeral. What was that if not cutting people off, after a fashion? "Do you think he'll be buried in the family plot with Nana?"

"Yes. He'd reserved space for us all in there."

Samantha looked down at her knees. "So we're in the same physical spot when we're raised up on the last day?"

Judith hesitated. "You might find it hard to believe, but he wanted us buried together out of affection. There was no religious motivation behind it."

"Sorry, Mum. I didn't mean to be unkind."

"I know."

"This is the first time I've been able to speak to you at home in a long while."

"Yes." She cleared her throat. "Samantha?"

"Yeah?"

"I understand how hurt you must feel. What happened hurt us all. But please don't judge your father too harshly over it."

"Mum... You've had to lead a double life since I got chucked out of the house. You snuck down the road to a pay-phone so you could speak with your youngest daughter. How messed up is that?"

"It's sad. Very sad." Her tone brightened. "When will you be home?"

"Home?"

"For the funeral."

Samantha cupped her brow in one hand. "Mum, I can't... You don't want me there."

"Of course I do. We all do."

"All?"

"Myself, Rachel, John and their children. Your sister and her family are coming over to stay for a few days."

"I'm guessing Rachel omitted to mention John has banned me from their house. Or from having anything to do with my niece and nephew. You don't need that kind of tension at home. Good job I'm not coming."

"Ah."

"Yes. I can't do the whole 'happy clappy' Charismatic church service. If it was a non-religious or calm funeral elsewhere, perhaps. But they'll want to give him their usual send-off. That was his life, after all. It's only fair. The entire crowd knows about my backsliding and dodgy spiritual practices. Either they'd try to cast demons out of me, or I'd get so mad at the back-stabbing, self-righteous arseholes talking behind their hands, I'd end up punching someone."

"Your view of the church hasn't softened then?"

"Why should it? It's the reason I'm cut-off from two sections of my family. And for what? Being honest is the real crime, when you get down to it. I could elaborate, but you're familiar with the whole story already. Next thing I'm like Lucifer, cast out of heaven."

"I know, darling. But I couldn't oppose your father."

"You should have been able to. This is the twenty-first century, Mum, not the Spanish bloody inquisition. Rachel's shaping up to have the same kind of relationship with her lord and master."

Judith sighed. "I understand. We'll miss you. Are

you sure you won't come?"

"When all this has settled down, I'll take a solo trip to Bath. We can visit Dad's grave together. You and I by ourselves. No church-types allowed. How does that sound?"

"Like a dream. Don't leave it too long. I miss you so much."

Samantha wiped a tear from one eye. "Ditto. I love you, Mum."

"I love you too, Samantha. I'm sure there's little I can do to convince you of this, but your father also loved you. One day, I hope you'll come to that understanding for yourself."

"Okay. Listen, if you need anything, please call. Day or night, pick up the phone."

"I will. Call me when you can."

"Bye, Mum."

* * *

William Acton secured the main double doors of his Kent auction house. The converted oast and attached storage buildings made for a picturesque commercial enterprise. One last staff vehicle pulled out into the lane, the hum of its engine fading to nothing in an instant. From a hill across undulating orchards, the bells of St. Mary's Church, Selling added a faint, melodious backdrop. William had been in the antique auction trade for the best part of his thirty-five-year career. Now in his late fifties, the man couldn't recall a time when being alone in his own establishment made him feel ill at ease. Not until the last week. Every once in a while something arrived ready for sale, that caused an odd internal sensation. There had been times over the years, when he could swear objects shifted from the spots he left them. He always dismissed this by reminding himself so many items came through for auction, it must be the product of a busy mind. How could anyone recall with total accuracy, the position of every new piece? Plus, his occasional staff could have moved some objects. Nothing to worry himself about. Assuming he didn't dwell on the handful of times he'd been certain where he'd left something, only to find it elsewhere, later on. Times when trade had been slack, and he'd worked alone. Yet this new experience was different. A pervasive dread settled on him after closing time each night. His cocker spaniel, Max - a bundle of mad, tail-wagging energy under normal circumstances - would be found shivering and whimpering as he curled beneath William's office desk. Large, terrified eyes peered up at him, whites exposed. The auction house owner had never been one to give much thought to ghosts. Even now he didn't know what he believed in relation to the subject. But something in the place wasn't right, and he didn't know how to address the problem.

The lights of the main storage building dimmed as William flicked a row of switches, one by one. It had been late by the time all accounting and sundry work was complete. From somewhere far back in the darkness, between aisles of shelving, a dragging noise cut through the stillness. The sound came heavy and set the man's teeth on edge. Shivers washed his form in icy waves. He reversed his switching action to bring the lights back up. A massive pine dresser stood blocking one of the access ways. There was no doubt about it: when four workmen delivered the cumbersome object, they'd placed it firmly against the far wall. Now it had moved twenty feet along one aisle, under its own steam. That or the agency of some unseen force William would rather not consider. A foul odour like stale sweat hung on the air. The auction house owner wrinkled his nose at the pungent, rancid smell. He checked his armpits for signs of perspiration. Clean as a whistle. It was a pointless, distracting activity, and he knew it. The stink became so intense, it couldn't originate from any ordinary human. A sharp report caused the man to jump and twist. About the same distance along another aisle, lay the sturdy glass remains of a heavy vase. William's mouth went dry as old leather. *Should I sweep that up now, or leave it until the morning when it's light, and the place feels easier?* As he weighed the choice, a china bowl began rocking from side to side on the same section of shelving. *What's happening?* The bowl stopped rocking. William gulped down viscous spittle; senses straining for any other disturbance. The same bowl slid along the shelf, as if dragged by a careless child. It reached the edge and hung in a precarious half-on, half-off position. The proprietor considered his likely insurance premiums after the owners of these items were reimbursed. It wasn't a pretty thought. So unpleasant in fact, it spurred his legs into action. William loped along the aisle, hands raised ready to secure the errant piece of chinaware. He reached it in time and lifted the bowl down, clutching it to his chest. Vibrations through his ribcage of a pounding heart, pushed against the delicate antique. A freestanding bank of shelves five feet away toppled forward, spilling a collection of glass and chinaware into a waterfall of smashing fragments. Flagstones beneath William's feet shook at the almighty bang, as the heavy storage rack collided with the floor and lay still. The damages were racking up. William fought not to add his own aroma to the prevalent grim body odour. His bowels clenched, holding back an evacuation fear insisted he let go.

"Hello?" To whom was he speaking? His voice came weak and pathetic, not even reaching the walls to return in sonic reflection.

Several aisles across, the dresser trundled forward as though dragged by an entire work crew. William placed the bowl back in place with shaking hands. He clambered over the toppled shelving and speed-walked away from the disturbance, not daring to look back. All lights died in the auction house without warning. The man fumbled his way along a wall in the blackness, navigating from a mental map to avoid a painful or expensive collision.

Upstairs in the main oast, Max whined and yelped.

William stumbled up the stairs, clutching onto the handrail. "Come on, boy." He opened his office door and fumbled in one drawer for a torch. Its beam fell on the terrified animal's face. Max wasn't going anywhere. William unhooked his jacket from a coat rack and pawed for a set of car keys. He stood in the doorway, rattling them at the dog. It was the daily signal they were off home. Another bang of toppling, sturdy racks sounded from the downstairs storage area. William turned and slipped down the staircase, panning the torch beam from side to side.

Faced with an obvious choice between remaining alone in his hidey hole all night with some unseen monster, or venturing out to escape with his master; Max shot out from beneath the desk. He almost took William off his feet on the last two steps down.

"Good boy. You don't want to stay here either, do you?" The man spoke under pretence of calming the dog. In reality, he knew the statement was a desperate attempt to resurrect his own flagging courage.

William Acton didn't bother setting the alarm that night. What was the point? With all that bizarre, psychic activity (or whatever the hell it was) taking place inside, the sensors would trip before he got halfway home. Then he'd get called out as key-holder by the police, to resolve the matter. William's car pulled away. Other than feeding himself and his dog, there was only one course of action left this evening: He'd go on-line and look for help. *How many wackos will I have to sift through, before finding someone with the skills and knowledge to solve the problem? Do I need a priest to perform an exorcism? Have these disturbances started because of something brought in for sale?* Too many questions, so difficult to answer.

In the boot of the estate car, Max whimpered to himself.

13

Going, Going, Gone

SAMANTHA RILEY, 2019.

"Lena? What's going on?" Samantha clambered up the last few, steep steps to the attic landing outside her Folkestone flat. Her Polish neighbour's face hung wan and stained with the telltale tracks of recent tears. A workman fixed new hinges to a battered door with splintered edges.

"Burglary, while I was at work. Kurwa! Some bezwartościowy człowiek broke in door and stole all my stuff."

"That's terrible. I'm so sorry."

"Not your fault. Landlord say there more burglaries, up road." Her grammar deteriorated further while under stress.

"It's not the best neighbourhood, is it?"

"So why steal from us? Why not pick rich people with big house and much money? Is shameful."

Samantha tapped the woman's forearm in solidarity,

then let herself into her own cramped lodgings. She took one look around. *I need to tidy up. Were it not for the fact the door is intact and my laptop still here, you wouldn't know if someone had burgled this place or not.* She laid a square, brown paper package next to the computer. Her mother's handwriting on the address and a Bath postmark left the sender's identity without question. It was a fortnight since she'd phoned Judith Riley. Most likely her father's funeral was over by now. There had been no further contact from Rachel, after that initial call with the tragic news. *Could Mum have told her to leave me alone, after she explained I wasn't coming? Perhaps John was so relieved or delighted, Rachel let me be without maternal intervention? They would have had their hands full anyway, what with the church crowd and everything else. What did little Jane and toddler Adam make of it all?* She put a carton of milk in the fridge, then unloaded some dried pasta and tins of tomatoes from a shopping bag. Her phone pinged an alert chime. Samantha lit up the screen and pulled down a memo notification. *Hmm, got that session at 'Acton Auctions' soon. Still hope I can find the place. What was it? Oh yeah, Selling. So what did Mum send me?*

She sat down at her desk and opened the packaging with tender fingers, as if it were a priceless artefact. A folded letter on her mother's favourite floral notepaper lay wrapped around a familiar jewellery box. Samantha left the container closed and unfolded the letter to read:

'My Dearest Samantha,

As I write this, Rachel, John and the children have left for Salisbury. I'm so glad to have had their company over the last week, and grateful to your brother-in-law for taking so much time off work. I know John can be a lot like your father, and that the two of you don't get along.

I found my greatest joy in the innocent comfort and affections of my grandchildren. It was fun to spoil them a little when John wasn't around. Is their upbringing stricter than it should be? Jane kept asking when Auntie Sam was going to get here. She misses you so; as do I.

Pastor Mike gave your father a beautiful send-off. His words were measured and sincere. For all his foibles, Mike Clarke mourns his friend Matthew. They built the fellowship up together, from a declining congregation in an old community hall to its present state. All that took decades of faith and hard work. No small amount of money, either.

The service was everything you dreaded. Not that I have a problem with lively worship, but there were times I'd have appreciated a quieter, more reflective tone. It was Charismatic Evangelical with all the bells and whistles: tongues, prophecy, interpretations, words of knowledge and power, and as much jumping and victory shouting as they could cram into the time frame. There were moments the coffin might as well not have been there, if I'm honest. As if that funeral were nothing more than an excuse for a mid-week meeting. Mike even took an offering, which rankled me a little. Those funds better go to the 'Matthew Riley Memorial Garden' he's planning in the car park, or I'll phone The Charity Commission.

The tone of this letter may surprise you, though we've spoken before about my growing doubts and questions. Since your father passed, I've ordered several books on Post-Evangelicalism. Why do I feel like a caged bird breaking free? I've lost the love of my life. Surely it shouldn't be this way?

One book arrived two days before your sister left. John caught sight of it and became quite steamed. We got into a debate about open-mindedness. Needless to say, he found my mind a little too open for his liking. It's encouraging to read about so many others who've taken this journey, and the various roads they've gone down.

I've asked Pastor Mike for some space to mourn my husband's passing. I have so many things to work through. Life will never be the same with my beloved Matthew gone. Now I need to decide what the rest of my time on earth should look like. I'm hungry for change and weary at so much in the church that has annoyed me for several years.

Oh how I wish you were here, Samantha. When Rachel and John came, I mentioned your banishment from their home. John flew into a rage about some dark spiritual force that rocked the house while you were there. I'd love to know your side of the story. I also want to hear more of your tales from the coma. What was your experience of God like? Do you have any more understanding about why you were given this strange ability?

Before I sign-off for now, I'm enclosing a gift. It's not a gift in the truest sense, because it already belongs to you. When I found your father face-down on the bedroom carpet, he was clutching your baptismal cross. On the day doctors told him his life would soon end, his foremost thoughts were of you. Yes, those thoughts were in the framework of religious dogma, but borne out of love all the same. I'm not excusing what he did. Even if this symbol no longer represents your view of God, I hope/pray/wish that it will one day remind you of the way your father loved you. According to a spiritual worldview, perhaps. But, still with his whole heart.

When you come to visit, I'll ask you to forgive me in person for not fighting your corner when he threw you out.

Maybe your memories of home are forever tainted and you wouldn't wish to return. But if you should, you are always welcome here. I have the strangest sense that I must cut some old binding ties, if I'm to continue on my present, spiritual trajectory. That could prove difficult and exhausting. Will I find the resolve alone? I need the strength and moral courage of my youngest daughter.

Please come home soon.

All my love,

Mum.'

Samantha's chest ached. Reading that letter, the world seemed to slow down. Her father's presence hung stronger than ever. She checked the time on her phone. "Shit. I'd better get going." Her words broke a silence that had blanketed the flat for some time.

Unseen by his daughter in that dingy rented bolt-hole, an agonised spirit looked on. Matthew Riley studied those grim surroundings and read the written words of his former wife. In that moment, his mortal existence took on the appearance of a sham. He'd hung on to save Samantha. To win her back to the Lord. Why did he now feel like some troublemaker or unwanted spare wheel? Was Judith going astray too, now he was no longer around? And what of his daughter and her supposed gift to see, hear and help earthbound spirits? That was what she once claimed. It must be nonsense. She hadn't noticed him standing over her shoulder as they read together.

Samantha stood, picked up her handbag and opened the door. She was halfway out, when the sight of Lena's flat brought back thoughts of the burglary. She leaned back inside and swiped the box and letter from her desk. *I'll read this again later. Maybe look at the cross. Maybe. But I'd better not risk leaving it here for now.* With that, she stuffed the items into her handbag and descended the stairs in a hurry.

* * *

"The next lot is a vintage charm bracelet in 14K yellow gold. 7.5 inch medium size length on a two mil chain with five charms. Do I hear twelve-hundred?" William Acton scanned around the seated throng of potential bidders. An assistant walked in front of his lectern, showing off the item for sale on a velvet cushion.

At the back of the oast assembly room, an ageing man with side tufts of white hair raised his auction programme.

"Thank you, Mr Jessop. Ever the shrewd customer with an eye for a bargain. Do I hear thirteen-hundred anywhere?"

A forty-something woman with red hair and freckles, waved her hand near the front.

"Thank you, Madam. At thirteen-hundred. Do I hear fourteen?"

No response.

"Thirteen-hundred for this premium item of jewellery. Quite a deal. Any advance on thirteen-hundred?"

Andrew Miles gazed out through Harold Jessop's eyes, but with a gift of vision the deceased antique dealer never possessed. William Acton's assistant wasn't the only person on hand near the lectern. Unseen by everyone else, a dejected woman around thirty-two with layered blonde hair and piercing green eyes, stood with her head bowed. Her wispy, shimmering, semi-transparent form almost floated. Gossamer strands woven together into a faded facsimile of who she was in life. Jessop's programme shot up again.

Acton raised his eyebrows, gavel held aloft. "Fourteen-hundred?"

Jessop nodded.

"Fourteen-hundred bid. Any advance on fourteen-hundred?"

The crowd remained still, except for the odd cough.

"At fourteen-hundred, are we all done?"

Silence.

"Fourteen-hundred, going once. Fourteen-hundred, going twice." He slammed the gavel down with a sharp crack. "Sold for fourteen-hundred pounds."

"Harold, how the devil are you?" William Acton caught the antique dealer walking out the door with his new purchase.

It was clear to Andrew Miles that the two were old acquaintances, if not full-blown friends. Acton's name was listed on the programme as chief auctioneer, so guessing games weren't necessary. "I'm well, thank you."

"That's a nice piece you've picked up today. Though I was surprised to see you go to fourteen-hundred. At twelve, you could have realised a tidy profit in the shop."

Andrew shrugged Jessop's shoulders. "True enough. I have something else in mind for this."

Acton grinned. "I should have known. You're purchasing the bracelet according to a client's brief. What will they end up paying?"

The antique dealer sucked his jagged teeth. "I can't go giving away all my secrets now, can I?"

"I suppose not. Listen, old man. How would you like to hang about for a dram? I've got some rare, thirty-year-old Glenmorangie in the office that's begging to be shared with good company."

"Why not? Let me stow this bracelet in my vehicle."

"Excellent. I'll see everyone else out, while my staff tallies up."

Samantha craned her neck over the Ford Ka's steering wheel, glancing from side to side. On her right sat a red brick pub called *'The Royal Oak.'* Dormer windows poked out of a Kent peg tiled roof. Rectangular, white painted sash windows ran along the ground and first floor frontage. Above and to the side of two carriage lamps decorating the entrance porch, broad-canopied oak trees on recessed painted inset backgrounds - most likely former windows - accentuated the hostelry's title. Samantha pulled over beside a low, white chain-link fence between some outside tables and the quiet country lane. It was the second time she'd driven past in her quest to locate *'Acton Auctions.'* She killed the engine and nipped inside the pub. *Someone round here must know the place.*

"What can I get you, love?" The proprietor wiped down a polished, semi-circular wooden bar top.

"Later, perhaps. I'm trying to find *'Acton Auctions.'* Can you help?"

The barman nodded and scratched some stubble with an unconscious hand. "Been in a circle have we?"

Samantha flushed.

He waved her discomfort away. "Don't worry, Miss. We get folk in here all the time who overshoot the turning. Selling is spread out in an odd shape. What with Gushmere, Neame's Forstal, Hogben's Hill and

Perry Wood all squished together, it's small wonder strangers get mixed up. Now then. Which way is your vehicle facing?"

Samantha indicated the direction.

"Good. Well, you're off to a great start. Keep going down the lane until you see a side road to your right, before the primary school. It's signposted 'St. Mary's Church.' Take that road. Keep an eye out for passing places. It's not busy, but you won't fit two cars side by side down there. It'll bring you out opposite the church. Go straight across, ignoring the T-junction sign. That's why many people miss the turning, I guess. William Acton needs to get permission for a sign at the crossroads. Anyway, at the end of the road, a gravel track will take you over two fields to a large oast house and outbuildings. Do you know what an oast house is?"

Samantha nodded.

The barman continued. "Good. Thought I'd check. That doesn't sound like a Kent accent."

"Somerset."

"Where the zoider apples grow?" He did an amusing parody of a West Country yokel pronouncing the word 'cider.'

Although she was running a few minutes late, the young woman couldn't hide the amusement in her eyes. "Something like that. I'm from Bath. A little more cosmopolitan."

"Right you are. Nice part of the world."

"Thanks for your help. I should be able to find it now. Last time I missed the turning and ended up going left, then left again. Wound up at a pub in some thick woods."

"That'll be *'The Rose & Crown.'* Wrong direction. So, take the next right and keep going straight." He turned his attention to a small group of new patrons, but kept his eyes on Samantha. "I hope we'll see you here for a drink later."

"Thanks. If time permits, I'll try to come back. Bye."

Five minutes saw her little motor crunching down the long, bumpy gravel track past a blue and gold sign bearing the name: *'Acton Auctions.'* The oast house, its assorted interconnected and random outbuildings formed a sizable complex. Only one estate car and a dark green Mercedes van remained in the vague parking area. Samantha locked the vehicle, swung her handbag over one shoulder and tried not to twist her ankle on the uneven surface leading to a set of doors.

"Hello?" She leaned her head into an empty assembly area. Piles of wooden chairs rose in neat stacks on the front window side of the room. In the far corner, a raised dais and oak lectern stood empty at a forty-five-degree angle to the principal space. "Hello?" Samantha called again. "Is anyone here?"

Upstairs in his office, William Acton leaned back with both feet on his desk. Ice clanged against the sides of a tumbler in his double scotch, as he waved it in a flourish while relaying an old tale of the trade to

Harold Jessop. The elder antique dealer sipped his smooth, thirty-year-old Glenmorangie. Sharon would have been nine years old when the spirit was laid down.

Max the spaniel lifted his head.

Acton halted the laugh that marked a punchline in his story and noticed the dog. "What's the matter, boy?"

The animal hopped up with no sign of fear. Tail wagging, he padded out the office door and ambled down the wooden staircase.

"Excuse me for a moment, Harold. I left the front doors open because I'm expecting a visitor. That might be her. Back in a second."

"Take your time. I'll keep enjoying this fine whisky."

William slid the bottle across to his guest. "Help yourself to another if you like. There's more ice in the fridge next to my filing cabinet."

The auction house owner descended the straight stairs to find an attractive blonde in her mid-twenties rubbing Max's tummy. The dog rolled on his back from side to side in a state of bliss. Tail wagging faster than an engine piston, his tongue lolled out of a mouth wide open in the smile only a happy pooch can make.

"Miss Riley?" Acton drew closer.

Samantha stood from a crouch. "Mr Acton?"

Max rolled onto his side, tail slowing. He looked from his master to the guest, wondering if the tummy rub might re-commence soon.

"Please call me William." Acton extended a firm hand, eyes evidencing relief that this recommended spiritual specialist looked like a normal person.

"Samantha. Pleased to meet you. I assume this is your dog?"

"Yes. That's Max. You already seem to be in his good graces."

Samantha crouched again for one moment to stroke the animal. "Hello Max."

"If you wait a while longer until the sun goes down, you'll notice a considerable change in his behaviour."

The woman straightened. "Your account of the activity here was quite alarming. Animals are sensitive to spiritual disturbances. More than most humans."

"He turns into a quivering wreck. After the incident with the shelving, glass vase, chinaware and a pine dresser, his master isn't much better. I'm so thankful you could come at such short notice. I was having a drink with an old antique dealer friend, upstairs in my office. Can I get you something?"

"No that's okay, thank you. I sort of promised the landlord of 'The Royal Oak' I'd be back for a drink later. He gave me directions here." Samantha glanced across the room to where a set of wooden stairs led to an upstairs office. Standing on a small platform balcony outside, a man in his mid-sixties clutched a glass of something or other. A flicker of electricity lifted the hairs on the back of her neck. That observer appeared solid and mortal enough, so why the sensual alert? Could it be general activity in the building? "Is that your friend?" She lifted her chin at the man on the landing.

William twisted round. "That's correct. Harold Jessop of *'Jessop's Antiques'* in Rochester. We've known each other for years."

"I see. Best to check. Sometimes I see spirits as ordinary people. Good to rule out anyone here."

William waved at Harold. "He's the only other one left. As to spirits: short of a bottle of Glenmorangie we've been imbibing..."

Samantha gave a polite snort at the quip.

On the balcony landing, Andrew Miles stared down through Jessop's eyes. *That blonde newcomer is a comely creature. What's Acton's interest in her?* Girl aside, another sight drew his attention. Standing two feet to her right (and unseen by either party), a grey-haired man with a thick moustache lingered. The fellow appeared connected via strands of vapour to the young woman's handbag. The antique dealer sipped his whisky and wandered back into the office.

"Can I have free run of the place?" Samantha peered down to one end of the assembly area, where a right-hand turn led into the large storage section.

"Yes, you may. I've left everything unlocked as you requested in our correspondence. Go wherever you wish."

"William?" Sam winced.

"Yes?"

"Whoever the spirit is, or spirits are (if there's more than one), they've already shown a predilection for breaking things."

"Hmm. I suspect I know where this is going. Look, the disturbances are getting worse. If breakages occur while you are 'at work,' they occur. Please try to lay this thing to rest. Then my business might stand a chance at remaining viable."

"Okay." She unhooked her handbag. "Is there somewhere I can put this out of the way? If things get physical, I don't want to swing it around and knock over a priceless Ming vase or something."

William reached out his hand. "Of course. I'll pop it in my office for now. Can't say I've ever had a priceless Ming vase in stock, but your concern over breakages is heartening. Please proceed at your leisure."

Samantha passed over her bag. "I'll start down in the storage area. Is it this way?" She pointed to the right-hand turn. The question felt redundant. Already her spiritual radar blipped like the announcement of an incoming air raid. Whatever lay in the room beyond, it was ready to play.

"That's correct." Acton looked at his dog. "Come on, Max. You won't want to accompany this lady where she's going."

Max remained stationary, legs rigid. He sidled up to Samantha in a protective manner.

The auction house owner shrugged. "Very well." he looked at the woman. "Don't worry if he turns to jelly and runs for his life, Samantha."

"Noted." Samantha patted the dog's head.

The pair sauntered off towards the storage aisles.

"Who's the young lady?" Jessop raised an eyebrow as Acton re-entered the office carrying Samantha's handbag. 'Moustache Man' floated beside him with a bewildered expression.

"You wouldn't believe me if I told you."

"How long have we been friends?" In truth, Andrew Miles had no idea. "Try me."

"Okay." Acton poured himself another dram and flopped down in his office chair. "We've started to suffer from psychic disturbances of some kind. Objects moving around in the dark when I'm here alone at night. Falling shelves. Breaking vases. Max hides under the desk in here after closing time, until we go home. I never used to believe in all that stuff. Over the last few nights, I've become a terrified convert."

"Really?"

"You're not pulling my leg like I thought."

Jessop rubbed his chin. "At my time of life, I've come to accept a few things I once scoffed at."

"I'll drink to that." Acton raised his glass.

Both men took a sip.

Jessop drew in a long breath. "So, what has the girl to do with all that?"

"She's some kind of spirit liberator. I know it sounds daft, but people I trust recommended her. Doesn't charge either, if you can believe it?"

"That must enhance her credibility."

"That's what I thought. She'll accept anything I give

in gratitude, or walk away with nothing."

"Sounds like my kind of price."

"You would say that, you tight-fisted old miser. If Samantha comes through, it'll save me from bankruptcy."

"Things are that serious?"

Acton nodded. "It's getting that way."

"You'd better give me her contact details, in case I need to invite her over to help me out."

Acton scribbled down the information on a pad and ripped off the sheet for his friend.

"Thanks, William. So, can she actually see the deceased?" One corner of his mouth raised in a sarcastic smirk at the sad soul attached to her handbag.

"As I understand it. She's helped several reputable contacts."

Down in the storage area, Max froze and growled.

Samantha sensed it at the same moment as the dog. Whatever 'it' was, the spirit had come forth. Just one. That much she could tell for certain.

"Easy." Samantha rubbed the spaniel's soft right ear between a gentle thumb and forefinger.

"Aaagh," a bloodcurdling male scream shattered what had been an eerie silence; its noise far more sinister. Naked bulbs hanging from flex cord in the high ceiling above, swung as if a hurricane had blasted through the building interior. Cones of light splashed back and forth across the racks of shelving, crammed with treasures awaiting sale. At the far end, the heavy dresser which had been moved back against the wall by William Acton's staff, juddered along the aisle.

Vibrations of energy coursed through Samantha's limbs. She had never felt this on-fire. Each liberation appeared to intensify her experiences, like the approaching zenith of some otherworldly mission.

"He killed me. My friend. He Killed me." The male voice - previously raised in a scream - shouted across the storage room behind the startled pair.

Samantha whirled on the spot, Max curling round behind her legs.

Thirty feet away, a young man about Samantha's age staggered from side to side. His skull was cleft down to the bridge of his nose. Eye sockets sagged and lolled in loose flaps of skin resulting from whatever opened his head. He flicked one hand across a shelf. Several porcelain ornaments dropped to the flagstone floor and shattered. "Why? Why did he kill me? Kathryn was mine. She didn't want him."

Samantha studied his clothing. He appeared to be some kind of eighteenth century agricultural worker. Given the recent development of these disturbances, she guessed he had nothing to do with the location. Sometimes there was a sense of an object to which an earthbound soul might be attached. Here again, she drew a blank. The storage space inventory hummed with the remnants of spiritual energy from previous owners. Could the collection have acted as a beacon to this wandering unfortunate? Some kind of attractive force?

Max whined and shivered against Samantha's calf

muscles.

The young woman stepped towards the agonised spirit. Her forearms pulsed with energy.

The dog's eyes widened in disbelief. Why was this friendly woman who gave such wonderful tummy tickles, walking into the jaws of terror? He fought against an inner quaking and shuffled forward on his belly to keep close.

Samantha spoke with resonant authority. "All their lives have passed now. Kathryn is gone. The man who hurt you is gone. Everything will be resolved in the world beyond." She reached her hands forward; the grisly, split head mere inches from her tingling grasp.

The man froze. "My life was taken from me."

Samantha's fingers touched his cheeks. With tender affection, she pushed the halves of his shattered head together to peer into the sad, tortured eyes of a handsome young man. "I know. But something better awaits." A glimmer of light pulsed and expanded ten feet behind. "Be free of your pain. The hurt ends here. There's only peace and love ahead." She twisted his head in a slow rotation, to fix on the expanding spiritual threshold.

Ghostly tears filled those sad male eyes, a mortal echo of physicality. It spoke of the relief already flooding his flickering essence. He stammered. "I... I can go?"

Samantha pursed her lips to kiss the air where his cheek might have been. Her mouth crackled with static at the sensuous impartation.

In the skies above St. Mary's Church, Selling, a warm summer's evening decayed into an unheralded thunderstorm. Dark clouds swirled out of nowhere, like billowing smoke from an oily conflagration. Wispy black streamers criss-crossed, angling up and down. They skimmed cottage rooftops before a gravel track leading to an old oast house complex.

"Cripes. Where did *that* come from?" William Acton slammed down his empty glass at the deafening boom. He pushed away from his desk and rose. "Hang on a tick, Harold. I'd better secure the front doors, before we get a gully-washer blowing through the assembly area."

"No worries." Jessop lifted two open palms, one eye drifting to where Samantha's handbag lay.

"Good man." Acton dashed downstairs.

Max barked like an erupting machine gun. The tragic agricultural worker had one foot across the astral doorway when the thunderclap exploded overhead. Rising dread - familiar from her dreams and that afternoon at the former asylum - sucked the joy out of Samantha's encounter. She placed both hands on the uncertain spirit's shoulder blades and whispered in his ear. "Go now. There are others far worse than the man who hurt you. They would hold you here forever. Be at peace, tiller of fields."

High windows set beneath the roof line of the storage room, blew inward. Showers of cascading glass rained down in a shimmering spray. The overhead lights swung again with the onrush of a howling gale. Streaks of inky black cloud slithered through the air like a python wrapping coils about its prey. A roar from some formless, unseen mouth echoed across the chamber, shaking ornaments.

Samantha willed all her gifted energy into the hands that held the confused spirit's shoulders. He took one last step across the threshold. The doorway closed in an instant, dimming the room. Above, the swinging bulbs shattered in a glittering explosion of sparks. The coils snaked around Samantha. Their slithering, negative energy rubbed against her body with evil friction. The roar sounded again and the streaks of cloud raced around the corner. They passed William Acton as he closed his doors, to zero in on the upstairs office.

Andrew Miles lifted the frame of Harold Jessop to his feet and wandered into the doorway. Something inside caused a sensation of fear. It went far deeper than any imaginings of eternal punishment, or separation from his beloved wife. Wisps of swirling cloud descended, forming into the rough outline of a faceless man. Devoid of features though it might have been, there could be no mistake the thing was studying him. Its gaze reached way beneath Jessop's outward appearance.

The Entity leaned closer to examine Andrew Miles' resident soul. He couldn't take this one to HER as a prize. She needed him for Her unfolding purposes. It lingered there a moment longer. With a deafening shriek of anger and frustration, The Entity forced Acton's recently closed front doors open again. Another squall of wind and it vanished into the night.

"Are you all right, William?" Harold Jessop helped the fallen auction house owner to his feet.

"I will be when I speak to Samantha about what's happening."

"It's wild. I had no idea all this was going on. Do you think that was the end of your problems?"

"I hope so. Are you off?"

"Yes. Much as I'd like to snaffle more of your wonderful whisky, I've still got to drive home. I'll leave you to your liberator woman. Thanks for an entertaining and informative evening."

Acton snorted. "You're welcome. See you again soon." He watched Harold Jessop climb into his dark green Mercedes van and drive off. Somehow the atmosphere in his oast house auction establishment felt right again. He mopped his brow, shoulders relaxing. "Right then. Where's that girl and my dog?"

* * *

Back at 'The Royal Oak,' Samantha settled down at a small corner table by herself. True to her word, she'd returned with her patronage. Plus, she needed a drink and a bite to eat after the events of the evening. It didn't take long to demolish the excellent pheasant and chorizo burger served up by the pub's friendly staff. Under normal circumstances, she wouldn't have splashed out on a meal. But William Acton's generosity proved considerable. His cheque rested on the table beside her, as she sipped a cola with ice and a slice. Samantha tucked it away for safekeeping, and retrieved the package from her mother. After another couple of readings, she folded the letter and lifted the jewellery box. *Am I sure I want to touch this? What could it hurt?* Tired fingers prised open the neat container. "Empty?" The thought came out aloud. *What on earth? Mum can't have forgotten to put the cross inside. Mind you, she's had such a roller-coaster of an emotional ride, I wouldn't blame her.* To be certain, Samantha rummaged around in her handbag, in case the necklace had slipped out. No trace. She closed the box again, put it in her bag and signalled to a waitress for the bill.

Later that night, Harold Jessop opened the wooden cigar box on his special warehouse table. A vintage charm bracelet joined that small, embroidered handkerchief inside. Watching in motionless apathy, stood the indistinct form of the thirty-two-year-old woman he'd seen during the bidding session. One more item went into the box: a small, silver cross necklace. Next to the vaporous woman, that grey-haired moustache wearing man stared like a solitary prisoner. An incarcerated spirit who didn't belong and wished to be anywhere but there.

14

The Invitation

SAMANTHA RILEY, 2019.

"Have you any idea how many entities have manifested at the warehouse?" Samantha paced up and down the limited space of her attic flat, phone raised. "Five?" Her blue eyes blinked and widened. "How large is the place?" She listened, lids half-closed. "I see. No, it can happen when you get a considerable number of old, treasured possessions together. Some people can't let go for various reasons. What about your shop?" She rubbed her brow with a careless hand. "That's one relief for you. Yes, I imagine you must have reservations about moving items out of storage and into stock. The first thing will be to isolate any items in question. If I'm able to guide all stranded spirits to the light, it won't matter afterwards. I clocked you from a distance at *'Acton Auctions.'* William mentioned you had a shop in Rochester. Is the warehouse nearby?" She strode two paces up to her desk and pulled a pad and pen from a cluttered drawer. "Okay. If you can give me the address, we'll sort out a date and time." As she spoke, hairs on the back of Samantha's neck rose again, like they had when she first noticed Harold Jessop at the auction house. He was courteous and smooth as glass to talk to. Yet something felt 'off' about the old antique dealer. Samantha clicked a ballpoint pen nib open and scribbled down the details relayed in her ear. "No, I don't know it. But if The Esplanade follows the river, I should be able to find the warehouse turning okay. Now what about your schedule? Uh, huh. Yes, he was desperate for help and I managed to fit him in." She sat down on the chair. "To be honest, I've nothing on tomorrow night. I know that's sad for a single girl my age on a Friday, but there it is." A half-smile crossed her lips at the caller's reply. "Shame younger men don't share your viewpoint. Most don't know I exist. I'm watching the pennies, so nights out are a rarity these days." She leaned back and listened. "That's right, he told you the truth: I don't charge. I'll accept anything you offer out of gratitude, but there's no invoice. It's complicated. Let's call it a vocation and leave it at that." She shook her head at his response. *This guy sounds like he's cheaper than a fake Rolex.* The job in question could be challenging, even dangerous given his wild stories about what rampaging spirits were up to in the warehouse. *Thank goodness the tightwad's friend, William Acton, had a generous nature which more than compensated.* "Nine PM will be fine. No, I don't know why some of these manifestations intensify after dark. Do you have any staff at the warehouse? Okay, good." Another bout of speech crackled from the handset. "That's an odd question. Are you worried someone will miss me if things take longer than expected? How sweet. No, I live alone and I'm a big girl. It takes as long as it takes. Since I don't bill, there's no extra charge." Samantha clicked the pen nib closed. "Okay, I'll see you there tomorrow evening around Nine. Goodbye, Mr Jessop." She laughed. "Harold. Okay, goodbye Harold." The call ended. Samantha keyed the address into an Internet map search on her laptop. The application informed her it would be a forty-two-mile journey taking an hour and five minutes by car. *I'd best leave around a quarter to eight, to be sure. Seems easy enough to find, but traffic's an arse on Friday nights. Gives me a ten minute leeway. The old boy sounds easygoing enough, if a little weird. Don't suppose he'll be watching the clock if I run late.*

Jessop's wrinkled hand deposited the sturdy, Bakelite phone receiver back in its cradle at the antique shop. He reclined in the high-backed armchair and studied the piece of paper with name and number William Acton had given him. Samantha Riley's body would provide a wonderful vessel for Sharon's spirit. Her firm, shapely curves more delightful than the flirtatious, older postwoman. What a joy it would be to connect sexually with Sharon through the soul chalice of that winsome young blonde. Assuming shock from their union didn't finish Jessop's body for good. The situation couldn't be better. As far as he'd elicited - without arousing too much suspicion - if the girl vanished, nobody would miss her for some time. There'd be no dead body to find, if all went well. The form of Samantha Riley would continue to populate the world of the living. With Sharon's spirit at the helm, they'd cut any connections to the girl's past, as if it were Samantha's whim. *Tomorrow night we'll see if those crusty old books contain more than folklore and ancient superstition.* Andrew pondered any negatives. *What's the worst that could happen? The ritual mightn't work. Then if Samantha got away, Harold Jessop would be looking at a stretch inside once she called the police. His body isn't in the best shape. Doubtful he'd survive prison. If he croaked, I'm no worse off than before the day I followed this curious antique dealer home. I've got to try. It's my best and only shot.*

* * *

Samantha fixed herself paella from a mixture of reduced-to-clear chicken and seafood she'd retrieved from the supermarket budget bin. The hob extractor wasn't any more effective than her bathroom one. Thus she opened the windows on both sides of the roof, allowing steam to escape. It was a sweltering Friday evening. The kind of oppressive heat where you don't want to occupy the cramped top floor of a tall building. As chicken stock and tinned tomatoes thickened into swelling rice, she wished she'd opted for a salad instead. Sweat caused her damp T-shirt collar to cling.

There was scant time for a shower, but at least the paella required little attention. *No way can I show up in Rochester like this.* Samantha lit her phone screen to check the time: Five to seven. Her clothes peeled off in an instant, as if someone had doused her in itching powder. She showered and emerged from the bathroom minutes later, rubbing her water-darkened hair on a towel. The pan of food heaved and bubbled in a less liquid state than before. *Oh, at last, it's ready to plate up.* She squeezed a finishing spray of lemon juice across the pan and pushed its contents onto a cheap white plate with a wooden spoon. After tossing the pan in a bowl of water, Samantha pulled on some fresh clothes and poured herself a glass of lemon barley to go with the meal. She sat down at her desk to eat. The spoon made it halfway to her mouth.

There came a knock at the door.

Crap. Must be Lena. Hope everything is okay. She yanked open the portal and came face to face with the dark blue gaze of her older sister. "Rach? What the…?"

"Surprise. One of your neighbours let me in the communal entrance. Hope that's okay? Is she Romanian or something?"

"Polish. Err, what are you doing here?"

"Aren't you going to invite me in?"

Samantha stepped aside to allow her sister access.

The older sibling looked around that tiny, L-shaped living/sleeping/kitchenette abode. Its single interior door (to what was obviously a bathroom) stood wide open, moisture from a recent shower still fogging the mirror.

Mindful of the time, Samantha picked up her plate and shovelled some paella into her mouth. She hadn't swallowed it all before speaking again. Manners would have to take a backseat for now. "You should have called."

"Have you just got in from somewhere?"

"The exact opposite. I'm on my way out."

"Drinks? I would say dinner, but well..." Rachel frowned at her younger sister stuffing food into her face like it was on a conveyor.

The girl shook her head as she swallowed. "Not that sort of 'out.' I've got an appointment over in the Medway towns."

"Appointment?"

Samantha fixed her with an emotionless gaze. "You know."

"Oh, I see. One of those."

The last of the paella disappeared down Samantha's gullet. She released an involuntary belch and covered her mouth. "Excuse me. I'm on the clock and time is tight. What are you doing here? Are John and the kids with you?"

"No." Rachel wrinkled her nose at the scruffy, unmade sofa bed.

Samantha followed her stare. "Sorry. I wasn't expecting company. Most days I leave it open like a bed and sit on my desk chair. I've time to fix you a quick drink before I leave." She drained her lemon barley and crossed the kitchenette to top up her kettle.

Rachel remained silent.

Samantha wheeled on the spot, kettle in hand. Her

eyebrows raised at the disgust writ-large across her sister's face. "It's okay, you're safe. I gave the cockroaches the day off. The weather's so nice out, they all took their towels down to the beach for a picnic."

Rachel flushed. "Oh, Sam. How can you live like this? After the upbringing we had, too. And our house."

"The one I was thrown out of, you mean?"

The visitor's eyes lowered. Her vocal tone followed them. "Yes, that one."

Samantha clicked the kettle switch and pulled two mugs from an overhead cupboard. "Tea?"

Rachel nodded but said nothing.

"I'm guessing you didn't drive all the way from Wiltshire to cast aspersions at my domestic squalor, Sis. So, what's going on? Your lord and master must have shit a solid gold brick when you told him you were coming to visit. And why no phone call? I may not have much of a social life, but I could have arranged to be home."

"I wanted it to feel natural. Didn't want you over-thinking what we might discuss."

"Oh? And what's that?"

Rachel cleared her throat. "Why didn't you come to Dad's funeral?"

The kettle clicked in an instant, the majority of its contents still warm from making up a stock cube. Samantha poured boiling water on two tea bags, her back turned. "You need to ask?"

"Would it have been such a strain to put up with a church service for Mum's sake?"

"It's not only that and you know it. Sooner or later there would have been a blow up. Sooner, with John there. Mum didn't need all that."

"She needed you more."

Samantha gulped. "I know. She sent me a letter the other day. It was supposed to contain my baptismal cross, but she must have forgotten to put it back in the box."

Rachel fondled her own silver cross necklace. "Dad was clinging onto it when he died."

Samantha handed her sister a mug of tea. "Mum told me."

"Do you remember what you said when you last came to Middle Woodford, about Mum having doubts over her faith?"

"Yeah, we've spoken about it on the phone once or twice." She motioned for her sister to sit down at the desk.

"I didn't want to believe it. Thought it was more of your anger directed at the church over what happened."

"And now?"

"Before we left Bath, John caught Mum reading what he calls 'backslider books.' You know, those Post-Evangelical self-help deceptions."

"Deceptions?"

Rachel gulped a mouthful of tea. "What would you call them?"

Samantha reached into her handbag and pulled out the package from her mother. "I suspect you'd dismiss whatever I called them, out of hand. Why don't you read how much they've helped Mum?" She unfolded the letter for her sister to peruse.

Rachel studied each line in silence. A single tear rolled down her left cheek. "She's walking away from God."

"No, Rach. She's walking away from a man-made religious system. Nothing more. Can you not hear in her words, how hungry she is for genuine connection with God? Dad would have put his foot down and stopped it. That's why she's like a caged bird breaking free."

"But she'll-"

"Go to hell? If you honestly believe that, the conversation might as well be over. Fuck your God and the donkey He rode in on. That's not the nature of The Divine."

Rachel clenched her teeth. "How dare you? Listen to your own words, Samantha." She clasped her necklace again.

Samantha sighed and placed her empty mug on the kitchenette worktop. "You know what? In that letter, Mum said she needs my strength and moral courage. Bullshit. Mum has both those qualities in spades. I died, Rach. I died and got a serious glimpse at what comes next. I stood in the presence of The Almighty and was sent back with this bizarre gift. It's not like I had a choice in the matter. There was no way I could continue dancing to the same old tune. Eventually, what happened was going to come spilling out. The whole deal with Tony was a distraction from the real issue. Sooner or later my experiences and abilities would have set me on an irrevocable collision course with Dad."

"But-"

"Let me finish. I ended up this way, because what I experienced was so bloody real and powerful there was no other option. Mum is exploring new possibilities without the benefit of those life-changing encounters. She senses there is something more. That *God* is something more. Judith Riley isn't losing her faith, Rach. She's got more faith than me with my experiences and you with your rules, fear and control put together."

Rachel stood on shaky legs. "Whether or not she's losing her faith, she may soon lose her mobility."

Samantha's eyes flashed, concern streaking her forehead. "What?"

"She hasn't told you, has she? Typical Mum, not wanting to be a burden."

"Told me what?"

"They've diagnosed Mum with Multiple Sclerosis."

"When?"

"She had the tests right before we left after the funeral. John and I insisted, when she kept falling over. The results came back yesterday. I spoke with her on the phone this morning."

"What's the prognosis?"

"Too early to tell. She might stabilise. A wheelchair could be an option in time. Managing the house will become an onerous struggle for her alone. John can't get a transfer to Somerset. So she needs Jesus. Without her faith, how will Mum cope?"

Samantha picked up her car keys. "She needs help of some sort."

"From you? Great. The blind leading the blind astray. You'll forgive me if I don't celebrate you wanting to drag her down with you, but she's MY mother too, damn you." Rachel's voice rose in pitch and volume. She stomped her foot at the last sentence. "She needs Pastor Mike and the church."

Samantha opened the door. "Why don't we let Mum decide who she needs?"

Rachel pushed past her onto the communal attic landing. "Judith Riley is confused, grieving and ill. We don't want you anywhere near her with your nonsense about a humanistic God, Samantha."

"*Now* I know why John let you come to see me. Did he put you up to this?"

Streams of tears ran unchecked across Rachel Saunders' face. "Why can't things be the way they used to? We were so happy." She span with a sniff and descended the stairs in a fresh flood of tears.

Samantha locked her flat door, head pounding from the tense conversation. It wasn't the best state to face a spirit liberation, but time was up and she had to go.

Samantha's Ford Ka lurched away from the kerb. Three parked cars ahead, Rachel watched her younger sister drive past. She couldn't leave Samantha like this and return to Wiltshire with everything up in the air. Somehow this matter required resolution, once and for all. Rachel keyed the ignition and put her Volvo estate in 'Drive.' Several minutes later, both parties joined the M20 on a route to destiny at an old Rochester warehouse.

15

The Warehouse

ANDREW MILES, 2019.

Harold Jessop's creaking form struggled to drag several splinter-rich, wooden shipping crates across the warehouse central atrium. Andrew Miles found the antique dealer's body less responsive by the day. Like a penniless worker living a hand-to-mouth existence and relying on a dilapidated car, there was no present alternative within reach. If the ritual proved a success, his next course of business would be a follow-up session for transference of his spirit to a 'sportier' male model commensurate with Samantha's body. He stood for a moment gazing up at the dirty skylight far above. *How the heck did I go from Medway carpenter to fanatical necromancer? Is love the answer? Love for Sharon? What about the moral implications of possessing the living?* Andrew shook the thoughts aside. The jagged edge of one crate left several vicious shards of wood embedded in his left palm, as he brought it to rest. "Ow. Bloody thing." He pinched the splinters clear with a bony, arthritic finger and thumb. *The girl should be here in about forty minutes. As long as she doesn't get lost.* He picked up the leather-bound occult volume in one hand. In the other he held a large stick of purple chalk. With a piece of timber as a straight-edge guide and twine anchored to a central point in the floor, Andrew inscribed a pentagram contained within inner and outer circles. Between the circumferences he copied long-forgotten runes from the printed illustrations, with great attention to detail. Next, five pillar-candles found a spot at each of the five points of the star. He'd already given some consideration to the artifice with which he would render Samantha Riley vulnerable. That girl was sensitive. The way she stared through the body of Harold Jessop like a searchlight falling on Andrew's spirit, left him uncomfortable. It was of paramount importance she not suspect anything until it was too late to react. He deposited the five ritual items on different floors of the warehouse and along its broad walkway platforms. They needed to look natural rather than placed, if his plan had any chance of success. He considered the effort it had taken to move a few empty crates. How would Jessop's body cope with hauling Samantha down several flights of stairs? Even knocking the young woman out on the ground floor and dragging her into place, would prove a struggle. It didn't bode well. A glimmer of fading sunlight reflected off something metallic, suspended above the central atrium. A hook dangled from a chain and pulley system designed to take the effort out of moving cargo between floors. He leaned against a cast-iron railing and peered down to the purple pentagram and circle. *If I attach her to the hook, it's only a matter of winding the handle down below to deposit the girl where I want her.* A satisfied, sinister grin - like some demented Cheshire cat on drugs - creased the antique dealer's sagging cheeks. He shuffled back to the ground floor, wheezing and panting for breath. Three incense burners joined the candles at the head and arm sections of the pentagram. Andrew rested a large dust sheet across the bizarre occult ritual space, careful not to smudge any chalk. A few more items of junk deposited around its edges, and the area became unremarkable to behold in that dingy, cluttered environment. To test his chain and pulley theory, he secured a rope to the old rocking horse and wound it up to hang mid-air at the top level. *So far so good. Samantha can follow it down, if all goes well.*

A gentle whine of metal on metal and ratcheting handbrake noise crept between the timbers of the double door. *Right on time.* Andrew took a deep breath, licked his lips and eased the right-hand portal open.

"Good evening, Harold." Samantha remembered the man's insistence she address him on a first name basis from their phone call.

"Good evening, Samantha. How was the traffic on Blue Bell Hill?"

"Not too bad." The young woman secured her car and sauntered across. Her padded but shapely backside moved in voluptuous, oily movements.

Andrew discovered Jessop's body still responded as hoped in some respects. He fought down a stirring of the loins. Now was no time to get distracted. "Have you had an encounter with the ghost there? She's famous in these parts."

Samantha shook her head. "No. I've not spent much time in the Medway towns since I came to Kent."

"Well, if you were to walk towards the castle and cathedral during daylight hours, I'm sure you'd find the precincts and Rochester High Street charming."

"I'll keep that in kind if I'm looking for somewhere local to visit. Thanks." She peered inside the tall, dim warehouse. "Any manifestations of activity today?"

"Not yet. I've been giving much thought to your comments on the phone. The ones about this situation not being unusual. You know: when there are a lot of treasured objects together in close proximity."

"And?"

"In the cold light of day - away from the scares - I realised that the odd happenings have taken place on different levels of the building. Could the haunting (or whatever you class this as) be localised to items in those areas?"

"It's possible." Samantha stepped inside. The illumination proved so sparse, Jessop's face became nothing more than a rippling shadow. Once again her neck hairs lifted like gold leaf to a carbon rod. Static flowed in waves along the fine hairs of her body.

Jessop closed the door with a bang that made the alert woman jump.

Outside, a short distance away, another car crawled to a halt.

Samantha took a few uncertain steps closer to the atrium. "Where has the worst activity occurred?"

"On the top level. That might be a good place to

start, no? Deal with the most troublesome area first."

The young woman craned her neck back to gaze at the skylight. "How do we get up there?"

Jessop pointed to the first of many rough wooden staircases. "This way. Watch your footing as we go. Most timbers feel firm enough, but the surfaces are uneven. I still trip on them myself, from time to time."

"Okay. Lead on." As she followed the shambling figure, Samantha glanced back over her shoulder. Against the far wall of the ground floor, the spiritual figure of a First World War soldier stood with his head bowed in silence. "Harold, have you had any trouble down below?"

"Not that I can recall. Are you sensing something?"

"Yes. As you say: we'll address the troublesome area first."

On the first level, there floated the apparition of an elderly woman. She hovered bent over at an almost right-angle, eyeing a shaped, wooden mantelpiece clock.

"What about the first floor, here?" Samantha studied the placid, dreamy old lady.

Jessop covered a grin with one hand, pretending to wipe his mouth. The impostor saw everything. "Only one time. After I adjusted the hands on an old clock I've been thinking of having refurbished for sale. That's one experience that got me pondering your assessment. The clock appears to have been the focus."

"You're right. I can see you've given this some thought."

"Mother always said I was spiritually sensitive as a

child," Andrew lied, coughing so hard Jessop's lungs burned.

Samantha gripped the handrail. "Do you want to stop and catch your breath? There's no immediate hurry."

Jessop batted her concerns aside by storming forwards up the next flight of stairs. Here again, the young woman picked up on a female presence, although the pair marched at such a pace she didn't have time to scan around. On the top floor, Samantha pushed herself away from the edge, spine flattened against the grimy brickwork. It was a long way down.

Jessop leaned over the railing, immune to any fear of heights or falling. "A touch of vertigo, Samantha?"

"I got dizzy. It happens when there's a lot of spiritual activity in an area. Didn't want to topple over the edge." Her eyes lifted to rest on a beautiful wooden rocking horse, swinging in a gentle motion from ropes attached to a metal hook. Astride the toy animal sat a girl of about ten, wearing a nightgown. She clutched at the creature's neck; soft, ghostly fingers stroking a mane of real hair in a manner powerful enough to cause a physical reaction. The hairs rippled up and down.

Jessop followed her stare with feigned ignorance and surprise. "What do you see?"

Samantha took a step closer to the atrium shaft. "A young girl." Vibrating energy rippled through her body. She walked around the platform to bring the child's face in line with her own, across the space and sickening drop. "Hey there."

The child patted her horse and lifted her nose. "Hello."

"What's *your* name?"

A soft, mournful voice lilted back with a slight echo. "Rosalind."

"Hello, Rosalind. I'm Samantha. I wonder if you can help me? I've forgotten the date. Can't even remember the year. Aren't I silly?"

Rosalind tilted her head. "I'm not sure either. It *was* 1815. But now I don't know."

Samantha swallowed hard. "Have you been playing with your horse ever since?"

The girl nodded. "Her name's Geraldine. Papa bought her for me when I broke my ankle and couldn't go outside." She buried her head back into the mane.

Samantha squatted to peer at the youngster through the railings and maintain eye contact. "Can you remember what happened next?"

"I was ill. A bad chest. That's what the doctor said."

Samantha noticed a few drops of blood near the neck of the girl's nightdress. She stood and called across to Jessop. "Harold, can we swing the horse over to the platform, please?"

The old antique dealer tried not to rub his hands with delight. Things were progressing. "Indeed. Wait right there. I'll winch it across to the other side." He stumbled over to a rusty handle mounted into an upright girder. With a grinding and tinkle of chains, the suspended beam swung wide to deposit the rocking horse on a nearby platform.

Samantha hurried round to the girl who still clung to

her toy. Power surged within the woman in a spike of energy. Further along the upper level, a growing orb of astral light twinkled like a blinding disco ball.

Andrew watched through Jessop's eyes. A sudden dread filled his stomach. *If she frees that child - or any of the other shackled spirits - this whole deal is over. I need five or I'm sunk.* He rummaged behind a pillar where he had earlier deposited a tool for the moment of truth. Gnarled fingers gripped a rough wooden cudgel. His shoulders pressed against the outer wall. Andrew shimmied round on reinvigorated, nimble legs.

Samantha knelt in front of the rocking horse, her back to the creeping form of the departed warehouse owner. "Rosalind. I'm here to help you. There's no need to be afraid, okay?"

Rosalind Layton pointed a short index finger across the young woman's shoulder. "I'm afraid of him."

Samantha didn't look back. "That's Harold. He won't hurt you, darling. We're going to reunite you with your family. Won't that be nice?"

The spiritual glimmer behind intensified. Above the skylight, a blast of lightning and immediate thunderclap shook the glass. What remained of sunset got swallowed up by dark clouds. They puffed and grew, forming like cancer cells filmed in time-lapse.

Rosalind's mouth turned down. She gripped Geraldine's reins. "I don't think that's Harold."

Samantha reached a tentative hand towards the child. "What makes you say that?"

The already shadow-filled warehouse became smothered in a suffocating darkness. Another flash of lightning shone through the skylight, illuminating the silhouette of one purposeful arm raising something sturdy aloft.

"Samantha, look out," Rosalind screamed.

The young woman half-twisted her head as Andrew's cudgel fell upon the back of it. Her unconscious body sprawled on the dusty, rough wooden platform.

As Samantha's eyes closed, the astral light faded back to nothing.

Rosalind cried and held tight to her horse.

Outside, Rachel Saunders crept around the warehouse perimeter. What few windows existed, were set way above ground level. Even had that not been the case, their coating of grime would deny the most ardent of busybodies a jolly good nose inside. With the first deafening eruption in the sky, the thirty-year-old woman pressed herself tight to the grubby wall. *Looks like it's about to tip down. I've got to get in there and see what Sam's up to.* Clouds descended, their shapes moving against the wind. A dreaded flashback to that terrifying night during Samantha's last visit to Middle Woodford, brought Rachel up sharp. *Oh no, not that again. What's she got herself into now? That thing almost killed her last time.* With legs empty and feeling like jelly, Rachel reached the west side of the building. Behind a large dumpster sitting at a jaunty angle, lightning flashes traced a low, vent window. She scrabbled forward on her knees; a woman on a mission. *If I can open this, it should be big enough to crawl through.* Her fingers yanked at the rusty frame. The vent window hung open on the first notch of a catch. It wouldn't budge. Rachel clambered up and folded over the dumpster lid. Another flash revealed a discarded, bent wheel brace. Seconds later, one end of the lopsided tool squeezed into the gap between window frame and wall. One foot pressing against the brickwork, Rachel levered with knuckles whiter than the overhead light show. A crunch of disintegrating metal and splintering glass disappeared beneath another boom from above. The window shattered and crumbled away. Flat on her belly, the woman pulled herself through that claustrophobic opening. Behind, those swirling clouds followed, engulfing the tiny space with an ice-cold presence like fingers of death. Rachel fought to get a handle on rising fear and tugged herself forward, her filthy outfit now redolent of a Victorian chimney sweep. The passage opened into the ground floor of the warehouse proper. Rachel clambered up to rest against a brick pillar near one corner, beneath a flight of wooden stairs. The levellers creaked in a sinister crescendo. Someone or something was coming down. Rachel froze, pressing her cheek into the cold brickwork. In the dim light of a few bulbs and the occasional flash from a skylight far above, she could make out a lumbering man around retirement age. He shoved assorted boxes aside from the middle of the floor. Two hands tugged at a grubby dust sheet, withdrawing it with curious care. Rachel gulped and reached for the next closest pillar near the stairs. Again she clung to it like a limpet, poking her head round every few seconds for a better look. The man stomped across to a table and returned with a box of extra-long matches. He squatted to light the wicks on a series of purple, pillar candles strewn across the space. Next, the match went into three pots of some description. Heady clouds of incense drifted upward several feet, then hung about shoulder height blending into an overpowering aroma. Rachel's nose twitched. She tried not to sneeze. *Phew, thank goodness. Oh no.* The twitch came back. She couldn't be precise about how far ahead of the next thunderclap her sneeze blasted, but the busy figure halted in his tracks. Rachel hugged the pillar again, holding her breath. The beating of her own heart appeared loud enough to betray her presence to the deafest of beings. All about her, streams of black cloud whirled along the interior walls of the warehouse. Spectators with no obvious intention to interfere. *Is this guy some servant of the demon? Where's Sam?* Concern stole away the big sister's fear for several tense moments. The figure resumed his activities, apparently satisfied nothing was amiss. Stomping footsteps pounded back to the staircase. With a series of unsafe-sounding creaks, the man ascended back to wherever he had come from.

Rachel waited until he started on the second floor staircase and his footfalls faded. Eyes never leaving the eerie, freezing clouds that continued to billow and slither, she edged closer to the candles. *Jesus, help me. It's black magic or witchcraft. John was right.* She studied the chalk inscribed circle and arcane runes. One hand reached into her back pocket to withdraw a smart phone. With the device raised between shaking hands, Rachel waited for the next pulsing flash of light from above. The phone's camera application snapped off an image, its shutter sound effect getting buried in the following report from the Rochester skies.

A clanging of metal and short grinding from close to the skylight, stopped as soon as it started. Something swung in a gentle rhythm far above.

The stairs creaked. Rachel nipped back to the shadow and relative concealment of that previous column. Eventually, the puffing figure made the ground floor again. He appeared more tired and out of breath with each step, gait evidencing a dragging noise like that of someone with a club foot. Near the table from which he had retrieved his matches, the man wound a large metal handle attached to a circular plate. Chains tinkled near the roof and the swinging object came closer.

After three minutes of vigorous winding, a child's rocking horse dangled above the surface of the floor. The warehouse owner detached it and positioned the toy next to one of the pillar candles. He rummaged around in a tabletop box, then hobbled over to place a delicate piece of fabric next to another, and something shiny near a third. When it became clear his intention was to make the laborious ascent once more, Rachel reached for her phone again. In a repetition of her previous, inquisitive attempt, she got as close as she dared. If the man peered down from one of the platforms at the wrong moment, he'd discover her.

Several clicks on the phone's zoom buttons, identified what appeared to be a handkerchief as the first new addition. At this range and in such low light, she couldn't make out any details. The second new object almost caused her to drop the phone. Still clutching hold of the device with one hand, she reached the other up to clasp an identical item hanging from her own neck: a small, silver cross. *It must be a coincidence. How many crosses are there in the world? Sam said Mum forgot to post it.* All the same, she took a snap with the camera. High above, something else swung out on a mechanical arm beneath the skylight. Rachel ducked and peeped up. *What's he bringing down now? Is that a person? Why haven't I seen Sam anywhere? She came in here.* The clumping footsteps echoed their creaking chorus on the wooden stairs. Halfway down, the figure broke into a bout of rattling coughs. When he came back into view, Rachel noticed an old mantelpiece clock beneath one of his arms. Something shiny hung from the fingers of the opposite hand. The figure added these alongside the two remaining candles. Back at the winding handle, he brought down the new, dangling object.

"Sam," the word escaped Rachel's lips before she had time to register her mistake. *She's trussed up like an animal and unconscious. What's going on?*

The lumbering warehouse owner unhooked Samantha from his pulley system, laying her on one side in the centre of that chalk pentagram.

Rachel thought fast. *This has gone far enough. I'm calling the police.* She hesitated. *But that will announce my presence. Whoever that vile man is, he appears to be alone. Please God, give me strength to hold him off until help arrives.* Nostril's flaring as she wrestled with erratic, fast-paced breathing, Rachel lifted her phone again and lit up the screen. An animated *'Low Battery'* symbol appeared, followed by a rotating circle. The phone powered off. *No! Lord, help me.* She tried not to hyperventilate. Adrenaline caused her spittle to clot like jelly in a throat with pulsing jugular.

From across the warehouse, the man's shadowy form lifted a book in one hand. He walked around the outside of the circle, reciting words in something that reminded Rachel of speaking in tongues. His other hand pointed a shiny object from side to side. It appeared to be a glinting letter opener in the shape of a medieval dagger.

All about the warehouse, those swirling clouds maintained a subtle distance. Their movement rose in intensity with each syllable spoken.

The icy touch of their growing excitement drew nearer to Rachel's hiding place. *Is he going to sacrifice her? No. No, I won't allow it. Whatever she's done, Sam's my sister and I love her. I've got to stop this, no matter the cost.* Rachel ran stumbling into a narrow cone of pale light from the atrium roof several stories skyward. Not a strong woman, she prayed forward momentum and her own body weight would be enough to topple the hobbling horror. Her shoulder connected with the small of Jessop's back. The pair tumbled into a pile of empty shipping crates. Dry rot caused their planks to splinter and snap about the collapsing bodies.

The warehouse owner twisted and winced. He clutched his back. From the shadows beyond, streams of cloud gushed forward. Like the blast of a fire hose they poured into the spasming form of Harold Jessop.

Rachel looked on as the old warehouse owner's body shook. His limbs stiffened; strengthened by some supernatural force. *The demon. It must be possessing him. Sam. What about Sam?* She forced herself up into a doubled-over run towards the pentagram. Samantha lay still. "Come on, Sam. Help me." Rachel tried to hook her hands beneath the motionless girl's armpits.

Across the room, Harold Jessop flew to his feet as if pulled up on strings like a puppet. It was an impossible ascent. Eyelids opened to reveal inky black clouds swirling over plain white orbs. That crinkled face twisted into a sneer.

"Sam. Wake up, Sam. We've got to get out of here." Rachel's voice trembled. The words tumbled out and fell over each other to spur her sister into action.

Jessop took a patient, casual step closer. He picked up the leather-bound book and knife.

Rachel supposed what came out of that manipulated mouth were words. The sound slurred and hissed in a deep, guttural timbre laced with eons of frustration and hatred. It appeared to be reading from the text. All about her, the chalk markings turned from purple powder to bright, neon light. The floor rumbled and shook. Inside the circle, air fizzed and rotated like a tornado of electricity. Something was rising from the symbols: a presence. It reached deep inside the siblings. Rachel took one long breath, hoisted

Samantha from the floor and pushed her clear of the ritual space. That final effort dropped her exhausted frame to the stone surface. She lay still, gasping for air. The probing, spiritual newcomer forced its way like a housebreaker, deep into the innermost part of her being.

Samantha stirred. Her head pounded at a tempo akin to a bass drum at a speed metal concert. Blurred vision in limited light adjusted to a sharper focus. She rested on the warehouse floor, hands and feet secured with rope. Beyond, lay a glowing occult symbol adorned with flickering purple candles. Alongside each stood an item and the spirit of a departed person. Moving from point to point on the star she saw: The rocking horse with young Rosalind; A handkerchief and that soldier she'd noticed on the ground floor; the mantelpiece clock and vigilant elderly woman; a charm bracelet and attractive blonde in her early thirties; and a silver cross necklace with... *Oh, my God. No. It cannot be.* "Dad?" The question sounded aloud in a sudden, retching sob. How did her baptismal cross and father end up in this place? Samantha thought back to the day she'd left her handbag in William Acton's office. How long had Harold Jessop been alone with it? *Jessop.* She remembered Rosalind's final words before she blacked out. The antique dealer stood off to one side of the circle, clutching an old book and knife. His white eyes - swirling with a disheartening and familiar black mass - fixed on the bound young woman. *The Entity. It's taken control of Jessop; whoever or whatever he was.* Those eyes turned to a fallen figure slumped in the middle of the glowing pentagram. It sat up with a snap to sweep straight, pale blonde, side-parted hair aside. *Rach? What the?*

Instead of the dark-blue gaze she'd known since birth, those eyes flicked open to sparkle with a malevolence beyond Samantha's imagining. A hideous cackle gurgled from Rachel's pretty mouth, setting her younger sister's teeth on edge.

The Entity knelt in Jessop's form before her, head bowed in reverence.

The creature at the centre of the glowing symbols floated to a standing position and threw back its head. Arms outstretched with index and little fingers pointing, she spoke with a blending of Rachel's voice and that of some otherworldly female, filled with venom and malice. "I have become flesh. Bow before me and tremble. The goddess of the sky form has come. I who work my will, shall steal earthbound souls to the underworld. No more will the restless dead find a path to the light." She lowered her head to fix Samantha with a stare of fathomless rage. One finger stabbed the air in the trussed-up girl's direction. She barked an order to the kneeling minion beyond the circle. "Kill her."

16

Mandate Discharged

SAMANTHA RILEY, 2019.

The ropes burned into Samantha's wrists and ankles. Even inching away like a worm didn't seem possible. She might roll, but not fast enough to escape The Entity bearing down on her in Jessop's creaking, unfit body. And where would she roll to?

All about the glowing ritual circle, The Shackled stood in a trance beside their respective treasures. Vague wisps of energy flowed from their flickering forms to feed the evil, female spirit gazing across the floor at Samantha with victorious glee.

The Entity lifted the blade high and tossed its book aside. Even with the use of a physical mouth, its voice boomed like the storm above. "Time to die, Pathfinder." It had taken on human form. For whatever reason, Samantha came to the realisation this being couldn't harm her during those earlier spirit liberations. Something held it back from completing that task. Yet its naked desire was never concealed. Now in mortal clothing, all bets were off. Restrained as she was, the vibrating energy still pulsed in her cramping limbs. In her immobile state, that energy was the only thing she could move and direct. Another few seconds and it would all be over, if she didn't try.

The bracelet-enthralled, thirty-something blonde shackled spirit was first to react as her energy stream cut-off feeding Rachel's possessor. Samantha concentrated on the others. The Entity was halfway across the atrium floor now. Nadine Evans left her mother's treasure, lunged forward and grabbed hold of Jessop's left leg. Her will manifested with enough force to slow the creature's advance. Sally Nelson - the old woman with the clock - took hold of the other, bringing Jessop to a staggering halt like someone wading through a quagmire. Matthew Riley left the cross necklace. His passionate spirit - still longing to save his youngest daughter - gripped Jessop's arms from behind. The blade clattered to the stone floor.

Rachel's face creased into an impossible scowl of torment and fury. "No." The force of her outburst blew out the candles at her feet.

Peter Haws lifted the peaked cap of his infantryman's uniform. As Rachel took a bold stride to clear the pentagram, the soldier locked her in an iron, restraining grip. Arcs of blue electricity danced between the figures. Rachel threw back her head with a roar. Peter cried in agony, his spiritual outline writhing for relief that wouldn't come. But he didn't let go.

At the head of the star, Rosalind Layton clutched

onto her rocking horse, terrified eyes flitting between the players in this tense stand-off. Across the atrium lay the bound young woman who had sought to set her free. Between Samantha and the thing controlling Harold Jessop's body, rested the solitary blade. Its double cutting edges ran with intermittent bursts of reflected light: those dancing above the skylight from storm-filled skies, and others flashing in blue pulses that encircled the soldier and female beast. Rosalind slipped her feet out of Geraldine's stirrups. One last hand held the reins until she had to release them or go no further. Wide, forlorn eyes brimmed with ghostly tears. The ten-year-old opened her timid mouth in a song of comfort and courage from her mortal life. That old melody of days gone by, grew in strength and purpose as she reached the fallen knife.

"*Courage, boys, 'tis one to ten,*
But we return all gentlemen,
While conquering colours we display,
Over the hills and far away."

She bent down with all her will, causing the knife to rise in the air as if clutched in a solid hand of flesh. The girl's emboldening voice gave defiant rebuke to Rachel's howls. She approached Samantha and knelt to cut her wrists free. The song flowed from her childish mouth as if accompanied by the ghosts of ten-thousand of the old monarch's loyal soldiers.

"*Over the Hills and O'er the Main,*

To Flanders, Portugal and Spain,
King George commands and we'll obey,
Over the hills and far away."

The ropes frayed and snapped. Samantha took hold of the blade to release her ankles.

Jessop's body staggered, wrestling against the three shackled assailants who sought to deny The Entity its murderous intent. Those white eyes, swirling with clouds, bulged outward - about to pop. The old antique dealer's swaying form crashed into the floor, shattering his jaw with a sickening crack. He twitched twice, then lay still.

Rachel screamed, the blue electricity stabbing at Peter Haws with renewed vigour. Her tone hissed a rebuke. "Release me, lesser creature of cowardice."

Peter's face darkened. "I'm no coward." He gripped tighter, causing the pain to treble. It was a pain that threatened to erase the very existence of his spirit energy. The essence of who he was.

From close to the skylight far above, a river of twinkling silver forms materialised.

Samantha watched the indistinct, black cloudy figure of The Entity pull away from Jessop's lifeless body. Another spectral figure dashed from the corpse, out of the atrium, to skulk in one shadowy corner of the building. Those silver forms encircled her malevolent pursuer now. The Entity writhed and struggled. Rachel howled. The dark, persistent menace of Samantha's prophetic nightmares rose like a netted fish. An explosion of light coated the warehouse interior with a surging roar of hot air. Assorted items in storage crashed to the ground and rolled about. The twinkling lights vanished, and with them their prisoner.

Peter Haws fought to grip tight, but his strength lessened as he vented more screams of pain. Seeing Jessop fall and The Entity imprisoned, brought an answer to his burning spirit. A helpless gaze looked past his quarry to the mortal girl on the floor, clutching the ritual blade. Every word he forced out cost him a hundred-fold in pain. "I can't hold on much longer. You've got to kill her vessel. It's the only way."

The truth of the soldier's statement stung Samantha's soul with the impact of a molten barb. Killing Harold Jessop while The Entity controlled him, somehow sacrificed its liberty to imprison, torment and have free rein in the half-light. Would the same be true of this female devil, whatever she was? Samantha looked at Jessop's body. Alongside it, Sally Nelson, Nadine Evans and Matthew Riley rested in a state of spent spiritual energy. There was nothing they could do to help. She staggered to her feet, fingers gripping the blade hilt. *How can I do this? How can I kill my sister?* One shaky foot went before the other in a heartless series of pigeon steps.

Rachel's possessed head lowered. Eyes of blazing hatred flickered with the faint realisation of a fault in its plan. The blue electricity ceased. Peter Haws collapsed in a heap. Rachel's familiar, pretty face lifted to lock onto her approaching younger sister. "Samantha? Thank goodness you're safe."

Samantha halted near the edge of the circle. "Rach?"

Her rigid, raised arm softened and relaxed its grip on the weapon.

Rachel's face convulsed and morphed into a facsimile so close to her own, Samantha felt as if she'd encountered her reflection in a mirror. The voice altered to mimic the younger Riley daughter. "Oh Rach. I love you so much. God is love, you know." The voice became guttural and mocking. "And that will be Its undoing."

Samantha's eyes reddened. "Let my sister go." She spat and lifted the blade to strike.

Rachel's body flew straight up in the air, the pause from its struggle with the spirit soldier enough to regain equilibrium and energy. Samantha snapped her head back as her sister's feet shot up to the skylight platform.

Peter Haws shifted onto one elbow. His voice whispered a hoarse lament. "None of us are safe while that creature walks the earth in clothes of flesh."

Samantha swallowed and took a deep breath. *No other choice. God forgive me, it must be done.* She ran for the creaking flight of stairs, feet thudding like a stampede as she ascended level upon level to the top. Clouds of dust puffed beneath each staircase at the power of her determined footfalls.

Glass panes in the dirty skylight cracked and tumbled inward. Samantha rounded the last half-landing in time to catch her sister's legs disappear through the rain-soaked opening. A torrent of water cascaded into the atrium. It formed into rippling puddles on the ground floor far below. They washed the fading occult inscriptions away, like some street artist's unwanted chalk pavement composition. Samantha slotted the knife into the belt of her jeans. She clambered out onto the pulley beam, clinging tight and trying hard not to look down. It took all her courage and resolve to force herself to stand on that narrow surface, so far above safety. There were enough broken skylight frames to get a grip and form a makeshift ladder onto the slippery clay roof tiles above.

Two forceful, feminine hands hoisted her up beneath both arms and threw Samantha across the saturated roof. Rain hammered down in unrelenting sheets. Another eerie cackle from her big sister's mouth, melded with a fresh clap of thunder.

Samantha slid down the western side of the roof, facing out onto the river. Her hands fought for a grip that wouldn't come. Fingernails dislodged crumbling loose tiles. They accompanied the frantic woman on her slide across the vertiginous edge. Metal guttering was the last hope of physical salvation. Samantha clung to the flooding half-pipe, its gushing and overflowing contents chilling her tired fingers. The woman's feet swung and scrambled in the air, searching for any extra purchase to support the weight pulling on her weakening limbs. Samantha winced. A clamping force pressed against her left hand, squashing the fingers and loosening her hold. She threw her head back to meet a gleeful light in her sister's eyes as the cackling woman twisted her foot from side to side. That shoe swivelled in the manner of a smoker putting out their cigarette, as Rachel's possessor sought to extinguish her younger sister's life. The weight on her hand held Samantha in a press of agony. But the point was it HELD her. *I must be quick. It's my last throw of the dice.* She released her right grip. The dangling victim swiped up the knife and jammed it through her sister's motionless, other foot. Its sinking blade tore the arch and sole with enough force to pin her in place. The pressing foot snapped away. Samantha clambered against the anchored leg to pull herself up. Rachel screamed without restraint, like a wailing banshee. Samantha fell on top of her, their faces mere inches apart. In the glare of sheet lightning, Rachel's pupils swam with particles like whirling star systems from some deep space galactic panorama. Whatever dwelt within her was old and powerful. The knife came out of Rachel's foot, held aloft by Samantha's quivering digits. Her sister's face returned to normal again, the voice a whimper.

"Please, Sam. Please don't kill me."

"No," Samantha cried.

That lapse of resolve was all the creature needed. A swift knee brought up with a jerk, forced Samantha over onto her back. The blade fell from her grasp, clattered down the rain-washed roof and spun through the air to disappear in an alleyway far below. Rachel jumped from the roof, Samantha's outstretched hand instinctively reaching to save her. Midway through that descent, the figure slowed to a gentle rate and glided to the ground unharmed. New energy seared through her injured body, causing the older woman to limp towards The Esplanade water's edge. Ghost lights flickered and swarmed down near the jetty. Samantha watched. *Earthbound spirits. She's going for more earthbound spirits.* The young woman twisted up to locate the roof apex. She had to get down there in one piece and stop it. Hand over hand, she forced her body up the tiles. Time and again, a foot or two of progress resulted in half that disappearing in another downward slide. *It's too steep near the top. There's nothing to hold on to.* That hopeless thought faded from her mind in a flash. A glowing arm reached down from above, pale fingers splayed.

"Dad." She stretched up. "It's no good. I can't make it."

Matthew Riley shouted above the storm, where he had appeared in the broken skylight. "You can, girl."

"I can't."

"Try. Never stop trying. God is with you. I don't understand it, but I know it's the truth." He fixed her with an adoring stare, like the day she came home from hospital as a newborn baby. "I love you, Samantha. I should have said it so many times and didn't. I'm so sorry for everything. Now reach."

She took hold.

With reserves of spiritual energy in physical manifestation running low, Matthew Riley drew his youngest daughter forward enough for her to grip the broken skylight frame. Samantha swung through the gap and dropped onto the top floor platform. Not pausing to recover, she ran headlong for the stairs, taking two at a time.

The front double door bolt slammed free on the ground floor and Samantha Riley emerged. She bounced from alley wall to alley wall, using each surface as a launchpad to bolster her flagging strength and maintain momentum. Down at the water's edge, an ear-splitting scream in the half-light realm cut Samantha to the quick. It had taken another one wherever those unfortunate victims went. Sister or no, this couldn't be allowed to go unchecked. Vibrational energy reinvigorated Samantha's body; the presence of earthbound spirits engaging the empowerment of her gift. Another scream cut through the lashing rain. Freezing droplets of water filled Samantha's eyes. Her sodden hair flicked from side to side as she ran. Ahead by the jetty, Rachel pointed a withering finger at another aimless spirit. Light flashed from Samantha's arms. She'd experienced nothing like it before. Crowds of The Shackled swarmed about her, the woman's new aura shielding them from the malevolent beast's diabolical machinations.

The Rachel creature sneered and twisted. A leering tone accompanied its scan of the cowering flock, lost in limbo. "How long do you think you can keep that up, Pathfinder?"

It was hopeless and Samantha knew it. Soon her energy would vanish. Then nothing could stop the monster having its way. More lightning flickered across the rippling current of the broad River Medway. Samantha released her draining emission of light. The spirits about her wailed in fear.

Rachel grinned and lifted both hands. "Now they're

mine."

There's a moment of clarity to be found, somewhere beyond the end of hope. Ask anyone who has crossed that final line and survived to tell the tale. They'll inform you of two things. First: The answer was simple and staring them in the face. Second: They would never have come up with it in a million years of pondering, had they not taken that last step.

Now Samantha found her moment of clarity. Pumping calf muscles drove her charge of total commitment onward. She slammed into Rachel, taking them both off The Esplanade wall into the murky, churning waters beneath. Rachel spluttered. Her head bobbed to the surface. Samantha kicked to stay afloat, hands pressing down on Rachel's shoulders to push her under. The sisters struggled and fought, their bodies bashing into the stone wall and wooden jetty poles with violent, bruising impacts. Down they plunged. Up they rose. With each crest, Samantha - always the stronger swimmer - took stolen breaths while denying her sister the same. Muscle memory worked in the younger girl's favour. Rachel's flailing limbs stilled. Samantha held her down a moment longer. That thing wouldn't get another chance to take advantage of her sisterly love. The current brought them close to weed-encased stone steps. Samantha reached for the slippery surface with one hand, her other pulling Rachel clear of the Medway's insistent, watery grasp.

"Rach," she half-gasped, half-sobbed. Her big sister's pale, lifeless body flopped onto cold stonework above the steps. Samantha rolled her over to push water from the woman's lungs.

Meanwhile, the river of twinkling lights reappeared in a sudden flare along The Esplanade. Something shadowy yet strong fled from Rachel's lifeless corpse. Its frustrated, wailing form was pursued along the bank by those same things which had stolen The Entity away.

"Come on, Sis. Don't leave me." Samantha pushed her mouth onto Rachel's, administering the kiss of life. She performed chest compressions, thumping and crying with equal force. "Jane and Adam need you, Rach. Don't do this to them. Don't do it to Mum." Her eyes lifted to the sky. "Please. Haven't I suffered enough to perform Your will? Please, God. Please don't take my sister now."

Rachel coughed. Filthy water trickled from one corner of her mouth like chocolate vomit. Weak eyelids flickered open to focus on the tear-stained cheeks of her younger sister. "Sam?"

Samantha lifted the woman's weak head and clasped it to her chest. Beyond, a gathering of glowing white shapes walked in a slow and respectful march along The Esplanade towards them. Rain eased to a faint drizzle and clouds parted in the night sky. One last rumble of thunder drifted westward above the hill across the water in Strood and went silent. Ghostly shapes formed a semi-circle around the embracing siblings. "Rach. There's something I have to do. We've got comp-"

"I see them." Rachel pulled her head away from Samantha's chest. She twisted from side to side, jaw stretched down in awe at the silent throng.

"What? Since when?"

"Since I woke up here." Rachel tugged her ear and frowned at her sopping wet clothes. A dazed look considered her sudden, unexpected outdoor relocation by the river.

"What about in the warehouse?"

Rachel touched her brow. "I only remember the weird old man. He wasn't a ghost, was he?"

Samantha tilted her head from shoulder to shoulder. "Not the bit you saw, I'll wager. It must be some residual ability from the possessing force, or-"

"The what?" Rachel lifted her left leg and let out a whimper. "My foot. I think it's bleeding."

Samantha bit her lip. "We'd better get back up to the warehouse."

"What about the old man?" Rachel grimaced through tears of pain.

"He keeled over. But there's something in there you need to see."

"I'm weak, Sam."

"Me too. I don't think I've much more than the energy to stand."

"What about these?" Rachel looked from side to side again. Then her eyes widened, and she blinked. "Oh my. I died. Sam, I remember."

Samantha gave her a squeeze. "Just for a moment, but yeah."

"How long?"

"Long enough. That's all that matters. What did you see?"

Rachel's pupils bounced around like ping pong balls in a rapid volley. "I... I can't begin to des-"

"Describe it? I know. Human language falls utterly short. There's no comparison with things on earth, because it's like nothing *on* earth." Samantha's limbs buzzed with spectral power, but something felt different this time. She closed her eyes and focused on the assembled crowd. A curtain of light parted along the jetty, as if a spiritual pleasure cruiser had tied up to take on passengers. One by one, The Shackled waterfront spirits formed an orderly line; stepping off the wooden platform on a journey to distant shores and endless, sunny horizons. When the last one had crossed over, the curtain drew back into darkness. A tiny flicker - like the last hurrah of a fading candle - glimmered in Samantha's core. "Come on, Rach. There's still enough left for one more liberation. Then I'm done." She stared skyward again. "At last I will have discharged my mandate."

The sisters leaned on each other for support, limping and hobbling back to the open warehouse door. Inside, Rachel saw Rosalind, Peter, Sally and Nadine for the first time. They lingered near their respective treasures, where once a chalk inscription marked the floor, now awash with pooling rain from the fading storm.

A man's voice she'd cherished since birth, rang out

across the atrium. "I knew your sister would save you. I knew she'd save us all."

Rachel let go of Samantha, staggering on with outstretched arms like an upset toddler. "Daddy? How can you be here?" She couldn't hold back a torrent of tears.

The shimmering figure of Matthew Riley took hold of his eldest daughter in firm but translucent arms. "Thank God you're safe, Rachel." He shifted his stare to what he had once considered his wayward daughter. "Thank God for your sister's obedience. How could I have been so wrong?"

Samantha wandered nearer to place arms around them both: mortal and spirit. "It doesn't matter, Dad. But you mustn't stay. The Divine intends no one to remain in the world between. That much I'm sure of. My gift is over. Finished. Those tormenting creatures are elsewhere, for now. There's enough latent power left inside, for me to crank the door open one last time. You must all be ready." She expanded her attention during this final line to the other four spirits, then turned to stare at one shadowy corner of the warehouse. "That means you too."

Andrew Miles' spirit stepped from the shadows, eyes downcast. The plump man wrung his hands. "I'm so sorry. I only wanted my Sharon back. What have I done?"

Samantha walked across and offered her upturned palms towards him. "Take hold."

Andrew recoiled. "I can't. I killed myself. In my grief and blindness, I raised that THING to wreak havoc on unfortunate souls."

"Artemis," Matthew's spirit responded.

Rachel stepped back from her father. "Like the deity worshipped at Ephesus in the Bible?"

Matthew nodded. "Or something like it. Artemis, Diana, Hecate - all the same. A Greek goddess and underworld spirit."

Rachel limped over to rest against an upturned crate. "How do you know?"

"She referred to herself as the *'Goddess of the Sky Form'* and *'She who works her will.'* They're ancient titles attributed to the same spirit." He turned to Samantha. "If any of that is real. Man-made interpretations and stories?"

The young woman stretched. "Doesn't mean they're devoid of truth, Dad. Ways for us to comprehend that which is beyond our understanding." She reached out to Andrew again. "Please. What are you afraid of?"

Andrew stammered. "Of being damned. Of never seeing Sharon again."

Samantha leaned forward and clasped the man's limp, wispy hands. "What's your name?"

His mouth formed into a soundless gasp.

From a new, glimmering light near the table by the wall, a woman's voice answered. "Andrew. His name's Andrew." A beautiful brunette with big brown eyes and a cheeky smile walked to the edge of an expanding astral doorway. She chastised her husband with a half-grin. "Look at all the trouble you've created, Silly Billy. I've been waiting for you to show up. What a mess."

Samantha glanced back over her shoulder at the

woman. "He's played an important part in something good, however dubious his actions."

"He was always clueless, but I love him." Sharon Miles offered an open hand.

Andrew let go of Samantha and stepped forward in a trance to cross the threshold.

As the figures embraced and faded, Samantha's attention turned to Sally. The old woman looked from her clock to the doorway, with pained indecision. The Riley girl placed a reassuring palm on Sally's shoulder. "It will tell time for another. But the hours of your life here are done."

Two male figures approached the threshold.

Sally lifted her focus from the mantelpiece clock at last. "Father? Granddad?" Without a further word she ran with spry abandon - an image of the schoolgirl she once was - straight into the light.

Nadine stepped away from her mother's charm bracelet. "I know what I have to do. Thank you, Samantha."

Samantha watched her walk into the welcoming embrace of her mother, Darcy Evans. When they had gone, she turned to the First World War soldier, now recovered from his agonising ordeal. "Artemis - or whatever it was - called you a coward."

Peter Haws sighed. "I was executed for cowardice near The Western Front."

"I can't imagine what you experienced there." Samantha motioned to those remaining in the warehouse. "None of us can. But I don't think you were a coward. If I've learnt one thing, it's that we become more of what we are in death, not less. None but the stoutest of hearts could have done what you did today. I owe you my life. Others owe you much more than that."

The soldier bent and picked up his embroidered handkerchief in almost solid hands. "My name's Peter. My wife, Mary made this for me as a keepsake. It's Gateleigh, our old home. I'd like you to keep it once I'm gone."

Samantha took the beautiful fabric treasure, still illuminated with stitched images of a Devonshire village and the letters 'M & P.' Her face shone with tender warmth. "Thank you, Peter."

On the threshold, a pretty, fair-haired woman with sapphire eyes approached. Behind, the faint outline of comrades from the Duke of Cornwall's Light Infantry clustered about.

Peter's brow raised. "It's Mary and my old pals. I can't wait to see my boy, Jack. I wonder what sort of man he became?" The soldier marched forward. On the cusp of transition he span to face Samantha. One hand raised to snap her a salute which softened into a gentle wave. In the blink of an eye he faded from view.

Rosalind Layton flung her arms around Geraldine's neck. Samantha crouched beside her and stroked the horse's mane. "She's been a fine friend and loyal steed, Rosalind."

The child burst into tears. "I don't want to leave her."

"But what of your mother and father?"

Rosalind nuzzled the wooden nose of the toy animal.

"Who will look after Geraldine?"

Samantha cast a glance at her sister. Rachel nodded her assent. Samantha cuddled the ten-year-old. "I have a young niece. She's only five, but she'd love Geraldine. Would you entrust her to Jane, to look after with her whole heart?"

"Is she kind like you?"

"Yes."

At the frame of the astral door, four figures stood waiting. Samantha lifted the girl's tingling, empty chin to point in their direction. "Some people have come to meet you."

Rosalind let go of the woman and tottered on the spot. "It's Mama, Papa, Cook and Ned the stableman." She began to run, then turned and hurried back. One last hug and kiss were given to the rocking horse, and a second to Samantha. The child skipped off into the light, bouncing with enthusiasm. Rosalind swung both her parent's hands. The group turned to walk away. Ned the stableman's voice carried through the door behind them. "Why, Miss Rosalind. Wherever have you been?"

Rachel stepped across the fallen body of Harold Jessop. "What about him, Sam?"

Samantha squatted to touch the man's neck. No pulse and cold as ice. "He's long gone. Somehow, Andrew hopped inside and manipulated his body for a time to bring all this about." She waved at the extinguished pillar candles and incense burners. Deep in her heart, the burning gift gave one final splutter.

"Dad?"

Matthew Riley reached for each of his daughters. "I know."

Samantha picked up her baptismal cross necklace and put it in her pocket.

Matthew watched. "I wanted to save you, Samantha."

The young woman nodded. "And you did. Rachel too. If I hadn't made it up that roof... And that's after you helped stop The Entity from killing me and holding others captive."

"What was my life about? Religion became everything, and now I have no idea what's true."

Samantha kissed him on the cheek, the static charge of spiritual energy crackling against her moist, physical lips. "Your life was a desire to connect with God. Religion might have clouded it a little, but you're about to connect in person. And, oh how I envy you, Dad. What I would give to go back there. One day I will, but for now Mum needs me. I love you."

Both girls embraced him.

"What a blessed father I am. Give your mother a kiss for me and tell her I'll always love her." He stared into the light, mouth agape, eyebrows lifting. "Is that the Lord? I have so many questions."

A distant, bright figure beyond the horizon, stretched wide two welcoming arms.

Samantha watched in silence. Did God appear in the manner desired and understood by Its creation? Who could fathom such a wondrous being?

Matthew let go of his daughters. With happy,

confident steps, he strode into eternity and never looked back.

Samantha and Rachel stood there in each other's arms, several minutes after the light faded. Now they were left with a saturated warehouse and a dead body.

Rachel sat down to take a load off. "What should we do about the man?"

"Jessop? I'll call an ambulance from a phone box."

"Anonymous message?"

Samantha scratched her cheek. "We can't leave him, can we? Looks like he had a heart attack or stroke. It'll be enough to get his body and affairs taken care of by the authorities. He might have a family."

"I hope you're right. After everything that's happened, I could do without being the subject of a police investigation." She paused and studied her foot. "Thank goodness my car's an automatic. Wouldn't fancy pressing a clutch pedal with this."

Samantha snorted. "We'd better come up with a convincing story before we get you to the hospital."

"You saw what happened. Can't we tell them that?"

"Err, no. Not such a good idea."

"Are you going to tell me what happened? Last thing I recall was tossing you clear of the circle. Then something reached up inside me. It was like a waking nightmare, but none of it is coming back."

"I'll tell you. But not right now."

Rachel accepted her sister's offered arm of support. "Sam?"

"Yeah?"

"I owe you an apology. More than an apology. Where do I even begin?" She shook her head. "I feel more confused about things than Mum must. What am I going to do?"

Samantha helped her from the warehouse. "One step at a time, like we're doing now. Let's get you to your car. Then I'll retrieve the rocking horse."

"Will you bring it over to Middle Woodford for Jane?"

"Am I allowed?"

Rachel screwed up her eyes. "This will be difficult."

Samantha sighed. "That's what I thought. Rach-"

"No. I'm *not* backing down. John will welcome you. I'll not suffer negative words spoken against my sister, anymore."

"To be honest, Geraldine won't fit in my Ford Ka. You'll have to take her laid flat in your Volvo. Will Jane ever learn where the rocking horse came from?"

Rachel drew herself up to her full height, then almost collapsed in pain. "All my life I've been an obedient lamb, because I thought that's how I should behave. Now I've some truths of my own to tell. That'll be one of them."

"I suspect John won't approve."

"He'll get it, nonetheless. Are you going home to Mum?"

"Yeah. I'll terminate the lease on my Folkestone flat tomorrow. Probably head back to Bath in the next week or two."

"She couldn't be in better hands, Sam. Now I know it's true."

17

A New Chapter

SAMANTHA RILEY, 2019.

The on-line version of a Kent newspaper scrolled before Samantha's eyes on her laptop screen. She paused at a headline that read: *'Antique Dealer suffers fatal heart-attack during freak Rochester lightning storm.'* The short article detailed how Harold Jessop of *'Jessop's Antiques'* had met a death by natural causes. The result of shock, when the skylight at his warehouse collapsed on top of him during the recent electrical weather disturbance in Rochester. Samantha knew that would be the last she heard of the story and the deceased antique dealer.

Police sirens wailed past her building, down below in the Folkestone street. Samantha stretched and powered off her computer. It had been a busy morning, pushing aside fresh attempts to secure her services as a spirit liberator. Having built up a reputation through personal recommendation and word-of-mouth, she now had to reverse that popularity. "I don't do that anymore." The words came out flat, to match her action of shutting the computer's lid. Still, earthbound spirits roamed the half-light. She supposed they always would. Such an idea caused no small amount of anguish to sting Samantha's heart. When you've been so close to The Shackled and seen them cross over with joy, it leaves an indelible impression. The thought of being powerless to help now, mingled sadness with relief. "I've done my part," she reassured herself again, while rising to look round the tiny attic flat one final time. At her feet, two bags sat stuffed full of clothing, toiletries and the sundry few items she'd either left Bath with, or acquired while setting up home. She tucked the computer under one arm and unfastened the door.

Lena stomped up the staircase with a bag of heavy shopping. "Ah, Samantha. You going now, yes?"

"That's right. Back to Bath."

The Polish woman's brow creased. "To have bath?"

Samantha grinned. "No. To BATH. That's my home city in Somerset."

"Ah, I see. I will miss you. You've been a good neighbour."

"Thank you. You too." Samantha dragged her bags out onto the landing.

Lena unlocked her own front door, dumped the shopping inside and closed up again. She reached for an item of Samantha's luggage. "I help you."

"Thanks, Lena. I was worried I'd drop my computer before I reached the bottom."

At the foot of the stairs, Samantha deposited her keys with the landlord. Lena helped her load up the Ka and the two women exchanged a friendly farewell.

As she left Folkestone for the M20, Cheriton Road Cemetery appeared on her left-hand side. Until those concluding events at the warehouse, Samantha would have avoided such a place. There were always confused, stranded and wandering spirits to be found flitting about between the headstones of a graveyard. With her gift still in play, such a visit could prove exhausting. The day after she said goodbye to her father, Samantha made a point of taking a walk there. A litmus test to confirm what she knew to be true deep inside: her unusual abilities had ceased to function. It turned into a peaceful stroll.

Samantha sighed and bid the coastal Kent town goodbye in her rear-view mirror. She joined the motorway heading west, accelerating into traffic.

Her intention was to remain on the M25 until junction 15 for the M4. She never made it that far. A nagging sensation wouldn't allow her mind a moment's peace. There was nothing supernatural about it. At least, not in the manner to which the young woman had become accustomed. Somehow she couldn't shake the feeling Rachel needed her.

At the exit for the M3, she took the plunge and signalled left. *Rach did say I was welcome. I can stop there for a cuppa and a visit with my niece and nephew. If John gets funny, I'll leave and head on up the A36 to Bath. It's worth a try to shake this sensation.*

Her normal, relaxed last few miles into Middle Woodford proved more fractious than usual. That insistent feeling caused Samantha to press her foot to the floor. She almost overshot the downhill junction near Rachel's house and ended up in the river. Black tyre marks bore testimony to her frantic recovery from a squealing skid.

* * *

"I've told you before, you're not going." John Saunders' furious, shouting voice dulled from the far side of the kitchen door at his Middle Woodford home.

"Try to stop me. I've had enough, John. I need some space away with the kids. And I need to spend time with Mum." Rachel's reply bore a commanding confidence her husband had never experienced before.

Two removal men humped a large box past a five-year-old girl and her toddler brother in the dining room. One signalled the kitchen door with his head and called to his mate. "Right old barney this pair are having. Hope she doesn't change her mind."

The other snorted. "Who cares? As long as they don't mess us around and the company still pays our wages. That's all I'm worried about." They continued out into the hallway, through the front door. The pair arrived at a medium-sized van already loaded with boxes, bags and a beautiful rocking horse.

Back in the kitchen, Rachel fished a six-pack of spring water down from an overhead cupboard.

John scowled. "Now what are you doing? Don't they have water in Bath or something? Makes a mockery of the name."

"It's in case the children or I get thirsty on the way. Trust you not to think of your own flesh and blood."

The man folded his arms. "They're all I *do* think about, Rachel. You're not taking my children away for that satanic bitch to influence."

"How dare you talk about my mother like that?"

John's knuckles whitened. "I don't mean Judith and you know it. She's going to be there, isn't she? Samantha?"

"Yes she is. Sam's moving back in to care for Mum."

"I don't believe it. I send you to Kent to warn her off from confusing your upset mother. You come back with a head full of deceptions and nonsense. Plus a rocking horse and some ridiculous story that it belonged to a ghost who left it to Jane. A ghost, Rachel? You know there are no such things. Then you fill our daughter's head with Samantha's poison too."

"Is that why you hit her?"

"When I caught Jane spouting those lies? She needed a short, sharp, shock to make her realise you don't say things like that. Proverbs twenty-three, verses thirteen and fourteen: *'Do not withhold discipline from a child; if you punish them with the rod, they will not die. Punish them with the rod and save them from death.'* Are you listening, Rachel? Save them from *death*. You want to damn your own children?"

"Death is nothing to fear, John; believer or not. Being with those transitioning spirits in Rochester showed me that. Being with Dad."

"There you go again. Samantha has you so bewitched by her black magic, you honestly think Matthew Riley spoke to you."

"He did. And the only thing I want to save my children from is *you*. Stand in my way, and we'll see what Social Services think of your *short, sharp, shock*."

Out in the dining room, Jane lifted her summer dress. Delicate fingers touched the angry, moist surface of a large bruise on her right thigh. The tiniest pressure brought silent tears of pain to her eyes.

From the other side of the kitchen door, her father barked an order. "Damn it, Rachel, you're my wife. I'm the head of this household. Ephesians 5:23 says: *'For the husband is the head of the wife as Christ is the head of the church, His body, of which He is the Saviour.'* You WILL mind me."

"Stuff your book, John. I'm going home and I'm taking my children with me."

A series of slaps were followed by a shriek from Rachel.

Adam dissolved into a bout of crying at the sound of his mother's distress. Jane left her brother and ran to push the kitchen door open a crack. The sight of John Saunders pressing his wife's head against a kitchen unit, sent her running for the front door.

Removal men on a fag break dived out the way, as a black Ford Ka slipped sideways into the Middle Woodford driveway. Brakes squealed and brought the vehicle to an abrupt halt.

"Bloody hell, not another one," one man grumbled.

Jane Saunders stumbled into the front garden as Samantha tore herself out from behind the steering wheel. The desperate five-year-old cried out in distress. "Auntie Sam, Auntie Sam. Daddy's hurting Mummy." She slipped over on the moist grass, her frock riding up to reveal the cruel bruise.

Samantha's eyes flashed. Fists clenched and nostrils blowing like a pawing animal about to charge, she stormed into the house.

If John Saunders underestimated the strength of his wife's younger sibling before that day, he never would again. The kitchen door banged open. With a shriek of rage, Samantha dragged him free of her screaming sister. The man toppled over and smashed his forehead against the washing machine. His assailant threw herself on top of him, fingernails like raptor talons, tearing at his face.

Rachel supported herself against the sink to recover her breath.

John gained the upper hand, rolling on top of the hated interloper who sought to destroy his Biblical Utopian existence. Fat fingers clenched around Samantha's neck. Breath blasting from gaps in his clenched teeth, he squeezed on her windpipe.

Jane screamed in the doorway. "No."

Rachel reacted on instinct. Both hands reached up to

unhook a cast iron pan from above the hob. Love for her sister caused the heavy object to feel weightless in her adrenaline-fuelled, swinging grasp. The pan's surface connected with John's head and knocked him out cold. Rachel flopped against a kitchen unit, feeling the full weight of her ad hoc weapon. Her foot was still in considerable pain from the knife wound. Another cause of tension with her husband. She let the pan rest as Samantha coughed and rolled John's unconscious body off her.

Rachel's facial expression pivoted on a dangerous cusp at the border of hysteria.

Samantha sat up to relieve the emotionally charged atmosphere. "Was that hollow 'dong' sound the pan, or the contents of his empty head?"

Rachel half-sobbed then fell into almost uncontrollable laughter. Samantha clambered up to hug her. "I saw the removal van."

"How did you know to come? Was it...?"

"No. A feeling. The kind we all get from time to time."

"I'm glad you listened to it, Sam." Rachel caught hold of Jane as she ran into the kitchen to clutch her mother's leg.

"Are you leaving John?"

"Yes."

"I saw the bruise on Jane's thigh."

Rachel fondled her daughter's hair. "Punishment for repeating the story I told her about Rosalind and the rocking horse." She pushed away from the side and hurried into the dining room where Adam still sat crying. "Hush now. It's all right. Mummy's okay."

The evening sky turned to a pastel swatch of orange and pink above the elegant city of Bath. A Ford Ka, Volvo estate and removal van pulled up outside an impressive old townhouse on an overlooking hill. Its broad front door opened before the vehicle occupants even decamped. Judith Riley flung wide her arms, then staggered to grip a wrought-iron railing near the two front steps. "My girls. Thank God my girls are home at last."

"Nanny, Nanny, Nanny." Jane ran from the pavement to steady and cuddle her grandmother.

Rachel helped Adam out of the back seat and walked round to place an arm across her sister's shoulder. "Welcome home, Sam."

Samantha gave her a peck on the cheek, then ran to embrace her mother as if both their lives depended on it.

* * *

"The Munchkin's asleep. That ointment worked a treat on her leg. Thanks, Mum." Samantha wandered into the kitchen where her sister and mother sat chatting over a mug of cocoa round the sturdy wooden table.

Rachel looked up. "Did she like her story?" Her eyes fell on the silver baptismal cross, now once again hanging from Samantha's neck. "Sam?"

Samantha followed her stare. She smiled. "I'm wearing it to remind me of Dad's love. Nothing more. Someone wise said she hoped I'd do that, one day."

Judith Riley rose and poured more cocoa from a pan into a fresh mug. "Come and have a drink with us."

Rachel sipped her own, then wiped away a chocolaty moustache. "I'm glad you and Dad found peace and reconciliation. I tried in vain to see a way out of our impossible relationship maze until that night at the warehouse."

Samantha sat down. *"And we know that in all things God works for the good of those who love Him, who have been called according to His purpose."*

Rachel almost choked on her drink. "Romans eight. You're full of surprises tonight, Little Sis. First wearing a cross and now quoting the Bible?"

Samantha shrugged. "Quoting a truth. There's much in there. I'd substitute 'Him' with 'It,' I suppose. The more I think about everything, the more I see another force or intelligence at work in all this. Why couldn't I see Dad's spirit until the ritual began? Why was I given my gift at the exact time negative forces sought to imprison and steal away those in limbo? Even that sad, funny guy, Andrew and his bizarre attempts to recover his wife. It all slots into place in a way only some outside director could orchestrate. So, I suppose God *worked for the good*. Whether those involved loved God, seems immaterial."

Rachel sat back in her seat. "You might be right. I feel like my brain is about to melt."

Samantha played with her necklace. "Christianity

isn't the enemy. I never thought it was. Its adherents are as numerous and diverse as the snowflakes of a blizzard. Some of their views and doctrines run a close second. I may not want any part of its beliefs and rituals, but the faith still opens the hearts of many to a relationship with God. That's something The Divine yearns to enjoy with Its creation, more than we'll ever know. I wish words could convey that intense desire I felt during my NDE."

Rachel tapped her fingers on the wooden surface. "All the same, I don't want John's flavour of it in my life. He used the faith to excuse his temper and abuse us."

Samantha nodded. "And to sate his need to dominate and control those he professed to love."

Judith stroked her eldest daughter's upper arm. "If you're unsure what to believe now, I know a place we might go?"

Rachel twisted. "Where, Mum?"

"Do you remember Virginia Leavers?"

"How could I forget? When she backslid from church, everyone in the youth group referred to her as 'Leaver Leavers.' We were cruel sometimes. Why do you ask?"

"I bumped into her in town the other day. She's part of a Post-Evangelical group that meet to share honest discussions about their views and experiences. If people want to pray, they can. But it's very free. There's a strict, no-nonsense policy over bigotry and absolutism. I wanted to go, but I'm nervous. My dodgy legs don't help."

"A support group for those *'in recovery'* from 'salvation?' Where do I sign up? Shall we go together?"

Judith beamed. "I'd like that."

Rachel looked at her sister. "Would you like to come, Sam?"

"No thanks. But it sounds like you'll be needing a babysitter." She stared out the back garden window into darkness. "Funny how the family name ends with us. No more Rileys carrying a torch for Christ and His gospel. This house has a lot of history in that regard."

Judith folded her hands. "And now it's time for a new chapter to begin."

*   *   *

"I can't believe you found this place, Sam." Rachel peered beneath the sun visor hanging over her Volvo windshield.

On the front passenger seat, Judith Riley twisted to wink at her youngest daughter and two grandchildren fastened in the back. "Samantha's always been resourceful."

Samantha watched Jane press her nose against the window glass. The girl studied sheep grazing either side of the long gravel drive to an exquisite, stately home. "Without a surname to go on, it was difficult. But, the Internet is a wonder. I'm glad the house is open to the public as a tourist attraction now. Plus, we needed to get Mum away from Bath. The break will do her good."

Judith adjusted her seatbelt. "Having my girls home

has already brought health to my body. The doctor thinks I could go into remission, of a kind. No wheelchair for me, if I can help it."

The Volvo rolled to a halt alongside a dozen or more other vehicles. A hundred yards ahead, a red-brick walled kitchen garden occupied most of this side of the driveway. On the other, tall trees and rhododendron bushes masked their view of the grand country pile.

Rachel was first out of the car. "Sam? It looks like there's a coffee shop or restaurant in the old stables. Did you want a drink first? It's been a long drive."

Samantha deferred to the eldest member of their party. "Mum?"

"Yes please. Coffee in a stable? What a delightful idea."

A white dovecote crested the roof line of the old stables. Grand windows spoke of great esteem for the animals once housed within. Now the stalls contained long wooden tables and bench seats. Samantha held her mother's arm as the pair ambled across a set of worn, uneven cobbles to find a place to sit.

Rachel studied a chalkboard menu. "They do coffee and a mini pastry for £3.50. Juice for the kids. What do you think?"

Judith and her helper muttered their assent, then got settled with the youngsters while Rachel ordered.

Samantha pulled out a glossy pamphlet they'd received at the gatehouse with their tickets. Above a sunny picture of the mansion in all its grandeur, flowing white text formed the title: 'Bridechurch.'

Jane tugged at her aunt's sleeve. "What does it say, Auntie Sam? Will you read it to me please?"

Rachel came back and settled down with her children, as Samantha unfolded the multi-panel document and began to read.

'The elegant home of Bridechurch was originally constructed by the Layton family in the early eighteenth century. It remained in the family for a hundred years until tragedy struck Lord Cecil Layton and his wife Barbara. Their only child - a daughter named Rosalind - died of consumption aged ten. Cecil and Barbara produced no further heirs to carry on the household line. After their deaths, Bridechurch was sold and remained in private hands until being opened to the public in 1977. Views from the property across nearby downland are breathtaking to behold. Along with formal gardens and an arboretum, there is a full kitchen garden with exotic fruit grown under glass. Amongst many striking features of this lovely old home, are a cantilevered staircase and fascinating, semi-subterranean kitchens. We hope you'll enjoy lunch or other refreshments served in the architecturally superb stable block and take a guided tour of the house. Please enjoy the grounds at your leisure.'

Jane took a glass of juice handed to her by a waitress. "Thank you." She looked at her mother. "Rosalind was the name of the girl who owned Geraldine, wasn't it?"

Rachel helped Adam with his juice, one eye on her daughter. "Yes, darling. This was her home, over two hundred years ago."

Jane gasped. "Is Geraldine as old as that?"

"Yes she is. All the more reason to take extra special care of her."

The girl nodded her head in furious agreement. "Oh, I will, Mummy. I will."

Suitably refreshed, the holiday party embarked on a guided tour with several other visitors. At the top of the portrait-adorned staircase, they were escorted through a master bedroom with bay windows modified during the Regency period. Several more chambers on, and the group came to a roped-off needlework room flooded with light from a west-facing window.

Their female guide paused. "If you'll come past this doorway one at a time, you can observe a fine area set up for ladies to spend their hours in sewing and embroidery."

A German tourist raised his hand. "Was it always used for this purpose?"

The guide made a chewing motion with her mouth. "It's hard to say. There may have been other associations down through the years."

"Like a nursery?" Samantha piped up. She had the strangest feeling, like butterflies in her tummy.

"Yes. That's possible. The room alongside was once a child's bedroom. It's believed it belonged to Cecil and Barbara Layton's daughter-"

"Rosalind," Samantha finished the sentence.

"Correct. I see you've read your pamphlet. Now, if

you'll all follow me downstairs, we'll look at the kitchen and butler's office."

In the kitchen, Samantha got that weird feeling again. It was pleasant, almost uplifting in a strange way.

The party finished their tour in the courtyard beyond the butler's office. Several of the group carried on across the cobbled space, for tea in the stables where Samantha and her family started out.

Rachel walked on ahead with Judith and Adam. Jane zipped from side to side of the courtyard, examining every nook and cranny of her toy benefactor's former home.

Samantha paused. She didn't know what had caused her to seek out this place, other than an indescribable affection for the little girl spirit and her wooden horse. Rosalind's presentation and the fact her mother and father were accompanied by a cook and stableman, got Samantha thinking she might have come from a stately home. A flush of heat followed the positive result of her extensive computer search. Events of recent years had left Samantha drained and lacking in joy and verve for life. Now, a childlike buzz of innocent excitement connected itself to her heart, as if left behind like some unseen present by the tragic Rosalind. Samantha bounced across the courtyard with a spring in her step. In her mind, she could almost imagine herself galloping as though on a pretend horse. The others disappeared through an arch that formed a tunnel between the stable and ancillary buildings.

Jane turned for a moment. "Come on, Auntie Sam. We're going to see the pretty flowers."

A cheerful ditty danced upon Samantha's lips. She hummed to herself and pressed on down the tunnel. At the end of that dark passage, new light, abundance and a brighter future awaited. It was a fitting metaphor for the life she had led and the one through which we are all passing. The sound of her unconscious melody reflected off the close brick walls. She smiled to herself as she recognised the tune: *'Over the hills and far away.'*

ABOUT THE AUTHOR

Devon De'Ath was born in the county of Kent, 'The Garden of England.' Raised a Roman Catholic in a small, ancient country market community famously documented as 'the most haunted TOWN in England,' he grew up in an atmosphere replete with spiritual, psychic, and supernatural energy. Hauntings were commonplace and you couldn't swing a cat without hitting three spectres, to the extent that he never needed question the validity of such manifestations. As to the explanations behind them?

At the age of twenty, his earnest search for spiritual truth led the young man to leave Catholicism and become heavily involved in Charismatic Evangelicalism. After serving as a part-time youth pastor while working in the corporate world, he eventually took voluntary redundancy to study at a Bible College in the USA. Missions in the Caribbean and sub-Saharan Africa followed, but a growing dissatisfaction with aspects of the theology and ministerial abuse by church leadership eventually caused him to break with organised religion and pursue a Post-Evangelical existence. One open to all manner of spiritual and human experiences his 'holy' life would never have allowed.

After church life, De'Ath served fifteen years with the police, lectured at colleges and universities, and acted as a consultant to public safety agencies both foreign and domestic.

A writer since he first learned the alphabet, Devon De'Ath has authored works in many genres under various names, from Children's literature to self-help books, through screenplays for video production and all manner of articles.

Printed in Great Britain
by Amazon

44689981R00199